Timeswept passion...timeless love.

LADY ROGUE

"I have watched you from the time you came and have known you were different, that you were sent here—maybe from the bastards who have perpetuated the beginning of the end of England at its greatest—but that you are not who you say you are."

"I'm Isobel, damn you! Jeremy's cousin and Lord Sheffield's guest."

"But is that all you are?"

He reined in the horse so suddenly she fell back against him hard. He lifted her and turned her around in the saddle so that she was close to him in ways that frightened her at the same time that they excited her. "We'll see about that," he whispered.

With one hand he captured her two hands behind her back; with the other, he gripped her head so that she could not move her mouth away from the fierce assault he was making on it. She let out a cry when his hand at her back gripped her even more tightly.

"Wherever they found you, my hat's off to them."

MOONSPELL

NELLE McFATHER

LOVE SPELL **NEW YORK CITY**

For my beloved son, Rob,
some lucky woman's future hero.

Acknowledgments

I am grateful, as usual, to Meg Ruley
and to Alicia Condon
and to Marlene Bush
and to Aleece Jacques,
the author of Jeremy's "Ode To Isobel."

Thanks to my cousin
and librarian at South Georgia College
Pat Hinson,
who was patient with my demands for historical detail.

Chapter One

London, Late Spring, 1990

Annabel Poe had felt the excitement of finally being in England from the first moment she stepped off the plane at Gatwick Airport.

Mastering the art of driving in heavy traffic to London was a challenge, but one which only added to her sense of adventure.

"I'm really here," she crowed as she made a jerky right turn from the unaccustomed left lane toward Belgrave Square and her modest little hotel. "I'm right smack in the middle of history. I still can't believe it."

She was also right smack in the middle of the wrong lane. The double-decker bus behind her nearly ran over her. "Same to you, Buster," she called back cheerfully when the driver shook his fist at her. "I got my training on the freeway in Atlanta. Where'd you get yours?"

A parking place miraculously opened up in front of the colorful Hansel and Gretel and Annabel whipped into it with an adroitness that amazed even her. "What, no doorman?" she murmured in humor. Her modest budget for this trip to England to pursue her graduate work had not included enough for a night at the Savoy.

She had explained her reason for the trip to her seat companion on the plane, also from Atlanta and a frequent traveler to England. Annabel had told him all about the small inheritance that had made it possible for her to seek her master's degree in English. "I quit my job at an insurance company and worked my fanny off for a year getting my course work at Emory University. Now all I have left to do is my thesis, but that's no small thing. It seems that there was very little available on the rather obscure romantic poet I chose to write about, so I had to come to England."

The man with whom she'd struck up the conversation was more interested in the warm, dark-haired prettiness of his traveling neighbor than in hearing about how Newton Fenmore had emerged recently as a poet to be compared with John Keats, but he was polite enough to pursue the subject. "Why not pick one of the old tried-and-true, like Poe or somebody?"

Annabel had laughed at that. The teasing about her name had started with her entry in graduate school and hadn't stopped. "Heavens, no. The trick in any dissertation is to choose a topic that very few other people know anything about. I was lucky, though. I wrote to the English Poets Institute in London and made contact with an actual descendant of my poet. He's going to be my thesis adviser and seemed quite excited about my interest. As it turns out, Newton Fenmore's collection will be presented at a special exhibition in England sometime this summer. The academics are making quite a fuss about him, as they did about Emily Dickinson when her unpublished writing surfaced in the fifties."

Annabel smiled as she signed the register in the tiny lobby of the Hansel and Gretel, remembering how hard the man seated next to her had tried to feign interest in the poems she'd recited from memory, starting with her favorite Keats ode, "To Autumn."

"Poor guy," she murmured. "All he wanted was a nice, normal pickup."

Her room was about the size of the cockpit in the 707 she'd flown in on, with a wall-to-wall bed, but Annabel's good mood would

11

not be spoiled by anything so unimportant as cramped sleeping quarters and a community bathroom three floors up.

She was in England, and the blood of her forebears was stirring deep inside her, thrilling her with the sense of somehow belonging in England.

She had a practical purpose in coming to England, but Annabel Poe knew that there was more to her being here than researching and writing about an obscure poet. Annabel vaulted over the narrow rail at the end of the bed and looked out the window at the moon, which made of the night an upended hollow log. "You, Moon, tell me. Why am I here? I know you're keeping something back. You were here through everything, every century, every war, every time. Tell me, Moon, will I meet that man, finally? The one that kept me from getting married all those times, that doesn't even exist except in my dreams? And not even there—he's just a faded image, part of that crazy dream . . ." Annabel sighed in exasperation, more at herself than at the uncooperative, uncommunicative orb in the London sky.

The dreams had something to do with it, too. Annabel had gone to a psychiatrist after her parents' death three years earlier, trying to deal with the shock of losing a mother and father simultaneously in a tragic auto accident.

The business about the recurrent dream had surfaced during the therapy. Dr. Wall had not accepted his patient's casual dismissal of the dream. He had questioned Annabel in detail, paying more attention to her guarded description of the dream's specifics than to her grief over her parents.

"You've had these dreams since you were how old?"

"Eighteen. I'm twenty-eight now." Annabel had refocused the session reluctantly. She was always uneasy discussing the dream.

"Describe it to me, with every detail you can remember."

Annabel had laughed wryly at that. "Dr. Wall, it is always exactly the same, always. People say they forget their dreams after they wake up. I always remember mine. At least this one." When the psychiatrist looked at her expectantly, she joked, "I thought you Freudian guys said that a person who dreamed she had died would never wake up."

"I'm not Freudian, I'm of the Skinner school, and I don't generalize about what goes on inside a person's head when she's unconscious. You're an English major. Remember what Hamlet said to his best friend."

" 'There are more things in heaven and earth, Horatio, than were ever dreamt of in your philosophy.' Well, Doc, I'm glad you're literary minded but I don't know where you're headed."

She found out when she finally described the dream. She told him how she was on a boat—a nineteenth-century English passenger vessel, she'd learned from research. "It's the same ship every time. And there's this captain . . . he's evil. The men hate him, he's cruel to his crew and scorns the passengers. He stares at me and I'm afraid."

"This man, does he attack you sexually?"

Annabel closed her eyes, conjuring up the images. "He wants to," she whispered. "He keeps telling me how pretty I am and how I can have a better place to sleep and eat if I'll be nice to him. I resist, because I'm going back to England, where I belong. There's a letter with a crest on it." Annabel squinched her eyes even tighter. "I can never make out the initials, hard as I try. But the miniatures I have of two men—one smiling, one stern and intense—haunt me, even burn my flesh where I hide them in my chemise."

The psychiatrist interrupted, "One of the men means a great deal to you for some reason."

His guess was on target. "Yes. The dark-haired one. I feel that I must get to him, no matter what. And then . . . and then . . ."

"And then what?"

Annabel's voice dropped to a whisper. "I am struggling on the deck with the captain. He's . . . he's pushing his hands into my skirts, trying to raise them, savaging my flesh, my breasts, my mouth, and I'm screaming silently for the man I'm sailing toward."

"His name?" Dr. Wall leaned forward as Annabel shook her head to and fro. "Your name?"

"I don't know," she whispered. "All I know is that I hear his voice calling me, saying we will be together forever, and then I'm in the cold water, being dragged down, down . . ."

"Then?"

Annabel raised her face, and Dr. Wall momentarily lost his professional detachment at the luminous yellow-green eyes staring into his with catlike mystery. "I didn't die," she said slowly. "I was floating beneath the sea, beneath the waves, calm and serene, somehow knowing it was not over, that I would complete my voyage. The moon looked down at me and I felt peaceful. The waves whispered my name. 'Isobel, Isobel.'" Her brow furrowed. "But that's not my name."

"It's the same every time, with no variation?"

"The same," Annabel said firmly. "No variation. Now it's your turn, Doctor. What does it mean?"

The psychiatrist shook his head slowly. "Period dreams with real people are the hardest to figure out. Have you ever heard of past life regression? Some people would say your dreams are actual events, experienced in another lifetime." He leaned forward, his personal curiosity overpowering his professionalism. "Would you allow me to hypnotize you to see if we can bring back more details to the conscious level?" At her vehement refusal he sighed. "Tell me, is there a chance you might go to England? Perhaps a trip to the destination in your dream would trigger further revelations."

"Not a chance. I was lucky to get any kind of job with my liberal arts major. My parents never had much money to live on, much less to leave to me."

Not many months after she left Dr. Wall's office for the last time, Annabel returned to her modest Northeast apartment to find a letter informing her of an education fund her parents had kept in force and which had matured in time for her to enroll in Emory University the following fall. . . .

She'd been destined to go to England. And here she was! Annabel heard a chorus of drunken Dutch tourists coming back from the nearest pub and smiled as she drifted into the dreamless, exhausted sleep of the overseas traveler.

"We made it," she whispered, her arm curling around her face to block out the light from the street. She was too sleepy to wonder about the significance of "we."

16

*   *   *

"So, you've decided to write your thesis on my ancestor and his poetry. I'm honored that your American Dean Pitts agreed to let me be your adviser. It's an unorthodox arrangement, but one that I think we'll both enjoy." Dean Morris Keller's smile revealed large, white teeth that made Annabel feel somewhat like a juicy T-bone steak on the verge of being devoured. "Especially now that I've met you in person." Mercury-gray eyes slid over Annabel's slender form admiringly. "So, tell me more about yourself and this decision of yours to come to England."

Morris Keller was a tall, muscular man whose good looks were accentuated by a shock of salt-and-pepper hair and an impeccably tailored suit that Annabel was pretty sure had not been bought in Cheapside. His manicured hands played with the papers in her file that lay open before him as Annabel responded, but his piercing gray eyes never left her face.

"Everything important is in my résumé." *Except my bust measurements which you've already figured out*, she added in her head. "As for coming to England, what student of English literature doesn't dream of doing that?" Annabel pushed a lock of hair off her face, wishing Dean Keller would stop staring at her. "I read about the exciting exhibition being held during the International Poetry Society's annual conference. How wonderful that the British government is releasing to your English Poets Institute a literary treasure that critics are saying equals Keats and Wordsworth in value and beauty! Of course, so much of this honor comes as a result of your own influence and academic prestige."

Annabel was relieved not to choke on the honeyed words. She knew that Keller was lobbying for the prestigious role of Director of the English Endowments to the Arts. His efforts on Newton Fenmore's behalf were not altogether altruistic.

Morris Keller did lower his eyes at her words, in what Annabel was sure was false modesty. "Well, I didn't feel my ancestor's genius should go unrecognized for another century. Too bad, isn't it, that most creative artists never live long enough to enjoy the fruits of their craft." He glanced at her file. "Hmm, I see from your transcript that you're well steeped in courses in the Romantics. That's good. My ancestor actually hobnobbed with the likes of Keats and Byron. Shelley, too, and his wife, Mary."

"Think of it," Annabel said softly, stirred by the thought of exploring the period that had been marked by the great Romantics in the very country where they had lived their explosive lives and careers. "Newton Fenmore probably heard Mary Shelley's own sweet voice discussing her classic horror novel."

"Well, *Frankenstein* has certainly endured. Now tell me." Keller perused her over pyramided hands. "What are your plans? As I wrote you, there are comfortable lodgings very nearby, in fact not far from my home on Downing Street." At Annabel's look of surprise, the dean laughed. "Yes, I live perhaps two blocks from the inimitable Sir Winston Churchill's enshrined office/home. In fact, you won't find many places in all of England that haven't some trace of a famous figure."

"Well, as I wrote back to you, I'd really like to stay in Kent, as near as possible to Sheffield Hall where your ancestor wrote his last two volumes of poetry."

The dean wrinkled his nose in distaste. "I shall never understand why the descendants of the family who acquired that place from Newton have let it come to such a disgraceful end." At Annabel's questioning look, he went on. "Newton was in Parliament during the uprisings over the Corn Laws. His part in bringing the leader of the insurgents to justice brought him the reward of the title to the leader's estate."

"That doesn't seem quite fair. But you mentioned a 'disgraceful end' to Sheffield Hall.

Has it been turned into a tourist attraction? A bordello?"

The quip went over the man's head. Annabel decided the only humor Morris Keller recognized was his own. "Worse. It was bad enough that Newton lost it due to his . . . er, insensitivity to pecuniary soundness."

"He put Sheffield Hall up against his gaming markers, if I remember my notes correctly," Annabel corrected mildly. "And then lost it."

The dean cleared his throat. "At any rate, the present owners have had the audacity to give a ten-year lease to some American engaged in one of those pugilist sports. I daresay you Yanks have a way of rewarding your athletes unrealistically. The man paid cash, I heard, some million and a half pounds, for the place."

Annabel was not a sports fan so she was interested only in what had become of the home of her thesis focus. "So this American jock immediately installed jacuzzis everywhere and painted the statuary McDonalds orange?"

"No. The chap turned the house into a pub. He actually has a sign on the road from Maidstone advertising the place." The wrinkles of distaste reappeared. " 'All Roads Lead to Roman's' or some such atrocity."

Annabel had to laugh. "Just be glad it's not a poster of Michael Jordan in jockey briefs. Now, shall we make an appointment to go over my thesis proposal?"

"Oh, we can do much better than that. You're in town, not knowing anyone, and I happen to be batching it this month while the missus is off to visit her sister in York. Shall we do a few pubs? Let me show you the real historical side of England."

I bet that's not all you'd show me before the night was out, Annabel thought with grim humor. This dean was as smarmy a character as she'd ever met. She hoped his ancestor proved to be more appealing. "Thank you, but no thanks. I'm still tired from the flight over, and since I'll be out early tomorrow looking for a place to stay, I'd better get an early night."

The dean looked more annoyed than disappointed. He wasn't used to being turned down by fresh-faced young graduate students, Annabel decided. Well, she wasn't the only one with something to learn.

"I'll have Miss Penbuckle make an appointment and ring you. You'll let me know if you change your residence from the"— he looked down at her note and said the name of her hotel with a noticeable sneer —"Hansel and Gretel? My dear, you really should have let me see to your booking."

"I'll keep you posted."

That night in her tiny room, after she'd had a couple of bitters in the hotel pub and watched a few minutes of British "telly" in the community lounge, Annabel got out her precious box of notes about Newton Fenmore's life and works.

As always, she lost herself in the lyric beauty of the earliest poems, cried over several in the middle period, many of which were dedicated to the tragic deaths of Keats and Shelley. And, as always, she puzzled over the abrupt transition to triteness and jagged rhythm that characterized the works in the last two volumes.

"Every genius has his dry spell, his writer's block. Why shouldn't Newton Fenmore? Poe, you just despise his descendant, that's why you're looking at this stuff differently tonight." Annabel closed the last leaf of the slim volume of the poet's last works. She must remember to ask Keller for copies of the actual manuscripts. Sometimes there were notes (such as Yeats's copious ones) that explained what the poet was experiencing when he wrote a particularly out-of-character poem.

She looked out her window, up at the purpling sky hung with the same moon and stars that had beamed down at Keats not far from here. "Tell me, Moon. How could a sleaze like Keller have a relative that could write 'To

Felicia, in Her Garden'? Tell me that, you big hunk of green cheese."

The moon didn't answer, but the wobbly chorus of Dutch tourists returning from a nearby pub filled the night air, and Annabel closed her window, grinning. "Guess that's my cue to go to bed."

She did not dream of the voyage across the ocean that night, perhaps because she was already in England and well on her way to her destiny.

By the time she'd had breakfast in the hotel's cozy dining room, Annabel had come to a decision. She was checking out of the Hansel and Gretel and would take her chances on finding a bed-and-breakfast in Kent, near Sheffield Hall. It was tempting to take in the sights of London, but Annabel thrust temptation aside. Harrod's, Buckingham Palace, the Elgin Marbles could wait (had waited). There was a little voice urging her onward to Sheffield Hall.

She paid her bill and set off for Kent.

The modern road to Dover was a far cry from the old coach roads that Newton Fenmore and his colleagues had traveled. The roundabout near Maidstone was like the Mad Mouse ride at a carnival. Annabel closed her eyes and darted off in what she hoped was the direction to Sheffield Hall. She ignored the tempting signs to Canterbury and Tunbridge Wells, focusing on her search for the turnoff to her destination.

"Well, he said the American has a sign. Stay alert, Poe. You don't want to wander all over Kent, beautiful as it is."

Then she saw it. "Why, that's not a tacky sign," Annabel said, slowing down to let a bullying Mercedes squeeze between her Toyota and an oncoming tour-bus. "Not tacky a bit."

The lane she turned on was well-kept and smooth. Annabel drove slowly, admiring the majestic evergreens lining the entry to the estate. When she turned into the stone-buttressed entrance, she caught her breath at the sweep of green lawn sloping down to the river. At the sight of the massive house looming into view, she let her held breath out in a whistle. "So this was your reward, Mr. Newton Fenmore. No rat-infested poet's garret for you!"

Then she saw the tower, its lonely grayness mossy with age and character, standing by itself like a forgotten sentinel of the main house's history. Annabel felt the goose bumps start at her ankles and ripple up to her ears. *That's the place,* the little voice said inside her head. *That's where you'll find what you came here to find.*

The turret looked abandoned. In light of all the improvements in evidence elsewhere, the trim grounds and well-kept road, Annabel found this curious.

But right now she was dry and hot. Maybe over a mug of ale she could find out more about Sheffield and its previous tenants.

First, she had to make the acquaintance of the newest one. "Roman's?" Annabel parked her car in the designated area off the front entrance to the house and smiled at the couple who were getting out of their car. "Am I at the right place?"

"Right you are," the young man told her, helping his companion from their car. "Love your boots."

Annabel looked down at her dyed-skin red cowboy boots. Maybe the boots, designer jeans, and silk shirt weren't just the ticket for the occasion, she worried. "Think I'm too laid-back for this place?"

The girl laughed. "Wait till you meet Roman! You look fabulous. We'll see you inside."

Annabel was right behind them as the doors to Sheffield Hall opened. The stunning impact of seeing the tower was still numbing, but her first meeting with Roman Forsythe made everything else history.

Chapter Two

Their eyes met across the immense space of the great room where the main bar was located. Even before the girl whispered, "That's Roman. Over there, behind the big bar," Annabel knew it was he. A strange wave of recognition passed through her, bewildering her at the same time that it brought a thrill. "Do you want us to introduce you?"

Annabel shook her head. "No, you two said you were meeting friends for dinner. Please don't worry about me. I've been used to managing on my own for a very long time."

"Well, we'll see you later, when the music starts. The dancing's really fabulous here."

"I'm sure it is." Annabel moved toward the

bar, feeling as though pulled by the gravity of fate. Just as she reached the bar, someone slid onto the last empty stool. The man behind the counter bent down and whispered something and the new customer hastily left, relinquishing his seat to Annabel.

"I told him dinner was on me if he caught the early sitting," Roman Forsythe said in response to Annabel's unspoken question. "What the devil took you so long?"

She knew what he meant, that he'd felt it, too—that sense of meeting someone long awaited. "I had a very long trip." She looked at the scar that ran from his temple to his cheek. He looked at the tiny star-shaped birthmark on her upper lip. Both felt the invisible touch of soft lips in fantasy. "Will it break the spell if I order a beer?"

He laughed and they were back to normal status, sizing each other up as any other attractive Americans meeting on foreign soil would. "You've got it. And I don't serve it lukewarm like most of my competitors." He reappeared quickly with a frosted mug and popped himself a root beer. "I like the way you wear your hair." He looked at the long wave of black sheen that hung simply across one shoulder.

"I like yours, too." She did, though some would say his sun-streaked, curly locks were unfashionably long. The broken nose was too humped to be naturally Roman; Annabel figured he'd had it broken a few times in whatever sport it was that he'd played. "I understand you're a famous athlete." She looked around the dim room, seeing now that the walls were covered with magnified black-and-white photos of all the major football players. "I don't know anything about football, I'm afraid. In college, I went to the Georgia Tech games and wore my big yellow corsage, but I never had the faintest idea what any of those fellows were trying to do."

Her host hid a smile, and Annabel saw with delight that he had a dimple. "Make a home run or a hole-in-one. Take your pick. Hey, where are my manners? I'm Roman Forsythe, former football jock and current owner of this joint." He held out his hand.

She put hers in it, feeling when it was gripped that she was safe from everything in the world. "Annabel Poe, from Atlanta. I'm in England working on my master's thesis."

"That's really your name?"

"You know Edgar Allan Poe?" Annabel's look of surprise was spontaneous. Football players weren't known for their rapture with things literary.

"Hey, don't be so quick to stereotype me as a bonehead. I majored in history, English history, and I've certainly read some poets in my time. Matter of fact, we're right in the middle of a real poet's background. Ever hear of a guy named Newton Fenmore?"

Annabel grinned. "I've . . . heard the name here and there." She burst out laughing. "Hell, I may as well tell you. That's my poet, the one I'm researching and doing my thesis on! That's why I came out here, hoping I could find a place to rent nearby, so I could be in the heart of Kent where he wrote his poetry."

"Well, I'll be doubledamned! Are you in luck, or what? It just so happens, I was planning to fix up that tower out there on the edge of the property and rent it out. I'm planning a long visit back home, and it sure would be nice to have somebody I can trust staying on the property while I'm gone."

Annabel's heart constricted. To stay in that turret, to live there! "Oh, do you really mean it? I can't tell you what it would mean to be able to live there. I saw it on my way in and I felt . . ." She stopped, not knowing if Roman Forsythe might withdraw his offer to rent to someone who occasionally ventured into the Twilight Zone.

He finished for her, quietly, without the teasing tone that had been evident in his earlier banter. "Felt that you'd been inside it sometime, somehow? Felt that it was waiting to be reclaimed by some human, the one it's been

waiting for?" At Annabel's look, he nodded.
"Me, too. I guess that's why I haven't been out
there yet, because I was afraid of what I might
feel if I actually went in the place.

"It'll need a lot of fixing up, if the outside
condition is any indication of the state of
repair it's in," he mused. Then he said with
finality, "But the cost will be no problem.
These two banged-up knees and this Mount
Rushmore nose may not be the prettiest sight
to behold, but I got well compensated for 'em
when I was out there bashing heads with those
three-hundred-pound linemen. Hey, bottoms
up. I want to show you this place. Then we'll
take a look at *your* place."

"My place. I like the sound of that already.
Yeats had his tower in Sligo. Now I'll have my
own in Kent!"

"It won't come without its price," Roman said
solemnly.

Annabel's eyes widened. "Oh, my gosh! I
hadn't even thought about the rent. Will it be
something I can afford?"

"How about your promise to fix a home-
cooked meal once in a while for a lonesome
ole boy from Dixie who is tickled to death to
have a real down-home woman to talk to now
and then?"

Annabel's smile was radiant, not just from
relief at learning she wouldn't have to bust

her budget paying for her new quarters, but because the prospect of getting to know Roman Forsythe was as exciting as the academic task ahead of her.

Maybe more exciting.

Roman turned over his barkeep duties to others and led Annabel out to the great hall and up the stone steps to the second floor. "Careful. There's been no renovation on the original masonry. Watch out for the dents and holes."

He went on with his lecture about the old "motte-and-bailey" structure that had given way to the "shell keep" in England, explaining that Sheffield was fashioned after the latter construction plan. "The timber 'fortress' atop the mound, or 'motte,' wasn't terribly practical for defense, they learned. The stone shell that replaced the old 'bailey' was much more effective."

"Hey, slow down," Annabel begged, laughing and out of breath at the fast pace of climbing and conversation.

"No way. You and I have some centuries to catch up on."

Annabel stopped dead still at that. "What did you say?"

"About the water closet that originally hung out over the old moat?"

"No. About . . . Aieee!" Something curled around Annabel's legs and she grabbed Roman's arm. "Oh, kitty, you scared me half to death."

Roman chuckled, enjoying the contact, and reached down to rub the silky black cat with the silver orb of fur on its forehead. "That's Moonbeam, one of the last real descendants of Sheffield Hall. Her family goes back as far as the old Sheffields. I found the old household accounts book, and milk costs for Moonbeam's forebears were listed right there along with the meat and cheese costs for the human residents."

"She's beautiful." Annabel stroked the cat and was startled when the animal turned her face up to stare right into her eyes.

"You've found a friend, it seems. Come on. Let me show you what I've done with the apartment that Newton Fenmore occupied while he was living here." Roman opened the heavy double doors to his rooms. A strong breeze rippled the tapestries at the glassed-in doors leading to the balcony overlooking the river. "Tremaine Sheffield's ghost, no doubt. They say that Newton often slept downstairs when he moved in here after the place became his. Eventually, he changed bedrooms."

Annabel rubbed her arms where goose bumps had appeared when she saw the rippling curtains. "What became of Tremaine Sheffield?"

"I'm not sure. When I moved here and got interested in the history of the place, I tried to find out. But the records were locked up in the old Newgate files with a 'No Access' seal that smacked of Parliament involvement."

Annabel lost her nervous feeling when Roman illuminated the room and she saw how he had decorated it. "This is wonderful!" She looked around the room at the eclectic combination of contemporary furnishings and Victorian antiques. "I could swear I've seen this room before."

"You probably did," Roman admitted a little sheepishly. "It was showcased in *Southern Living* about a year ago."

Annabel felt inordinately relieved. So that's what the déjà vu was all about. She'd seen him in a magazine she subscribed to. "Well, so I'm visiting with a celebrity."

"Hardly." Roman got them drinks from the chrome and mirror bar that held a collection of old cut glass decanters. "I got coerced by a writer friend of mine in Atlanta. She was doing a piece on the so-called ten most eligible bachelors in town and . . ." Roman shrugged, looking on the verge of blushing. Annabel found that endearing.

"My, my. I'm surprised. But you're in England and not Atlanta. How did you qualify?"

"That was before I moved over here. For a while I had homes in both cities and spent part of the year in each. As for the article, it

Chapter Three

"It's beautiful. It's just beautiful."

Annabel stood with Roman Forsythe as the Kent countryside sunset imbued the newly painted tower interior with a rosy glow. She still couldn't believe they'd gotten it all done and that the results were so close to what she'd envisioned when she'd first seen the historic edifice.

"I think the color turned out great. I can't wait to see it in the moonlight."

Annabel turned to Roman, her face shining. "I can't begin to thank you enough. I've never seen anybody work as hard on anything as you did on this place."

"You wield a pretty mean putty knife and paintbrush yourself, chum. As for thanking me, I seem to remember you promised me a candlelight dinner in that haunted turret of yours. Is that still on?"

"You'd better believe it! Come on, let's have that champagne while I play the mistress of the tower. Does this place have a name, by the way? I keep forgetting to ask."

"Hmm. Should have, a place this interesting with all that history. I don't know, to tell the truth. What would you call it if you had the choice?"

Annabel took a little skip around the room. "Well-l-l, something to do with the moon, I think, since every time I've been out here, everything looks silvery, and my first night sleeping upstairs I kept waking up to see the moon looking down at me."

"That ole black magic. How about Moonstone? There's a rock down there by the river that has been polished by the water for so long that it gleams in the moonlight like the real thing."

"Oh, I love it. Moonstone." Annabel peeked into the small bedroom, still awed at how nice it had turned out, with the chintz curtains and spread and the rug they'd found at an auction in Maidstone.

"You know what they say about moonstones. . . ." Roman said.

"No, what?"

"It's supposed to be a very magical piece of jewelry. I'm an amateur gemologist, by the way, and don't ask me to explain how that fits with pro football or anything else. I just got interested, that's all, when I was tracking down some amethyst lodes in north Georgia."

"I'm learning never to be surprised about anything you do. Come on, the moonstone. Dinner's cooking and so is my curiosity."

"Well, there's not much to tell, actually. It comes from India, from Sri Lanka, to be exact, near Dumkara. All precious and semiprecious stones have legends attached to them. It's said the moonstone always brings good fortune to its wearer and arouses passion in lovers."

"You made that up."

"No, I didn't. There are two things about me you can count on. I don't play games and I don't tell lies." Roman poured them more champagne. "Shall we go up and watch the last of the sunset from on high?"

"I'd like nothing better. You do know by now that I'm in love with this place."

"It did turn out well, didn't it? We make a good team in this decorating business." The lighthouse prints that Annabel had ordered from a friend on St. Simon's Island in Georgia had arrived that morning, and she had surprised Roman with them when he'd arrived. "I think the prints will go great on the landings, don't you? I really like the silver gray color, too. Thanks for steering me away from the beige."

"Beige is too neutral for whoever stayed here. Who did, by the way? I know that the Sheffields were here from medieval times up till Newton Fenmore took the estate over in—1818? 1819? But who lived in this tower? It reeks of history, emotional and otherwise. I swear, when I was cleaning the windows in the turret, I saw pictures of the past, of swans swimming . . ."

"Of lords leaping . . ." Roman laughed as they reached the top of the tower. "Oh, boy, does something smell good. When my chef told me you'd ordered something special for tonight, I knew I was in trouble."

"Armand and I worked out a wonderful menu. I hope you like it." Annabel lifted the top off the chafing dish she'd had set up along with a bowl of tossed salad. "Voilà! My famous shrimp, artichoke, and cheese casserole. Your chef says he's planning to add it to the menu at Roman's."

"I'm beginning to think you have my entire staff wrapped around your little finger." Roman touched a finger to the savory dish and licked it. "Umm. The Romantics would have loved this."

"Byron especially. Of all of them, I guess he's my choice for the one I'd like to have met in person. What a life he led! That crazy mother, making him drag around his poor deformed foot in a great iron box, the women who camped outside his apartment in London, even Shelley's sister-in-law Clare and maybe his wife Mary, too . . ."

"Hey, I'm getting jealous. Come back to the present and this wonderful food. And this."

Roman gently took Annabel by the hand and led her over to the glassed-in window seat that they had covered in rose and teal chintz that depicted swans and English hunting scenes.

"Look at that river! Oh, if it could only tell its stories. If this tower could talk . . . Roman, stop that. Nibbling is for the casserole, I'll thank you to remember."

"It's not easy," Roman murmured, his lips at the neck of the soft voile Victorian dress Annabel had donned to be in keeping with the mood of the evening. "There seems to be some magic working in this place. I find myself wanting to . . ."

"Eat," Annabel said firmly, handing him a plate off the fine hunt table they'd found at the flea market in Maidstone. "You're leaving for the States tomorrow for two weeks, remember, and this may be the last real meal you'll get before landing in Atlanta."

Roman loaded up his plate, carefully counting out his share of the shrimps and artichokes. "I wish I didn't have to do this, but there's no way I can get out of it. That old coach was good to me, mighty good to me, and I can't miss the retirement wingding they're throwing for him. He'd be real hurt."

"Oh, you." Annabel laughed. "I still haven't gotten over you telling Morris Keller those dreadful redneck jokes when we had lunch the other day. He must've choked five times, I swear."

"That man's a snake with shoulders," Roman said, suddenly going serious. "Annabel . . ."

"Drink," she told him, handing him a glass of wine.

After dinner, they had coffee and brandy on the window seat, counting the stars until Roman would have no more of putting off what lay between them. "Enough astronomy and star-gazing. I want you to gaze into my eyes and tell me how much you'll miss me."

She did as commanded—and more. Roman drew a deep breath at the shy kiss on his scarred cheek. "You don't know what that does to me."

He took her in his arms and proceeded to show her.

"Wow," Annabel said, emerging shakily from the most thorough kiss she'd had since high school necking days. "I think you could call that a completed pass."

"You're finally getting the terminology of my game," Roman whispered, going back for more.

His lips claimed hers, gently at first and then with a ferocity that made her cry out. "I would never hurt you, my darling," he said, taking the combs from her hair so that the captured dark tresses spilled onto her shoulders. "My God, you are so beautiful, so delicious . . . Annabel, Annabel, where have you been all these years? It took me so long to find you. I knew you were there, I just couldn't find you."

The muscled bulk of him held her safe against the world, against the loneliness that had haunted her. As Roman caressed her, kissed her, began the preliminaries to passion, she closed her eyes, feeling the magic of knowing a familiar love. The room was a carousel of emotion, of feelings pent-up for centuries. Annabel could no more have stopped it than she could have flown to the moon.

"I'm not hurting you, am I?"

"No, it's just that I haven't been in a man's arms in such a long time that I'd forgotten what it felt like."

"I hope it feels as good to you as it feels to me."

Annabel lifted her face for a tender kiss. "It does," she whispered. "It really does. And to have this happening in this place . . . !" She looked around the room, marveling that the moon had embellished the soft candlelight with silver. "I feel that this turret holds magic, not just for me but for you, too."

"I'm holding the real magic in my arms," Roman murmured, his lips trailing down from Annabel's lips to the low vee in her gown. "You should have kept on your paint-spattered cut-offs. I can't resist this nineteenth-century delectability."

"I don't really want you to," Annabel whispered. She was feeling a pressing in from the room, a sense of history repeating itself. She closed her eyes to revel in the potent sensuality that filled the air like the scent of magnolias.

Roman was a surprisingly gentle lover. When he bent Annabel back on the moonlit couch, he was exceedingly careful not to overwhelm her slender frame with his weight. "You're so fragile," he whispered. "I want you so much but I'm afraid I'll crush you."

"I'm not afraid," she said, looking up into his eyes as he leaned over her. "You're my protector, not my enemy." She kept saying that, not knowing where the term was born. "My protector," she whispered. "Love me."

He kissed her, his own body trembling now as hers had earlier. "I spent a big part of my life protecting the man carrying the ball. Now I feel somehow that I'm supposed to protect you."

"Speaking of which . . ." Annabel laughed softly and traced his scar with her finger. "Can I count on you for that?"

"You can count on me for anything," he told her huskily. He took the precaution to which she referred and was soon back to resume where he'd left off.

Annabel knew from the moment his hands burned her tenderest flesh that this was the man she'd waited for all these . . . centuries? That was scary, too scary. She caressed Roman's body, keeping the delicious sensations he aroused in her in the present, not to be wasted on the past.

Her breasts enchanted him. When he freed them from her gown, he kissed each pink-tipped mound lovingly. "If I only were a poet," he murmured, savoring the reponse she made to the sweet tugs. He stroked her with maddening slowness, loving the arching moves of her thighs as he aroused her.

"You are a poet, just without the words." Annabel caught a glimpse of the stars beyond her lover's shoulders and thanked them for sending Roman to her. "You hold the rhythm of the universe inside you and I feel it in my blood. Hold me, hold me, never let me go." The room echoed their impassioned breathing, their love cries and moans, and Annabel knew at last where the seat of poetry lay. . . .

He tangled her hair in his hands as their need for more closeness reached a crescendo. Annabel felt that the turret room was swirling with her feelings, that the velvet night outside the window was a soft blanket around her nakedness. She heard herself saying things she'd never even thought as the intensity within her deepest being mounted unbearably.

Roman was moved by her vulnerability to him. "Are you sure, my darling? Are you sure this is what you want?"

"Yes. Yes!" Annabel was so sure that she helped guide him to the moist haven awaiting. The room seemed to sigh when they united, though Annabel did not hear for the sound of her pounding heart.

"Oh, Roman, Roman. I never knew it could be like this."

He held her tight. "It's never been that way for me, either. It's like . . . well, like I've been waiting for you for a long, long time. I know that sounds corny, but it's true. Annabel Poe, I can't believe I've found you at last."

"It's this room," she said, her words muffled against his chest. "There's something here that was waiting for both of us. Don't you feel that?"

"I can't feel much of anything except pure wonder at having you in my arms. Thank God you came here, for whatever reason."

She pulled his hand from her hair and kissed it. "I thought it was a professional reason. Now I'm not so sure."

"Whatever reason, you're here now. Damn, I hate leaving you!"

"You'll be back."

"Promise me you'll be here waiting for me."

"Only if you promise, cross your heart and hope to die, that you'll come back to me. Hold me," she whispered. "And swear it, that you'll come back to me."

"I swear it." Roman's mouth sealed the promise and assuaged Annabel's hunger for assurance. Their lovemaking this time held the intensity of two people committing to each other for a lifetime.

Annabel held the gaily wrapped package that her lover had slipped into her hand as she was seeing him out the door. "The darling." She started unwrapping the box, smiling at the memory of how romantic Roman could be.

The black cat came up to Annabel as she was going back inside. "Well, hello there, Moonbeam. You're such a pretty pussy. Want some leftover shrimp? Oh, dear, there isn't any. Milk?"

The creature wound itself around her legs when she brought a bowl of milk and placed it on the stoop, ignoring her offering. "Oh, you're an indoors kind of cat, are you? Well, I don't know what my landlord will say about taking on a roommate but I happen to have plenty of room . . ."

She let the purring animal come inside with her. It waited patiently while she locked doors and turned out lights.

The feline demanded that Annabel stop all the fuss and pay attention to more important matters—such as her.

"Oh, you! What a lover you are." Annabel stroked the silky fur and looked into the yellow-green eyes that held the uncanny knowing that some felines have. "Don't get too attached. I won't be in England forever, you know."

The cat left her and started for the stairs to the turret room. It waited till she reached the landing to her bedroom, then darted higher. "Oh, no, you don't. I'm off to bed, we'll clear up that mess first thing in the morning."

The cat stood and looked at her expectantly.

Annabel laughed. "Well, have it your way, then. I wanted one more look at the river by moonlight, anyway. Oh, aren't you fast on your feet!"

The cat bounded ahead, stopping to look back from the top landing, to make sure her newly adopted human was following. "I'm coming, I'm coming!"

Annabel smiled at the mussed pillows on the window seat, remembering their amorous activities there. "Sweet," she murmured aloud. "So very sweet."

The moonlight was eerily brilliant in the room. Outside, the owls hooted and a soulful loon gave off its plaintive cry. Annabel wondered if her body in its new sensual awakening was more attuned to the night. She felt tingles everywhere, from her scalp to her toes, as though she were on a liftoff to the stars. Then she missed the cat. "Where are you? Where are you, puss? Don't hide from me, now."

The cat jumped down in front of her, startling her. "Oh, so there you are." Annabel reached down to pet the animal, but it swiftly moved away and prostrated itself on the small rug in the center of the stone floor.

"So you want to play," Annabel said, laughing and getting down to combat the batting, playful paws. "Ouch!" She licked her finger where the cat had caught her.

The cat was disdainful of the wound she'd inflicted, instead applying her energy to pulling the small fringed rug away. Though Annabel scolded, the cat persisted, pulling the rug completely off the stones it covered.

While Annabel watched, the animal stuck her slender paw into the crevice around a loose stone and then looked up at Annabel, her expression clearly communicating that she had done as much as she could and it was now up to Annabel.

Annabel cursed as one of her nails broke when she tugged at the stone. "I don't know why I let you talk me into this, cat. Oh . . . there it is. It's coming! Oh, dear Lord. What is this?" The stone was lifted, and Annabel's heart pounded when she saw the sealed packet stained with age. Gingerly she lifted it out, almost afraid to open it for fear of what she might find.

The wrapping of oilskin was mottled and musty. Annabel brushed her hands on her skirt as she carefully untied the packet.

"What's this?" The crackly paper that lined the packet was discolored and fragile. Annabel lovingly smoothed out the parchment and pulled the candle over closer to peruse the spidery writing that filled the page.

She gasped when she saw a faded note in the margin. "John Keats! Keats wrote on this! Oh, God, cat, what have you uncovered here?"

The cat had since discovered a cricket and wasn't interested in Annabel's find.

Annabel felt awe as she softly read the words:

To Isobel in Her Garden

Thou lady with voice of cooing dove tone,
Thou step-sister of nature and healing time,

Moonspell

Flower nurturer, who can thus write on a green-
    ing tale more nicely than our rhyme—
What leaf-arbored legend murmurs about thy
    shape of night love or noon dally, or both?
In dreams or the dales of fantasy?
Are we gods or men, thou maiden both
To answer pursuit with struggle to escape?
What face seest thou in wild ecstasy?

Ah, happy, happy maid! Thou will not lose thy
    bloom, nor ever bid thy youth adieu;
And, happy gardener, mayst choose
Forever budding blossoms over new.
For life is love, happy in a better shape of love,
Sun everwarming, a heart to be enjoyed
Forever gentle, and forever young,
Thus breathing human passion far above
A dimmer soul rich only in restraint and cloyed
With coy refusals and denying tongue.

What? Mayst not thou be lured to the dear
    sacrifice
On some green altar? Oh shy priestess
Tending thy garden under amber-lit skies,
All the silken lips of flower-kind speechless
With yearning of untold joy thou yet resists.
My pretty poesy is writ to spell
A freer time with love in careless morn.
And yet will thou turn away unkissed
Will silent be, and not a soul to tell

59

Nelle McFather

Why thou art weeping, weeping amongst the
willow fern.

For my darling cousin

Jeremy Harker Simmons

Annabel sank to the window seat, overcome
by the emotion she felt upon reading what she
knew to be the original of a poem she had
perused numerous times. A poem by Newton
Fenmore. "But what does this mean? Newton
Fenmore's poem was to his sister, Felicia.
Something's crazy here. Isobel! Who's Isobel?
For that matter, who's Jeremy? Oh, God, what
am I expected to do? I feel a presence; I feel you
calling to me, depending on me for something.
What? What can I do? How can I help you?
Isobel! I feel your sorrow as though it were
mine! You're the one I dream of. What became
of you? Why did I come here? Dear God, what
is happening to me?"

Trying to hold on to the reality of the moment,
Annabel clutched the present that Roman had
given her. "What's happening to me, darling?
Does it have something to do with you and me?"
She shakily opened the lid to the box and cried
out when she saw what lay inside.

It was an old moonstone pendant whose
gleam matched the moonlight. She put it to

60

her burning cheeks and then with shaking fingers put it around her throat.

The turret seemed to be spinning, with her at its vortex.

The gray sea swept her on a watery passage through time, toward a past destiny that would become her future.

The dizzying tunnel of waves ended where it had begun, at Sheffield Hall, only the time was not Annabel's, it was Isobel's.

And Annabel somehow knew she was being transferred to that time.

"Isobel! Isobel, where are you?" She heard a voice calling, a man's voice. Annabel heard the voice and fought her bewilderment.

Annabel had no choice. Whoever Isobel was, she was at the center of this mystery, the mystery that was propelling Annabel into the past. Whatever was happening, for whatever reason, Annabel had to go along with it and hope for the best. She reached up to touch the moonstone and found it gone. The window to her own time had apparently been shut behind her.

As the gray sea of confusion receded, Annabel found herself still standing in the tower room, but it was morning now, and the man's voice was louder, nearer, calling, "Isobel."

Chapter Four

There was a pounding of feet on the stairs, and the turret door flew open. Annabel was clasped in a warm bear hug by a tall, blond young man. Her utter confusion went unnoticed in the exuberance of his welcome.

"Oh, look at you, my darling cousin, more beautiful even than your sainted mother. Isobel, Isobel, why did you not wait for us to meet you, to bring you here from the boat? A lone girl like you, so very pretty, how could you be so brave as to travel here all by yourself?"

"Who . . . who are you?" Annabel asked, breathless from the hugs and the overpowering shock of finding herself in another century.

"Your cousin Jeremy, of course. Don't you recognize me from the miniatures we sent you? I saw a light in the tower, a very bright light, and then it went dark. When I caught a glimpse of a woman at the window I guessed it must be you, though I couldn't imagine how you'd gotten here. Tremaine's gone to London, you know, to meet your ship."

"Tremaine?" Annabel asked weakly.

"Yes, my stepbrother. Oh, if you knew how thrilled we were to get your letter saying that you were coming to England for a visit. When your mother married and moved to America, I was only six, but I remember how beautiful she was and how my own mother grieved that her sister was going away. Then you were born, and somehow the years just went by and . . . oh, Isobel, how I wept when I got your letter. My joy over your saying you were coming was great, but how sad that you lost both your parents. It was a miracle that you escaped the fire which destroyed your home."

Annabel was paying close attention to the account. It was important to learn about this Isobel for whom she was apparently being mistaken. "It was a very sad time," she said.

"Oh, yes, but now you have me, you have Tremaine, and of course Greymalkin, my crazy old nanny, for what that's worth." Jeremy didn't know that with the mention of his step-brother's name, he had stirred turmoil in her heart. Was he the man Annabel had dreamed of so often? "That's a miniature of Tremaine over there on the dresser, isn't it?" It was a replica of the one from her dreams.

"Notice I have the one of you that you sent us positioned cozily between the two of us. Funny, the picture was dampened and blurred in the post, but I recognized you right away."

"You're not a bit alike, are you?"

Jeremy smiled as he looked at the miniature. "Except for our builds, which are similar, we are exact opposites. Look at Tremaine, scowling even when he's being painted, so dark and commanding. In contrast, look at me with my mother's lamblike look of innocence, all blue-eyed and blond-haired, like an Eton schoolboy."

"I think you are marvelously handsome," Annabel blurted out honestly.

Jeremy laughed, but she could tell he was pleased with the compliment. "Well, it's the fellow in front who has to put up with my looks. Which brings me to a compliment of my own—for you. How on earth did my tiny blond aunt with her blue eyes and white skin produce a raven-haired, voluptuous, green-eyed daughter with skin like a sun-kissed nectarine?"

Annabel let herself be guided to the mirror atop the dresser, where she could compare her own looks to the woman in the painting. The dark hair was truly close to that in the dim miniature. Eye color was not discernible in the picture, but the match was near enough. Whoever Isobel was, Annabel's looks were similar enough that Jeremy had mistaken her for the cousin he'd been expecting from America. "A raven's nest is closer to the proper description of my hair. My, it's a mess."

"Greymalkin has a magic touch with coiffures. She'll fix you up."

Jeremy was so elated about seeing his cousin that he hadn't noticed some of the oddities about her presence. During the middle of his excited chatter, he stopped suddenly and asked, "Where on earth is your valise? Your trunk?"

Annabel's heart beat fast as she struggled to come up with a good reason for her lack of baggage. "There was no trunk, Cousin." She lowered her eyes in sadness. "Almost everything I owned was destroyed in the fire. As for my valise with its poor pitiful contents, some unfortunate who stole it while I was negotiating for a carriage to bring me here is probably even now throwing it in the Thames in total disgust."

"Oh, I'm sorry." Jeremy was abject at the thought that he might have humiliated his cousin. "Well, we'll outfit you properly as soon as we get you settled, you can count on that. Now, dear Isobel, shall we have tea? Cook will be sending Greymalkin to fetch us to breakfast soon, but right now I want you all to myself."

Annabel took the steaming cup of tea gratefully. It had been a cold passage, she thought, shivering at the memory of the waves that had seemed to engulf her. "And I want to learn everything there is to know—about you, about Tremaine, about Sheffield Hall. There is so much to catch up on." Just a couple of lifetimes. "Start with you. Is this where you live? I saw a bedroom on my way up." Actually, the bedroom she'd seen was in Annabel's time, not Isobel's, but there was a good chance that much hadn't changed.

"Well, yes, you might say that. I sleep over here when I'm working late so I won't disturb the people at the Hall with my ungodly writing habits."

"So you're a writer." Annabel leaned forward eagerly. Maybe she and Jeremy actually were soul cousins! "What do you write?"

Jeremy said modestly, "Well, not much of anything, really. I'm doing some . . . political writings that would bore you to tears."

"And . . . ?" Annabel prodded.

"Well . . . I write a little poetry now and then. Nothing to get excited about, you understand," he added hastily, seeing his cousin's eagerness.

"I would like nothing better than to be allowed to read some of what you've written."

"Oh, you wouldn't like it. Keats says I'm coming along, but that I've got to stop being such a dreamer and work harder."

John Keats. Annabel caught her breath. "See, you show your work to others, after all."

Jeremy's face showed the awe that his companion was secretly experiencing at the thought of her cousin knowing the greatest poet in England's Romantic period. "But Keats is a poet himself. He understands the agony of seeking the words one wants and the ecstasy of finding them. Isobel, something just occurred to me. Why on earth did you come up here instead of to the main door?"

Careful, now. "I . . . got out at the main gate to see if I was at the right house, and that dreadful coachman just drove off, leaving me there. This was the first place I saw, and the door was open, so I came on in. Oh, Jeremy, you have to overlook my gawkiness. Just chalk it up to my being American. I'd never seen anything like this before." *Well, not until years later*, she justified to herself.

Jeremy grinned. "It's quite a place, isn't it? Actually, I fell in love with Sheffield Hall the first time I saw it, not just this tower but the whole place. My mother came

Annabel's look. "Well, he *did* have a few reservations about a young American lady fitting in here. I mean, we hear all these stories about wild Indians and women who shoot rifles to protect their families and who work out in the fields side by side with their men and . . . damn it, Isobel, stop looking at me like that!"

"When can I meet your friends?" Annabel made a mocking curtsy. "That is, if you think my manners are up to snuff."

"Sooner than you think," Jeremy said enthusiastically. "As soon as Tremaine gets back from London, we plan to have a lovely party for you. How you'll charm them! I can hardly wait."

"Neither can I. I presume you'll include some of your writing friends, such as, perhaps, this Keats person you mentioned?" It was very hard to keep the question casual.

"Oh, I should like nothing better, but poor Keats's brother Tom has been quite ill, and John is only waiting for him to rally somewhat before taking off on a very long tramp with a dear friend."

"I should very much like to meet your friend Keats if there's any time before he leaves."

"Well, of course you shall, and his friend Brown and his fellow poets Byron and Shelley, too, if we can make a trip to Italy as I've planned for you. Oh, Isobel, I have so much planned for your stay! Please say that you'll not return to

America for a very long time."

"I can't make any promises about that," came the truthful answer. "But I can tell you this much. I won't leave this place without seeing those friends of yours, and you can go to the bank with that."

"I beg your pardon?"

"Oh, just another of our little American sayings. I meant that you can count on my staying until I've had a chance to meet your poetry-writing colleagues."

"To call them 'colleagues' is an injustice to them. If you could only read the draft of 'Endymion' that Keats honored me by showing me in its early stages, you'd know that my poetry is mere doggerel."

"Who else might be at the party, if I might be so bold?" Isobel looked at her cousin teasingly. "Besides all the young women around here who are in love with a certain handsome young man."

"Oh, you've got me confused with Tremaine, who's the real Don Juan of the county. Felicia Fenmore has been after him since she and her brother took the old Scott house. She and Newton moved out here from London where he's a member of Parliament, they say to avoid the hustle and bustle of the city."

This was interesting news! "This Newton Fenmore, is he also a writer?"

Jeremy roared with laughter. When he finally stopped, he said, "I'm sorry, I should not be so hard on poor Fenmore. He has such an exalted opinion of the little rhymes that he's always writing—and reading aloud whenever given the slightest encouragement."

"Well, I shall certainly avoid doing that at the party."

"No good, he always sees to it that someone clamors for a reading of his latest 'poesy.' I heard a rumor that he plans to have one of his poems dedicated to Parliament orally and written into the minutes."

"Dear Lord, what a menace. So he's really, really bad?"

Jeremy looked thoughtful. He was a kind man, too kind to be mean-spirited in talking about an aspiring poet. "Well, I tried to be generous when he asked for criticism. But Keats said it best after he'd met Fenmore. (The chap kept pestering me to let him go along with me on a visit and I finally gave in.) Keats said after hearing 'England, Dear England' that he hoped that Fenmore was better at drafting Parliamentary laws than he was at penning rhyme."

They had a good laugh together over that. Annabel was getting an introduction to the poet she'd chosen for her thesis topic that was altogether different from her expectation.

Chapter Five

Annabel was glad when Jeremy was sent word that breakfast would be served shortly at the great house. She was starving. The tea had only whetted her appetite.

As she and Jeremy walked across the broad expanse of grounds, she marveled at the view of the river, at the terraced lawns sweeping down to a small dock where boats were moored for the pleasure of the Hall's guests. "It's so beautiful," she said, pausing to admire the colorful summer gardens that flanked the many walkways. "I like your tower best of all, though." She looked back at it. "Just look at it, like some sentinel lighthouse guarding Sheffield Hall."

Jeremy took her hand and led her up the broad stairs to the entrance of the manor. "Now who's the poet? Stop here a moment on the buttress and see if you feel the ghosts as I always do. Greymalkin's cat always perches here and gazes into space as if she sees amazing things."

Maybe she was seeing people coming in from Roman's parking lot. "I'm not particularly psychic."

"I beg your pardon?" Jeremy laughed. "Oh, another of your Americanisms. Perhaps you can teach me the modern English language."

"I don't think you want to know some of it. Oh, Jeremy, can it be . . . is it really . . . that's a *maze!* A real maze! Oh, do tell me there's some secret at its center."

"All I'll tell you is to stay out of it unless you want to spend a very long time finding your way out. Oh, here's Greymalkin now." The front door opened just as Jeremy's hand enclosed the knob. "You've not met. Greymalkin, here's Isobel come from America."

Bright sunken eyes penetrated Annabel's as though they were looking clear through to the girl's soul and the secrets that lay there. "Yes, Jeremy, I know the visitor's name. Welcome, Lady, to our home and to England. I'll be helping you with your things after you've had a bite."

Jeremy whispered to the old woman about his cousin's dilemma, and the wrinkled eyelids flew open. "So we'll be using some of my mother's old things until we've had a chance to get to London."

"Miss, you were very quiet with your coachman from London. I can hear my cat snap a mouse's neck from my bedroom but I heard nary a sound of your arrival this morning."

Jeremy brushed that off, eager to get his guest fed after her harrying journey. "Dear lovable crone, don't stand here prattling about what you heard and didn't hear. We both know that your ears are no longer as sharp as they used to be, though they're still just as pointed."

The two laughed together, and Annabel knew that Jeremy's banter, sharp though it seemed on the surface, covered a deep affection for the woman who had been his nanny. "My cat's been missing these two days and nights, Jeremy, and I don't know where to find him."

Jeremy whispered to Annabel as they went in the house behind the old woman, "Tremaine swears he's never seen both of them at the same time."

There was a cat in the tower, all right, but from which century? That was too mind-boggling to ponder.

*   *   *

It was strange seeing the great hall as it had been during the Sheffields' ownership. After breakfast Isobel was invited into the kitchen for a little tour with Maude and Todd, the cook and butler.

She was delighted to find that the couple drank coffee and carried mugs of the thick brew with them. "And you'll be having it with your morning breakfast from now on," Maude promised, nodding so vigorously that her gray-blond curls bobbed under her cap. "Todd'll bring it up to you without fail. I've never been a tea person meself, neither."

"So you made another hit," Jeremy told Annabel later when he collected her for a ride about the grounds while her room was undergoing final preparations. "Todd says you're 'a bit of all right,' and Maude says it's a shame you're blood since you'd be the perfect wife for me."

Annabel had to laugh. "I haven't done anything to deserve all this affection, I swear."

"Well, no matter, it's yours. And once Tremaine sees you, you'll have yet another admirer. By the way, he sent word that he's on his way home. Would it overwhelm you, dear cousin, if I had the gala we planned for you tomorrow night? Tremaine will be here tomorrow afternoon. He was making a stop or two on his way, or he'd be home tonight."

"That's fine. Tomorrow night's fine. Just remember how limited my wardrobe is at this point."

"Oh, that's all taken care of. Lady Felicia Fenmore has already gotten the word—via the maids' grapevine, I suppose—that you're in rather a bind with regard to your wardrobe, but she will see to it that you're dressed fittingly."

I just bet she will. Maude and Todd had let drop enough little tidbits about the venerable Lady Fenmore to complete a picture of a young woman who would brook no competition from the upstart cousin from America. "I'm sure she will." Annabel wished that the moonstone, Roman's gift, had made it back with her so that she could wear it to the gala. "I just wish I had some fancier jewelry." The image of the necklace flashed through her consciousness. When would that magical ornament show up again? she wondered.

"Come on, you don't need jewelry. Your eyes are like peridots, your hair shiny ebony, your ruby lips encase a smile of pearls that light up any room you're in like diamonds in the sun." Before she could protest such effusive praise, Jeremy laughed at his own excess. "Never mind telling me how poor that imagery is. Shelley has told me enough times that I need to let the reader draw his own elaborate picture from sparse description."

"Shelley?" This weakly. "Percy Bysshe Shelley?"

Jeremy nodded. "I thought I mentioned him to you already. He's a fine poet, but totally overwhelmed with awe at Byron. I suspect it's because Byron has women camping on his doorstep at all hours, longing for one word from his lips."

"I loved Shelley's poems, too."

Jeremy looked at her with the same puzzled look she was beginning to get used to. "You surprise me."

"Enough so that maybe you'll allow me to see some of your writings?"

"Maybe. Come on, we have time for a ride along the river before lunch."

"We just finished breakfast!" Annabel wailed. "And besides, I can't ride in this."

"Greymalkin's laying out a set of my riding clothes from when I was fifteen. You'll look adorable in them. And besides, the horses don't care what you wear, and I certainly don't."

Annabel was glad she was an accomplished horsewoman, though she didn't ride English style. But by the time she emerged looking surprisingly dapper in the sage green riding pants and jacket and a small black derby that matched the jabot at her throat, she was looking forward to the experience.

Thank goodness for all those hours she'd spent at the stables when she was growing up. No doubt Isobel, with her background, had been an excellent horsewoman.

"By Jove, you ride like a highwayman outrunning the sheriff." Jeremy caught up with his cousin and let his horse along with hers catch a spot of drink at the river's edge. "Where on earth did you learn to ride like that?"

Annabel dampened the pretty handkerchief she'd found in the jacket pocket before answering. "It's just something American girls like to do. Everybody in America rides. But our horses were never so blooded as these." Annabel patted her sleek black mare. "Lady Godiva here is a real trouper. We understand each other very well."

"Then consider her yours while you're with us. Tremaine likes that wild-eyed stallion that you saw pawing and stomping around the stall when we saddled up. Don't ever try to ride that horse. That's how Tremaine had his accident. Or so he said at the time."

"Accident?"

"Trey never liked talking about it, so I suppose I shouldn't." Jeremy changed the subject, pointing out a flock of swans swimming toward them. "If I could ever capture the grace of those birds with my poetry, I would write about them, but I never can match some things in nature."

Annabel remounted Lady Godiva and gave dutiful attention to the swans, but her mind was on what Jeremy had just told her about Tremaine. He would be home the next day, and deep in the heart of her, she knew her life would never be the same again.

After lunch, Annabel retired to the room that Greymalkin had made up for her and slept for four fitful hours till she heard the bell for tea.

"All these people do is eat and drink," she moaned when the knock came at her door. "Come in. Oh, Maude, how wonderful. You brought my coffee up. Does that mean I don't have to go down and gorge myself again on whatever delectable confections you've loaded on the tea tray?"

"It means that Master Jeremy thought you'd had quite enough doings for one day after your hard ride. He said Lady Fenmore sent word she'd be over about ten in the morning and you're to sleep late and ring for your breakfast. Lord Tremaine will be coming in tomorrow a bit late-ish, but you're not to worry about presenting yourself till right before the party."

Annabel yawned and pushed her hair away from her face. The coffee was wonderful and so was the rich Devonshire cream. "What's he like, Maude? Really, I mean."

"Lord Tremaine? Ah, he's a hard man to figure, always has been since Todd and I first came here when he was small. I know he was born to money and rich blood, but there was always something about him that spoke of more than that. Like a prophet, if you'll excuse me. He said there would always be an England, but unless some changes were made and made soon, the England we knew wouldn't be here."

"Jeremy said he had some sort of dreadful accident, something that involved that beautiful horse he rides."

"Mordred? Aye, there were those who couldn't believe Lord Tremaine didn't put the horse to death after that, but he wouldn't have it."

"After what?"

"Ooh, you're getting some fine color in your cheeks after that nice ride and your nap. I'll report back to that anxious cousin of yours that you're doing just dandy and will be seeing everyone all bright and bushy-tailed come morning."

"Maude . . ."

"Good night, Miss. Sleep tight and don't let the bedbugs bite."

Annabel hugged her knees in exasperation, wondering if anyone was ever going to give her a straight answer about Tremaine Sheffield's accident.

Maybe he would.

*   *   *

Annabel awakened the next morning to a bright English morning, an acute sense of excitement, and the delicious smell of coffee. On the other side of the huge silver tray being held at her nose was a beaming Jeremy.

"Top of the morning to you!"

"And to you. Umm, what a wonderful way to wake up." Annabel sat up in bed, almost swallowed by the nightshirt Maude had lent her. "Not fresh hot cross buns!" she said after a big sip of coffee and a look under the silver-domed dish from which an incredible aroma was drifting. "And marmalade and kippers and eggs . . ." Annabel covered up the tempting dish and looked at her cousin accusingly. "Lady Felicia has no doubt put you up to fattening the American up like Gretel for the wicked witch."

Jeremy laughed. "Felicia is considered a beauty, which she's never been heard to dispute, but her face and figure don't hold a candle to yours. Come on, eat up. We've a busy day and night ahead and not a minute to waste if we're to get you ready for your English debut."

Annabel dug in, "I'm not sure I like that terminology. You're not going to make a fuss about introducing me formally or anything, are you?"

"I won't have to. Everyone's dying to meet

you. Newton Fenmore has sent a note begging for the honor of having you at his side at dinner. He sent flowers as well, which I took the liberty of passing along to Maude for arranging. You must be careful of the man. He's a legendary womanizer, though frankly I can't see what any woman would see in him."

"Then you can be sure I won't, either. Jeremy, has your stepbrother come in yet?" Annabel lost her appetite as she thought about what Tremaine would say about not finding her on the packet. Would he expose her lies about how she'd gotten here? Throw her out as an impostor?

As if in answer to her worried speculation, Jeremy said, "In fact, I had breakfast with him before his ride on Mordred. He looked a little funny at me when I jumped in with my babble about you and your mishaps, and said very little except to ask if you were as pretty as the miniature you sent us. I said, even prettier, and he looked even grimmer, as though he didn't know quite what else to say. I think he's probably in love with you already, Cousin."

"Not likely," Annabel said. It was more likely that Lord Sheffield was keeping some very serious suspicions to himself until he had a chance to meet the vagabond American cousin in the flesh. "Now, let me get out of bed and dress before our visitor arrives. I shouldn't like Lady Fenmore to catch me at a disadvantage."

When Jeremy had left, taking the tray with him, Annabel looked in the mirror, wondering if Tremaine would go along with his stepbrother's acceptance of the American cousin who had appeared in such a mysterious way. She hoped so, though she had a feeling that Tremaine wasn't the pussycat his half-sibling was.

The rumble of a carriage and a woman's carrying voice giving directions about boxes brought Annabel back to the business at hand: preparing to meet Lady Felicia Fenmore, whose Lady Bountiful role was no doubt an excuse to have a good look at the visiting cousin before the evening gala.

Annabel barely got her hair pulled up in its ribbons and a touch of powder to her nose before her boudoir was invaded by servants laden with boxes, and right behind her entourage, Lady Fenmore.

Over more tea that Jeremy had sent up before leaving for a ride with his stepbrother, the two women took careful stock of each other.

"Well," Lady Fenmore said, looking Annabel up and down. "I expected someone strapping and plain, but you could be one of us."

Annabel laughed at Lady Fenmore's patronizing words, though she didn't much like the implication about women from her country. "My dear Lady Fenmore, you must remember that those of us who settled in north Florida and Georgia came of good English stock. The idea your people have of scalawags, criminals, and riffraff populating the colonies has some basis in fact, but there were many good men— and women—who had the courage to pioneer a country filled with 'savages.'"

Annabel's history lesson went unappreciated. Its object was more interested in assessing her new rival. "You're actually very pretty." Lady Fenmore circled Annabel like a predator deciding where to take the first bite. "The hair's not a wig, I take it. And you're not wearing stays." Sharp hazel eyes took in the fall of soft dark hair and expertly assessed the size of Annabel's bosom and waist.

Annabel looked at the impossible dark red of Lady Fenmore's piled masses of curls. Henna had been known for centuries, and this woman had apparently taken advantage of it. "Good gracious, no. I don't even wear a bra when I can help it."

"Bra?" Thinly arched eyebrows lifted.

Annabel lied hastily, "A short term for the corsets and stays that some of my compatriots use to lift their bosoms and press in their waists. Oh, do let me see what you've got there." Annabel changed the dangerous subject, pretending interest in the array of dresses the servant had spread out on the window seat. "How pretty." She lifted up a shimmery crimson silk gown lined with beads. "This is just my color. May I try it?"

"I think that would be wrong for you, now that I've seen you. Too vivid. Try this one."

Annabel smiled secretly on seeing the plain, buff-colored frock that Lady Fenmore was holding out. "Wouldn't the high neck and tight long sleeves be inappropriate for a festive evening such as Jeremy says we'll be having?"

Lady Fenmore tossed her head. "Oh, that boy is such a romantic, one can't listen to what he says. Actually, Tremaine is rather stodgy and enjoys convention."

It was Annabel's turn to raise her eyebrows. Why had she gotten a very different impression of the man who would be her host at the dinner-dance tonight? "Really? Well, if I may ask, what are you wearing?"

The woman had the grace to blush. "Well, there are so few social events out here in the country. I have a gown that was specially made for me in Paris which is a bit on the daring side, but since I've nothing else to wear . . ."

Annabel said wickedly, "You could take the buff-colored gown. It would match your . . ."

she didn't say "roots," as much as she would have liked ". . . skin tones, which are quite lovely."

Lady Fenmore hadn't paused in lifting the gown in question and waited a full minute before responding. Her smile would have made the leading actress at Drury Lane look unskilled at the art of dissimulation. "Oh, and aren't you kind! I can see that you and I shall have an . . . interesting time together." The smile got wider and more artificial. "Now, when was it that Jeremy told me you would be going back to your brave little colony in America?"

"I love England so much, I may just stick around for the next century," Annabel said devilishly.

Felicia Fenmore looked momentarily startled but pressed on with her notions of the New World. "We have heard so much about the beasts charging around on your prairies with the savages running about and those men on horses saving women from being scalped and worse."

"Lady Fenmore," Annabel pointed out gently, "I think you've got us mixed up with the wild wild west. I have never laid eyes on a buffalo, and while we did . . . do still have Indians who occasionally go on a binge after drinking too much firewater, the ones I've met wouldn't know what to do with a scalp." Annabel was glad she'd seen so many John Wayne western movies.

"Maybe you should try on the crimson dress. I didn't realize that Gwen, my maid, had included that item with the collection we brought for your perusal. It has a special history, that gown."

Annabel waited until the other woman had turned away to pull off the gown she was wearing and don the shimmery crimson dress. "Tell me about it. I love stories about England and any kind of history."

"Well, I don't know if this story is really historical, but those who passed it along seem to think it did occur. 'Twas during Tudor times, in Kent, when the notorious Henry the Eighth was ruling, when enclosures caused hard feelings. A legendary highwayman, said to be a nobleman, raided the shipments of wool bound for Calais and other parts. Well, Lord Blackheart fell in love with a beautiful miller's daughter and kidnapped her, making her part of his band."

Annabel's instinctive dislike for Lady Fenmore was momentarily derailed by her love of romantic history. "He gave her this very dress?" She smoothed out the folds of the voluminous material that was sliding down her hips like a man's sensuous hands. "But how could it have been preserved so many years?"

"That's part of the story. Lord Blackheart did present the crimson gown to his lady love. She wore it in their hideaway in the weald, but the gown was lost after her death. It was so much a part of the lore of the weald, though, that it could be reconstructed in every detail."

Annabel smoothed the fabric around her waist, glad she'd resisted the second hot cross bun. "I don't understand. This is not the original dress, then?"

"No. The one you're wearing is a copy of the one Lord Blackheart's sweetheart wore. At a Guy Fawkes celebration masquerade, I wore this dress, which I'd had made to commemorate the legend. My brother Newton wore a replica of Lord Blackheart's usual costume, with his black hood and dark clothes." She giggled. "He's a bit too plump to carry off the role of a dashing rogue, but he did so strut about that night."

Annabel felt a ripple of goose bumps along her arm. There were so many ghosts in this countryside! "I'm sure you made quite a pair."

"It was a lark, all right. Heaven knows we have few enough diversions in this provincial wasteland. That looks quite charming, I must say. Don't let yourself be seen out on the byways without someone to protect you. We have our own buccaneer who rides the roads by night."

Again, the prickles. "Lord Blackheart rides again, almost three centuries later? I thought

91

the problem of the enclosures was no longer an issue."

"There's always a new cause among English peasants," Lady Fenmore said with a sniff. "The one that has involved the Falcon in a series of strikes on royal favorites living in the counties is the Corn Laws issue. Perhaps you didn't know, you being off in America, about the law that was passed three years ago. Poor people, tenants and laborers—and some landowners—want it repealed and are passionate about it."

"Ah, yes. I . . . have heard about it." Actually, Annabel had learned about the controversial act which favored large British landowners, most of whom had power in Parliament, in her English history class in college. "Let's see, the laws were revised to prohibit import of foreign wheat until the British produce reached . . . I don't remember, but it was a very high price during hard times. After all, your people were . . . are just recovering from the impact of the Napoleonic Wars."

Lady Fenmore was apparently not sympathetic to the poor. "Eighty shillings. Hmph. High bread prices aren't nearly so distressing as rabble trying to dismantle sensible practices that have been in England longer than they have."

"Let them eat cake?" Annabel asked gently.

"Why . . . yes!" Lady Fenmore looked pleased. "I could not have put it better."

Nor could I, Annabel told herself, with apologies to Marie Antoinette for her plagiarism.

Chapter Six

Lady Fenmore left Annabel after one more futile attempt to persuade the American that the plainer gown was more becoming. "Well!" she said, departing in a huff. "I have my own preparations to see to. No need staying around offering good advice where it's obviously not wanted."

Annabel's thanks were brushed aside, as was her offer to share her room at the Hall should Lady Fenmore desire to dress there. "Certainly not! I must have my maid dress my hair. I find your Southern custom of staying at parties overnight quite unseemly. I daresay invitations there are given sparingly, since Southerners,

95

from what I hear, never know when to take their leave."

"Is that another subtle way of asking me when I'm planning to go back to America?" Annabel found the Englishwoman's airs more amusing than annoying. Lady Fenmore was definitely a woman of her century, she decided. "If it is, I have to content you with a vague answer. My visit will end when it . . . ends."

Lady Fenmore rolled her eyes at that. Annabel was glad she couldn't hear the comments the lady was making on her way down to her carriage where her servant patiently waited.

"And the same to you, sister," Annabel muttered as she gathered up the crimson gown to hang it in the wardrobe.

The house was throbbing with the activity of preparation for Lord Sheffield's return and the festive evening ahead.

"Oh, my God! Greymalkin, you scared me half to death."

The crone had entered as stealthily as a cat. She had appeared at the foot of the stairs just as Annabel was headed for the kitchen. "Nervous, are you? Over the master coming back and you never having laid eyes on him, or nervous over all the folks coming to look at you tonight?"

Annabel saw no need to answer that. "There are some boxes in my room. Would it be too much trouble to unpack them for me?" The less she satisfied the old woman's curiosity, the better. "Are Maude and Todd in the kitchen? I'd like to check on the dish they're preparing from my recipe."

Greymalkin's yellow-green eyes sparkled; her snaggle-toothed grin spread over her face. "Twarn't easy, talking 'em into cooking fowl like you wanted 'em to, but Maude and Todd is both taken with the American lady. You've got your ways, Miss, of winding yourself about a body like a cat wanting a new home."

"Thanks . . . I think." Annabel wondered if she would ever know what the old woman thought of her.

As the woman started up the long winding stairway from the hall, she stopped and asked, "Will you be wanting me to dress your hair? I always did your mother's 'fore she run off to London."

Annabel was pleased at the offer. Greymalkin had extended very few signs of friendliness since her arrival. The old woman spent most of her time around Annabel staring, muttering under her breath, and—Annabel was pretty sure of this—crossing herself. "Why . . . that would be very nice. I'd be honored to have my hair dressed after the fashion of my mother's."

The toothless grin widened, and Annabel had a wild hallucination that was as brief as it was startling. For a moment, Greymalkin's humped, aged appearance had melted and a beautiful young woman was smiling down at her.

Annabel stood transfixed for a moment as Greymalkin hobbled up the stone stairs. Then she headed for the kitchen to see how her English replication of Southern fried chicken was coming along. Getting the cook to use buttermilk instead of Devon cream had been a real feat.

"It's beautiful, Greymalkin. It truly is. You've got a magic touch with hair, no question about it."

The old woman stood back from Annabel and admired her handiwork. "My, it does look pretty, if I do say so. And pretty just isn't the right word for you, Miss Isobel." Greymalkin looked at the image in the glass, at the satiny ringlets that topped a vision of crimson and gold and cream. "I just wish you had a proper piece of jewelry to top off your beauty."

Annabel thought with a sigh of the moonstone pendant. It would have been perfect. "Well, I certainly wouldn't be able to match Lady Fenmore in the jewelry department, so I suppose it's just as well that I go plain."

The tap at the door startled them both. "What, is it time already?" Annabel felt her insides churn at the idea of finally meeting Tremaine

Sheffield. He'd been built up so much since she'd arrived that she was actually scared to meet the man behind all the legends.

"No, it's something for you." Greymalkin came back after opening the door and taking the small box that had been brought. "It's a parcel that was left at the far gate with your name on it. Todd says he didn't see who brought it, nor was there any name on the outside except yours."

The moonstone? Annabel banished that fantasy. She knew innately that when the moonstone was presented, it would not be presented anonymously and without ceremony. Her ticket back home would be returned to her at some point in the future, and she must allow that future to unfold.

She unwrapped the package and lifted out the contents. Ornate earrings spilled into her hand, with a necklace of the same design.

"Oh! How very beautiful. But who? . . . Greymalkin, are you sure Todd saw no one?"

The crone stared at the cascade of garnets encrusted with pearls. Then her eyes narrowed and she said in a sly voice, her long, curling nails grazing Annabel's earlobes as she fastened the jewels to them, "No, but they say the Falcon leaves pretty trinkets for ladies he fancies. Perhaps he's caught sight of you in the garden or riding by the river with your cousin."

Annabel's heart leapt. Ever since Lady Fenmore had brought up the name of the Falcon, she'd had that mysterious name in the back of her mind. *Silly,* she admonished herself. *You may be caught up in an amazing situation, but you're not the heroine in some swashbuckling romance.*

"Perfect." Annabel turned her head from side to side, loving the rich color that matched her dress and brought out the color in her cheeks. "If these are a gift from the Falcon, I hope I get a chance to tell him how much I admire his taste in jewelry."

"Pardon me, Miss Isobel." Todd, no phantom, was at the door, and he had a message from a very real person. "The master says he'd find it awkward to meet you for the first time in front of all his guests. He begs that you favor him with a visit on the balcony adjoining your bedroom and his."

"That's Lord Sheffield's bedroom, the one next to mine?" Annabel's eyes widened. "Oh, my Lord, Greymalkin. Is that proper in your England, for an unmarried lady to be staying right next door to an unmarried gentleman?"

Greymalkin's eyes twinkled. "Ah, if it's the master's wish, it is. But you mustn't worry, Miss, the master's too much the gentleman to take advantage of such an arrangement. I expect he wanted a chance to get to know you better."

But how much better and how quickly, Anna-bel worried. Her heart was tripping as she walked toward the double glass doors that Todd was holding open for her.

"Here goes nothing," she murmured as she walked out into the night to meet the lord of Sheffield Hall where she was a prisoner of time.

The dark figure at the end of the balcony looked larger than life in the moonlight. When Lord Sheffield turned to greet his guest, the light from his open bedroom doors fell upon his face, and it was all that Annabel could do to keep from letting out a cry.

A long, jagged scar ran from one temple, out-lining the left cheek and ending at the bottom of the strong jaw. As the man approached her, Annabel gathered her shocked wits the best she could and managed a shaky, "How do you do? I'm Jeremy's cousin from America." Well, sort of. Lying was getting easier. She thought fever-ishly about curtsying and then decided against it. She might get tangled up in her voluminous skirts and lose her balance which was already precarious.

"Introductions are redundant, don't you think, since I was the one who booked your trip here to England? But since we're being proper and formal, I am Tremaine Sheffield, your abject servant."

"Abject" was the last word that one would ever apply to this man. The elegant bow he made was half-mocking, Annabel decided. Tremaine Sheffield did not strike her as a man who would bow to many people. "It's very kind of you to have me here. I love England already and feel very much at home at Sheffield Hall. And getting the chance to know my cousin Jeremy is something I am deeply indebted to you for, Lord Sheffield."

Tremaine kissed the hand that Annabel held out daintily. She felt the edge of the scar against her flesh and shivered inside. Instead of revulsion, it made her think of . . . ? *Roman.* But the two men were centuries apart and had nothing to do with each other, she reminded herself. She'd had an immediate reaction to the man in her own century, she remembered, confused and unsure about what was happening to her now. Annabel didn't want to think about the reaction that she was having to this man whose presence seemed to overpower the night, whose aura bore a sense of reined power and strength that made her feel weak.

For God's sake, girl, don't swoon. You're a modern woman, remember, and men do not sweep us off our feet at first meeting.

"Then let that debt include a more intimate relationship with your cousin's best friend and patron." The man's smile widened at

Annabel's reaction to the word "intimate." "Call me Tremaine if you will. 'Lord' is not an earned title and you need not call me by it. Now, I noticed your surprise when you first laid eyes on me. Jeremy did not tell you about my disfigurement, did he?"

"Not . . . exactly, Lord Sheffield . . ."

"Tremaine. Well, that isn't surprising since the fellow has such a generous heart. He never thinks about my . . . hideous side." He walked over to the table and poured two goblets of wine. "Here." He handed her the cup and stood deliberately in the light so that his scar was easily visible. "Some women have told me this makes me even more romantic a figure, as Byron's limp makes him. Do you agree?"

Annabel wondered if she were being put to some kind of test, one whose failure would mean her immediate expulsion from Sheffield's largess. "I wouldn't put it exactly that way, though I do find the scar mysterious and would like to know how you got it." She waited, but when he said nothing, she continued. "You're a handsome man, Lord . . . Tremaine, and the scar certainly does nothing to take away from your appearance." She looked at the thick dark hair that reached broad shoulders, at the strong nose that had a hawklike hook, at the wide mouth whose touch on her hand had made her quiver, and said truthfully, "You rather remind me of a famous football player I met once . . ."

Annabel realized her slip even before Tremaine jumped on it. "Football player? Is that a reference to a gaming person?"

"Oh, that's just a figure of speech that's purely American. It's not worth explaining." Annabel took a hasty gulp of her wine. She had to be more careful about what she said if she wanted to remain welcome as Isobel. "Tell me, do you like the dress your friend Lady Fenmore kindly brought over for me to wear?"

Tremaine took the goblet from her hand and lightly twirled her about, making Annabel feel giddier than she already was. "Quite lovely on you; the color suits your hair and skin." He touched her hair lightly and let his hand trail down her cheek. "Very nice hair and skin. Until I saw the miniature of you, I thought most American girls were rawboned and freckled, especially those from the Southern colonies where even the women work the crops."

Where had these people gotten their ideas of American women? Isobel wondered, a little miffed. She pulled away from him. Lord Sheffield needed a couple of centuries of education about women, especially American women, she decided, but it was not her place to teach him. "We wear sunbonnets," she said sweetly. "Tremaine, I know we mustn't linger much longer, pleasant though it is, since your guests will be arriving shortly. But I must ask about these fascinating tales I hear of a man called the 'Falcon' who goes about the country raising Cain over the Corn Laws."

"Raising Cain?" Tremaine's good eyebrow peaked. "Another American expression, I suppose. I rather like it. Why on earth would you think that I might be familiar with romantic gossip of that sort? I'm a landowner with heavy responsibilities both here and in Calais and London where I maintain small business offices. The Falcon?" He laughed. "No doubt some puffed-up, disgruntled tenant who's trying to revive the old Lord Blackheart legend."

"This dress is a copy of the one Lord Blackheart gave his true love while they were hidden away in the weald."

"Know your history already, do you?" Tremaine reached out a finger and touched one of the dangling earrings Annabel was wearing. "Those are very pretty. Similar, in fact, to some that were stolen from the wife of Parliament member Lunsford last week."

Annabel put her hands over both her ears. "Oh, my lord! Stolen? I mustn't wear them, then. Dear God, what should I do? Stolen!"

"Did you steal them?"

"Of course not!"

"Then by all means wear them. They look

much better on you than on the Lady Lunsford, believe me. How *did* you get them, by the by?"

Annabel told him.

Tremaine was thoughtful. "Hmmm. So this so-called Falcon is moving into our territory, getting closer. Interesting. Well, little American mouse, it might behoove you to be more careful when you go out walking or riding. It sounds to me as if the Falcon has his eye on you as a tasty morsel and might swoop down upon you at any given moment."

"I thought you said all of this was just gossip."

"Isn't gossip the smoke of truth? Ah, they are arriving downstairs in droves and we must join them, as much as I hate to end this tête-à-tête. May I have the first dance? And the last?"

"I'll check my card," Annabel said, still unsure as to whether this man had been pulling her leg about the earrings or not.

She would hate to wind up in Newgate Prison on her first trip to England.

Chapter Seven

Newton Fenmore, Felicia's brother, made sure that Annabel's dance card was filled. He was one of the first men introduced to the American visitor and was already making a nuisance of himself as far as Annabel was concerned.

She didn't like anything about him and told Jeremy so at the first opportunity. "Jeremy, you've got to rescue me from this man! He hasn't let me take a breath since I got down here, and I'm sure once the dancing starts I'll never get away from him."

Jeremy, tall and handsome in his formal attire, grinned at his cousin. "You've really made a hit, not just with Newton, but with every other eligible man in this room." He eyed the row of dowagers with their charges, all sipping punch and looking over the room's pickings while trying to act blasé. "I've seen many a fierce, if admiring, glare from the marriage-broker corner. Dear cousin, I hope you do realize that young Newton is an heir apparent and quite ripe for a young wife."

Annabel fanned furiously, ducking behind Jeremy when she saw the man in question heading her way. She really couldn't abide the man's looks, his curling pinkish hair, which was matched at his nostrils and ears, the hint of a paunch, and above all, his fawning over her as though she were the last layer of a delicious trifle that he was trying to get to the bottom of. "He's so ripe, he smells. Why doesn't he pick on one of those unfortunate hopefuls lined up behind their mothers?"

"Because, dear Isobel, he has taken a fancy to you. Felicia told me so, in fact. She said her brother has never behaved like this about a young woman."

"She just wants to make sure I'm kept away from Lord Sheffield." Annabel hadn't missed the entrance of her host and the way Lady Fenmore had immediately attached herself to him and hadn't left his side as he moved through the ballroom greeting guests.. "It apparently runs in the family, this business of attaching oneself where one isn't particularly wanted."

"Why, Cousin, how ungracious of you! Was it not the Lady Fenmore herself who accommodated you with that most exquisite dress? The earrings, too, I wager?"

"You lose," Annabel said quickly. "The earrings were a gift from an unknown admirer, sent by an unknown messenger."

"Ah, so that was what the dogs were making such a fuss about down at the front gate early this evening. Todd said someone left a package, but no one saw the deliveryman." Jeremy's eyes gleamed. "My dear cousin, you seem to have stirred up quite a romantic porridge here in our stodgy old Kent. I see Tremaine's taken with you, too. He keeps looking this way as if at any moment he might make a break for it."

Annabel looked down at her card which Newton Fenmore had tried to fill with every vacant dance. "Are these things carved in stone? I mean, if I change my mind about dancing with someone whose name is on here, will I be drummed out of British society?"

"You promised me the first dance, as I recall," a deep voice said in her ear. "Newton shall have to find another partner."

Annabel looked up at Tremaine Sheffield who was holding his hand out to lead her onto the floor. In a daze, she heard the music, which she recognized as Schubert's "Erlkönig," which had been composed only two years before.

When she was in her partner's arms, she managed to catch her breath enough to comment on the piece. "I understand you've actually met Schubert."

"Oh, you know Franz? I've not seen him in a while, but between you and me, he cannot touch Ludwig in musical talent." If he noticed his partner's sharp intake of breath at the mention of the great Beethoven, he didn't acknowledge it. "Imagine, being able to compose such inspired music when the man cannot even hear what he writes." The heavy, rich music ceased and a lighter melody ensued. "Ah, we're going to do the quadrille. You know it?"

Only through college dance class, Annabel thought as she was swung into the graceful, mannered dance that had reached England recently.

Annabel was having no trouble with the dance steps but she was having trouble acting normally when people casually referred to greats such as Schubert and Beethoven. "I'm afraid he won't live to be old enough to finish all his wonderful symphonies, as Keats won't live to write all his poems. It's such a shame, all that wonderful talent lost at such young ages . . ."

She realized that Tremaine had come almost to a stop and was looking down at her with a very odd expression. "Are you a seer, by any chance?"

Annabel gave a light little laugh. "But of course! I see my cousin Jeremy getting into trouble because two young ladies both want the next dance with him, and I see you trying to figure out how you can dance with me the last figure when Lady Fenmore has put you on her card for the next six, and I see—"

"You see too much," Tremaine said in a tone that was not joking. Annabel felt his hand at her back holding her like steel and could not shift her eyes from the iron-blue stare that bore into her very soul. "Who are you, Isobel—really, I mean?"

"Really?" The repetition came out like a squeak.

"Yes, really. Are you just the simple country cousin who's come to England to get acquainted with her long-lost kin, or are you some little husband-hunting, fortune-greedy urchin ready to take every advantage of an impulsive invitation?"

Annabel's laugh was genuine this time. She'd expected some very different accusation and was vastly relieved. But when the words sank in completely, relief turned to indignation. "Well, I never in my born days heard anything so insulting, *Lord* Sheffield." She flung her hands from his as though from a hot stove and, eyes blazing, turned on him. "Get this through your blue-blooded skull, mister, once and for all.

I don't need your cotton-picking money, or house, or anything else. I especially don't need or want a husband, thank you very much! By the way, you could use a couple of lessons at Fred Astaire. You're not only insulting, you're a damn lousy dancer!"

She left him standing there looking totally perplexed—and somewhat amused, she realized with fury.

She was too angry to hear him repeat softly, with bewilderment, "Fred Astaire? *Cotton-picking?*"

Actually, she'd lied about his dancing ability, a prevarication that was underlined by her turn around the floor with Newton Fenmore. The "Pink Man," as she was beginning to call him privately, held her in a waffle-iron grip and steered her into other couples, when he wasn't bumping into tables on his own.

Annabel felt as if she had earned a medal of honor when she finally retired from the floor.

"May I have the last dance?" Newton wheezed, wiping sweat from his neck and brow as he bowed before his battered partner.

"You just did," she told him. Then she smiled sweetly and explained, "I shan't be dancing any more tonight. Someone scrunched my little toe—"

"Not me, I hope!"

"Oh, no, I could not blame you for my American-sized feet which kept getting in the way. And the bruise from the punch table hardly smarts at all now that I've sat down. In fact, you are such a . . . dancer that word has gotten around. That very pretty young blonde whispered that she thought you were the best dancer on the floor."

Annabel's fingers uncrossed after Newton, straightening his cravat, strutted over to the hapless lady in question.

She would send her a package of Dr. Scholl's bandages the next day, Annabel justified to herself. But then, Dr. Scholl had not yet been born, so she would just have to perform some sort of penance later.

Right now, she was glad to be by herself and able to seethe in private about the insufferable remarks that Tremaine Sheffield had made to her.

How dare he insinuate that she had come to England to find a rich husband? How could a man so boorish exact such devotion from the likes of Jeremy? Annabel just wished that she could take Tremaine Sheffield back to the twentieth century for just one humbling interlude.

But Roman would be there, and that could lead to all kinds of complications. Annabel was getting very confused about her mixed reactions to a man who was much too old for her. About two centuries too old.

After dinner, at which her Southern fried chicken was an enormous hit, Annabel politely excused herself from the partners on either side of her and glanced about the room to be sure that Tremaine wasn't watching her. The last thing she wanted was his following her to bombard her with more insults!

As she was about to leave the dining room, there was an announcement that told her the other man she was avoiding was safely engaged.

"Ladies and gentlemen, we have a special treat tonight before we say our good nights. The Honorable Newton Fenmore has offered to read some of his latest poetry."

Annabel stopped at the door to the terrace. She caught Jeremy's eyes on her and made a little face. He rolled his eyes heavenward and mouthed something that was probably British for *Get out while you can.*

That Annabel did. After only one couplet of Newton's poem, she knew that she would get sick if she stayed to hear more.

Outside, under the stars, she thought about Newton Fenmore and what part he might play in the scenario involving her cousin's poetry career.

There was no longer any doubt about it. Newton Fenmore was many things, but he was not a poet. Of that much she was certain.

Annabel had not meant to wander so far from the house. She could hear voices as guests made their good-byes and realized that she was remiss in not being present. But the river looked so peaceful in the moonlight, she hated to leave. Newton Fenmore would search her out if she went back now and probably coerce her into some future engagement. "Jeremy will forgive me, and Lord knows it's Tremaine who should be asking forgiveness for his bad behavior, so mine should go unnoticed."

The bridle path was well-worn and tempting. Annabel wandered along it, enjoying the freshness of the air and the nocturnal sounds. Somehow the night melted away the century and a half between Isobel's and Annabel's times. The latter might be strolling from dinner at Roman's, the cat walking with her could be the one who'd led her to the hidden poem. . . .

"Cat!" Annabel froze at the touch of soft fur on her ankles. "What in the world? Moonbeam, surely you didn't come back here, too."

The cat at her feet mewed between purring noises, and Annabel reached down to pet it.

115

"Oh, thank goodness, you're not the one from my world after all. My cat had a bump on its tail. You're the eighteenth-century cat."

The faint sound in the distance was evident to the cat first. Its ears twitched, eyes widened, and then with a quick bound, it was off in the brush, leaving Annabel standing in the path wondering what had spooked the creature.

Before she could turn around, there were thundering hoofbeats almost upon her. With a little cry, she started to run, but the horse was bearing down on her rapidly and she almost stumbled.

A strong arm went around her waist and she was lifted into the saddle.

Like the wind, they rode through the night. Annabel felt muscled arms guiding the horse along the path to a wider road that led deep into the woods, and at last she had the courage to open her eyes.

"Oh!" She closed her lids against the specter holding her. The half-hood with a falcon's head embroidered on the forehead blocked out the moon. Annabel felt like a woodmouse trapped by the bird of prey, and just as helpless. "Where are you taking me? Why are you doing this? Please let me go!"

"Be quiet. You'll spook my horse." The muffled voice held no compassion for her fright.

116

This angered Annabel, and she started flailing with her fists.

"Stop it at once!" A steely hand held both of hers until she quieted, realizing she had not enough strength to make an escape.

"I won't hurt you. I'm just taking you with me to a gathering that you will find interesting and enlightening. You mustn't cry out or make a fuss. People don't wish to be recognized at these meetings, so be careful not to ask questions or look at faces. Just listen and learn."

"Why me?" Annabel heard the jerkiness in her voice that meant she was on the verge of tears. She would not cry, she determined, since this man would never be swayed by feminine devices.

"I have watched you from the time you came and have known you were different, that you were sent here—maybe from the bastards who have perpetuated the beginning of the end of England at its greatest—but that you are not who you say you are."

"I'm Isobel, damn you!" she swore, hoping he'd believe the lie. "Jeremy's cousin and Lord Sheffield's guest."

"But is that all you are?" The hand slipped up her waist to cup her chin. Annabel stiffened. "Whose Isobel? Lord Seymour's? That pompous ass Boynton's?"

"Nobody's Isobel, damn you!"

He reined in the horse so suddenly, she fell back against him hard. He lifted her and turned her around in the saddle so that she was close to him in ways that frightened her at the same time that they excited her. "We'll see about that," he whispered.

With one hand he captured her two hands behind her back; with the other, he gripped her head so that she could not move her mouth away from the fierce assault he was making on it. She let out a cry when his hand at her back gripped her even more tightly.

"Wherever they found you, my hat's off to them. You are not only a dead ringer for the real woman, you're absolutely delicious. Your mouth tastes like raspberries with the dew still on them, and the rest of you promises even greater delight." Annabel felt his stiffening against her and struggled.

"Don't do that, little bird. The net only gets tighter. Surely the embrace of the Falcon is more appealing than that of whatever fat, balding policymaker sent you to spy on me."

He pushed her back against the neck of the horse and tangled her hair with that of the rough black mane. "I shall ride you one day, too, only to ecstasy," he whispered between kisses. "After that, I'll defy you to tell me that Boynton or whoever your lover is can make you feel the way I can make you feel . . ."

Annabel rallied her strength and reared forward, rubbing her freed hand harshly across her mouth. "You chauvinistic son of a bitch," she spat at him. "To think that you would imagine I could desire a man who's too cowardly to show his face and stand up publicly for what he believes!"

She had shocked him into letting go of her. Annabel took advantage by yanking her dress back to more decorous array.

"Chauvinistic son of a bitch? Is this a new London street way of speaking that I haven't heard about?"

"It means exactly what you think it means, understand it or not," she said bitingly. "Now, if you're through mauling me, I'll thank you to take me back to Sheffield Hall and I will consider not having you arrested for attempted rape."

"The Falcon arrested? Believe me, little bird, when they got through with you, it would probably be you who would wind up in jail. Prostitutes don't fare well in our courts, as you probably have already learned firsthand."

"Look, we need to get something straight. I am not a prostitute. I am not a spy for one of your political enemies. I'm not . . ." Annabel stopped, knowing she could never explain her bizarre role to this Falcon. She couldn't even explain it to herself.

". . . a very good liar, whoever you really are. Who are you?"

Annabel's laugh was wild. "You, the Lone Ranger with a falcon mask, are asking me who I am?"

"The Lone Ranger?"

Annabel laughed again, even more wildly. It could be that Annabel, aka Isobel, was rewriting the English language long before Americans ever got around to it.

While Annabel was having her startling first encounter with the legendary Falcon, another rendezvous of a different sort was taking place at the center of the maze at Sheffield Hall. The hooded swirling cape of the one who'd arranged the meeting hid the identity of the wearer, but the dark figure who joined the first knew who it was.

"So you finally heeded my message."

"I told you how dangerous it's becoming to spy on those meetings for you. At the last two, I'm almost sure I was spotted."

"By the Falcon?" The voice was sharp with anger. "I told you to hide that blasted hair of yours and stay on the edge of the crowd."

Felicia Fenmore flung back her hood and glared at the man who was menacing her. "Well, why don't you ask your dowdy wife to do your spying for you, Lord Lunsford? I'm sure no one would notice *her*."

The man adopted a more conciliatory tone. "Now, now, my love. No need to bring Elizabeth into it. I've told you, as soon as the whispers about you and me have died down, I'll bring you back and set you up in the most expensive house on Kew Street."

"And allow me to entertain the way I like?"

"With accounts at every establishment, your own household staff and dressmaker . . ."

Felicia turned her pouting lips up so he could kiss them. "And jewels to rival the Queen's?" She opened her eyes suddenly as the man's mouth was moving from her lips to her throat and said slyly, "Like the ones you bought your wife for her birthday . . . the ones that were stolen?"

Derek Lunsford's lips froze at the tip of her ear. "The Waterson garnets? How did you know about those?"

"Oh, I know a lot of things that you don't know I know." Felicia caught the tip of her lover's ear in her sharp white teeth and he yelped. "Sorry, love, sometimes the faithful lapdog forgets what sharp little teeth it has. How did I know? Because you gave them to her at that huge party you had at Claridge's in honor of her birthday—the night of the same day that you paid off my brother's bills and gaming debts on the condition that he move me out here to this godforsaken, boring county." Her voice rose with her pique.

"Now, my love, now, now. I told you it would only be temporary and that if you helped us uncover the identities of the rabble-rousers, the rewards would be great. And they will." The ear-nibbling began in earnest. Lord Lunsford had a late supper engagement back in London and had little time to waste in subtle wooing. His hands were already busy at the opening of Lady Fenmore's gown, which was conveniently covering only the slightest of underthings.

He had already loosened his trousers and now let them drop, making the object of his impatient lust giggle. "If I take your pants right now and leave and remove the markers I left for you to find your way through the maze, what a story for the London mob!" She had pilfered the map to the maze and copied it.

Lord Lunsford said gruffly, "I would have you spitted and roasted on a slow fire, and you know it."

Again, the giggle. Felicia was thinking about the jewels she had seen at the neck and ears of the upstart American and was thinking how she could use that information to her advantage. "And then would you eat me with Yorkshire pudding and mint jelly?"

Breathing harder with desire, Lunsford swore under his breath at the impediment of her cloak ties. He finally solved the problem by breaking them.

"Oh!" Felicia's breath started coming as heavy as her lover's. The snapped cord let the cloak fall to the grass near which a statue stared at them with pupil-less eyes.

"You little trollop," he growled into her shoulder as he clutched at her. He clasped one of her breasts and slurped at it hungrily while Felicia, secretly smiling at her power, moved tauntingly.

"You say the nicest things," she whispered, trailing her long nails along his backbone and stopping to dig in at the back of his neck.

"You know you love it, my saying what you are while I'm pleasing you. You shouldn't have been born to the aristocracy. You should have been a Nell Gwynn, giving pleasure to your man behind the scenes."

"You know me better than any man ever has."

Lunsford raised himself up and looked down into her face. "It had better stay that way, love, or you and your ass of a brother will wind up begging on the back streets of Piccadilly."

Felicia's smug smile disappeared. "What do you mean?"

"I mean I've heard that you've started cozying up to Tremaine Sheffield, and it's no secret that you've made it clear you wouldn't say no to being the next Lady Sheffield. See, I know things, too, love."

"I've just been cultivating his friendship to win over the people around the country. They all look up to him."

"There's some speculation in my circle that he may be the Falcon."

Felicia pulled the man back down to her and opened her mouth to let her tongue circle his. His hand she guided to a breast, not crying out when, in his renewed lust, he squeezed and kneaded the soft flesh. "Tremaine Sheffield, the Falcon? Don't be silly. Love, I'm only using the man to keep me from going raving mad out here in this provincial purgatory."

"I'll drive you raving mad. Ah, how you do open up to me, you little tramp. Whore, move those thighs wider, I need a woman who can take all of me." His pride in his sexual bulk had made available mistresses scarce since few could handle the roughness. But Felicia was as insatiable as he, and Lord Lunsford could pound her into the grass knowing she was his equal in appetite.

The signal whistle told Derek Lunsford that it was time to go. He saw the marks of his seed on Felicia's thighs and briefly thought about having a bastard by the trollop. She had good bones and blood, and heaven knew the son he'd fathered by his wife was sickly and stupid.

But, no, then she would have a hold over him and a claim to him beyond the time that he planned to use her. "You were splendid, my darling. I shan't be able to get you out of my mind until I see you again."

He was dressed now and impatient with Felicia for fumbling at the ruined ties. "Oh, do hurry, there's no need for worrying about those damn strings. No one will see you when I drop you off at your house. It's after eleven."

She obediently made do with pulling her cloak around her and followed Lord Lunsford out of the maze, stopping when he signaled her just inside the final arch. "Shh. My driver can be trusted, but the night has eyes and ears. Stay here till I tell him I'm on my way."

A moment later, he stalked back to the woman waiting inside the last hedge of the maze and delivered a backhanded blow that knocked her to the ground. "Bitch. I knew I couldn't trust you to live up to your part of our agreement. I ought to have you packed off to one of those Shanghai markets where they love pale-skinned whores."

Felicia struggled halfway up, putting her hand to her mouth and staring at the blood when she took it away. "Wha . . . Derek, I don't understand. What have I done? Why are you so angry with me?"

125

"While you were dallying with me here, the Falcon was holding one of the largest rallies ever staged in this county. My driver just heard about it from one of his cousins whom he visited while I was with you. Damn you, you were the one who should be giving this report to me, along with the bastard's identity." Lunsford drew back his hand for another blow, but Felicia, her face pale and hard, caught his wrist.

"Never do that again," she said in a low, fierce voice. "You can do what you want when we're making love, I've never liked namby-pamby sex, but don't . . . ever . . . hit . . . me . . . like . . . that . . . again."

They stared at each other, knowing what they were and that both meant what they said. Lunsford was the first to bend. "I'm sorry, love, it's just that if word gets out that I was actually a few miles from one of the Falcon's rallies and didn't even know about it, I'll look foolish."

"Well, the fact that we're here and the Falcon is there, even as we speak, gives us a golden opportunity to find out if the speculation you've heard is true."

"That the Falcon is really Tremaine Shef-field?" Lunsford did a little dance. "Now, there's my smart girl. I knew I could count on you."

As much as I can count on you, Felicia told herself, putting her hand to the tender flesh where her lover had struck her. She followed

Lunsford through the shadowy grounds, stopping him well away from the balcony which she knew led into Tremaine's private bedchamber. "That's his room," she whispered. "His light's on. He never goes to bed before two in the morning and always comes out on the balcony about this time."

"How do you know all that?" Lunsford saw the warning glint in Felicia's eyes and hastily dropped that line of questioning. "Look, I see someone moving about. Yes. He spoke to Parliament last year. I can't see him clearly, but it's Sheffield, all right. I recognize that arrogant strut that would have you believe he's the king of the walk. There he comes; he might see us. I'm satisfied. Let's go."

The pair skulked away, Felicia turning her face away from the kiss her lover would have planted on her bruised mouth as they climbed into the carriage that would bear Lunsford back to London.

"So much for your brilliant theory," Felicia said bitterly, wondering how she was going to explain her physical condition to her brother the next morning.

She didn't have to. He was waiting up for her when she got home.

Newton Fenmore was less horrified by his sister's appearance than by his fear that she might have offended their benefactor. "My God, Felicia, you know how violent the man's temper is, why on earth would you choose to insult him?"

"I am his mistress and his spy, brother mine. I shall not add to that the role of his punching bag. Well, at least he won't be taking tales to those slimy friends of his about how Tremaine Sheffield is really the Falcon."

Newton waited until the sleepy-eyed maid who brought a pan of water and a white cloth had left before hissing, "What do you mean? Everybody thinks Tremaine is the Falcon." He jabbed at the cut on Felicia's mouth in his agitation, making her wince. "He's a traitor to his country, that's what he is, and once he's found out, he'll pay dearly."

"I know how much you lust after the Sheffield estate and holdings, but depend more on one of those rigged card games of yours to make your fortune, little brother. Tremaine was safe and sound in his mansion whilst the Falcon was out spewing fire and brimstone in the countryside."

"You saw him yourself?"

"I saw him."

"Oh." Newton's hand paused in its task of washing Felicia's cut. "The man's a brute. Not Tremaine, though I don't like him, nor that cocky Jeremy who never misses a chance to mention that he knows Byron personally. Was the girl with him?"

"With whom?"

"With Sheffield, ninny. Was Isobel with him when you saw him tonight?"

"No. The little prig, I doubt that she's ever been in a man's bedroom in her life."

Newton brightened. "I say, have you ever seen a prettier piece of work? I wish she hadn't missed the last of my poems. I expect she'd think more highly of me had she heard 'Lady, Who Rules my Heart, be Fair.' "

"Perhaps it's best that she didn't." At her brother's chiding look, Felicia amended quickly, "I only meant that Americans haven't the taste for eloquent poetry, darling."

Felicia was to regret the kind words, for her brother was eager to try out his newest rhyme on someone and she was the unfortunate victim.

While her brother's voice droned on, Felicia distracted herself by wondering if Derek Lunsford was even now at a romantic assignation as she suspected. The bastard, she swore silently, not angry anymore. She touched the cut on her face, remembering the passion that had preceded it. Her nipples stung at the memory of his relentless use of them; a warm rush went over her as she thought of the powerful organ that had pinned her to the damp grass . . .

129

The bastard was probably doing the same thing to some cheap wench right now.

Well, turnabout was fair play. She would seduce Tremaine Sheffield and maybe even marry him and show Lord Lunsford and his oversized . . .

"Felicia, you're not even listening!" Newton's whining reprimand, on top of his horrid poetry and everything she'd been through that day, was the last straw. Felicia leapt up and, without so much as a good night to her brother, went to bed.

Chapter Eight

On the balcony of the second floor at Sheffield Hall, the robed figure whom Felicia and her companion had seen listened as the clatter of horse and carriage faded and chuckled wickedly.

"More spies trying to trip up my brother," Jeremy said, pulling off the dark wig he'd borrowed from a Drury Lane impersonator and abandoning the distinctive carriage Tremaine was noted for. He leaned on the rail to watch for his stepbrother's return. He'd seen the figures emerging from the maze and had put the plan that he and Tremaine had worked out into place.

"I just hope he was careful to see that all

the guests were safely gone before he left for the rally. Poor Tremaine. He's going to be exhausted when he finally gets home." Jeremy was tempted to step across the balcony and see if Isobel was still awake, but changed his mind. Her room was dark and she was no doubt in a deep sleep by now after all the excitement. He was just glad she hadn't wandered onto the balcony as he was pretending to be his stepbrother. She might have been frightened and ruined everything.

In fact, Annabel was at that moment far from frightened. She was mad as a wet hen over the Falcon's high-handed treatment of her and didn't stop telling him so all the way to wherever it was he was taking her.

She figured that the place they came to was between Maidstone and Canterbury. The field was thick with people, most swathed in disguising scarves and low-slung hats and most of them men.

When the Falcon rode into their midst, the crowd cheered and chanted, "No more Corn Laws! No more Corn Laws!" The Falcon raised his hand in salute and rode up to the huge bonfire near which a rough platform had been rigged. He handed Annabel over to two waiting men as though she were a sack of corn. "Watch her carefully and keep her hidden. And for God's sake, hide those jewels."

Annabel's retort was muffled by a callused hand. Its owner was polite but firm. "The Falcon's about to speak, Miss, and we don't need nobody distracting folks from hearing what he has to say."

"All right, you people of England, as Cobbett said before he was run off to America to escape persecution, it's not the price of corn we're worried about—it's the burden of taxation!"

The din of cheers and clapping hurt Annabel's ears, but she was fascinated in spite of herself. She was in the middle of England's most important agricultural uprising against oppressive laws. The man who was its spearhead, Cobbett the Radical, was not here, but the Falcon was filling the void. She strained to make out the hoarse words thundered through a bullhorn.

". . . and they say the nation must keep faith with its creditors, but if, as Cobbett tells us, the farmers are ruined, this will profit the landlords little. Whose pockets will jingle? The fundholders and stockjobbers of the great 'Wen.' With ruined farmers, we'll see vacant farms and no rents. We'll see the beginning of the end of England as we know it, the passing of the land from old aristocracy to the 'ragrooks,' the paper money men who've grown fat through the Pitt system. New gentry will inherit old estates from old blood which has fed the farmers and the laborers. The new landlords will suck the land dry without replenishing it or nurturing its laborers."

In spite of herself, Annabel joined in the loud cheer of approval.

The man who was guarding her grinned and said admiringly, "You can see why the people look to the Falcon to help them fight for reform. Wait till you hear him tell about the inflated currency, the pensions, the swelled-up army, and the huge war debt. Oh, it'll make you cry!"

She gave a loud whoop when someone in the crowd yelled, "It's the high-handed legislators and the Government who's to blame! Let's get those rascals out!"

From somewhere the Falcon got a horse for Annabel and led her out to the main road which would lead her directly back to Sheffield Hall. "It's dangerous for you to be seen with me, and since I suspect you're not who you say you are, it's dangerous for me to see you home. Free the mount after you dismount and someone will see to getting him back to his owner."

"If you think I'm someone who can't be trusted, why the dickens did you bring me out here to hear your speech?"

" 'Why the dickens.' I do love your turn of phrase, though some of it puzzles me. Dear

Isobel, if that is indeed who you are, I have learned the hard way that keeping one's enemies to one's bosom is the best way to know what they're up to. Now, when you go back to that house and go to bed, do one thing for me that will set my mind at ease about your arriving safely. Put a candle on the balcony post, betwixt yours and Sheffield's bedrooms."

"You speak as though you know the household very well."

"I make a point of it. Now go! I shall see you to the bend of the road, and then a quiet sentinel will watch you to the main gate of the Hall." He grabbed her rein. "But first—tell me what you thought of this night?"

"Of your speech? Your politics? I have to confess I saw a good deal of common sense."

"I mean of what lies between you and me," he said, his hand gripping her wrist and sending goose bumps all over her body. "I don't know who you really are, Isobel, or what you're up to, but I will find out."

She looked into the glittering eyes behind the mask and quivered throughout her being, knowing that whatever her destiny was, it involved this man.

"I hope you will," she whispered. Then she wheeled her horse away down the road to return to Sheffield Hall.

It had been a night to remember, her

first night with the Falcon. She remembered just before she drifted off into exhausted slumber to put the candle on the balcony. As she did so, she heard someone moving about in Tremaine's bedroom. So much for her suspicions about the Falcon's identity!

Jeremy was working at his desk in the turret when he heard the small pebble hit the window. Then another. He went to the window and made a motion, then bounded down the stairs to let his late night visitor in.

"Tremaine? Good Lord, you must be nearly dead. I was waiting at the house, then decided to come up here to finish that piece I'm working on." Jeremy helped his stepbrother off with his cloak and took the mask from a weary hand. "I'll get you something to eat."

"No. No, just some ale. And be sure that Mordred's sister Vivien gets a good rubdown before she's let out to pasture." Tremaine sank onto the bottom stair. "I shan't go up, I don't think I could. I just wanted to let you in on the rally."

"I've already had a report which I'm writing up. Everybody says it was the best one we've had in the county, or in several counties, for that matter. And I have some news for you. You know that leak from London that let us

know you were under suspicion as the Falcon?
Well, tonight I got a chance to throw them off.
Someone was spying on the house, no doubt
someone who knew about the meeting and that
you couldn't be both places at once. I have got
your swagger down to a fare-thee-well, brother, and the black wig was, ahem, the crowning
touch."

Tremaine threw back his head and laughed.
"Jeremy, you never fail to astound me. Some-
times I think it should be you who is the real
Falcon instead of me."

"Which brings me to a point. Your effective-
ness lies in the fact that the people look on you
as a symbol, a spiritual entity, not some poor
chap who's burdened with family and taxes
and day-to-day drudgery. We must keep the
Falcon removed from those things, must maintain his indestructibility, his elusiveness."

"And from that gleam in your eye, I suspect you have a plan for accomplishing that."
Tremaine lounged back, swirling the ale in his
goblet as he eyed his stepbrother, who was
pacing back and forth in his excitement.

"Yes. We make him ubiquitous. People see
and hear the Falcon here, and then, lo and
behold, he's there, miles away, and the legend
grows, his listeners swell in numbers. No one
can pinpoint him, be sure that he'll be one
place, or another."

"I can't be more than one place at a time, little brother."

"You were tonight." Jeremy sat on the stair beside Tremaine. "I carried it off, and I can do it again—and again. Think about it. I can imitate your persona, the Falcon's voice. I help write your speeches. I can be you one place, then you can be you another place. It will awe your followers, add to your legend, befuddle the enemies who are trying to trap you."

Tremaine thought about it. "I must say that it sounds like a good way to throw off those who would bring me down. The thing I don't like is the potential danger to you. Already, that underground writing you're doing could do to the editor of *Legal Watch* what Cobbett's *Political Register* almost did to him."

"Tremaine, I'm committed. I know poets make rotten politicians, but I'm a writer and I believe in what you're doing."

The older man embraced him, overcome by his love for this bright young man who'd looked up to Tremaine as a hero from the time they'd first met. "I just don't want you to get hurt. And that brings me to a really touchy subject, your cousin Isobel. Be careful about her. It could be that she's not what she appears to be. There are some things still unexplained, things I won't get into until I'm sure, but be careful. Don't tell her anything about our talks, about the

Falcon, about what we do, until we're sure we can trust her."

Jeremy laughed. "I wondered if you'd gotten the report about an alleged spy in the ranks, and I guess you have. Well, I can assure you that my darling cousin is innocent. God, Tremaine, how could she be in any way involved with that London mob? She only got here this week."

Tremaine thought about his talk with the port authorities about the packet that he'd met, expecting Isobel to be aboard, and the story that Jeremy had related about the girl taking a different boat. "All I'm saying is that I don't want you confiding in her about our activities until we've had a chance to know her better."

"I shan't. She's more interested in my poetry than in anything else. Oh, what fun we shall have reading together, taking long walks and rides and visiting Keats in London, before we meet Shelley to take Byron's daughter Allegro to Italy."

Jeremy didn't miss the jealous look on his stepbrother's face. "Oh, so your suspicious nature hasn't precluded your noticing how lovely my cousin is, and how charming! Well, you shall have to be on your mettle. Newton Fenmore has set his sights, and it will take our combined efforts to ward off his suit."

"I'll take my leave now," Tremaine said grimly, "Before I get vulgar and tell you what I would like to do with Fenmore."

The leisurely days that followed her great adventure made Annabel wonder if she'd dreamed the whole thing. Immediately upon waking the next morning, she hid the jewels, which she suspected were stolen. She vowed to have them returned to their rightful owner as soon as she had a chance to talk to someone in the constabulary at Maidstone.

She loved morning at Sheffield Hall, with her tray of coffee and delicious breakfasts in her room, usually in the company of Jeremy. On one such morning, almost two weeks into her visit, she expressed guilty feelings about being such a lazy guest, involved in only hedonistic activities and no tasks. "I'm not used to being so useless, Jeremy. Please tell me what I might do around the house to help earn my keep."

Her cousin kissed her hand. "Your mere presence earns your 'keep,' darling Isobel. I vow I've never enjoyed the country as much as I do on our strolls and madcap rides along the river. Maude and Todd were telling me only this morning that they'd never seen me happier and they knew it was due to you."

Annabel set down her cup with a clatter. "Well, they certainly can't say that about your stepbrother! The man avoids me as though I had the pox and barely speaks when we do meet, which is very rarely. Has he said anything to you? Why does Tremaine dislike me so?"

Jeremy turned his head but not in time to conceal the look of distress that Annabel was sure had to do with her and Tremaine's distrust of her. "He's never been a lighthearted person, Isobel, and the times weigh heavily on him. He feels that people like him must take back our country before it's too late, before the greedy politicians and legislators ruin England forever."

"That sounds like what the Falcon believes." She had finally told her cousin about her strange night in the company of the county's mysterious hero. Annabel sat up suddenly, disturbing the cat who had been sleeping with her since the night she'd come back from the rally. "Are they one and the same, Jeremy? Tell me the truth, they are, aren't they?" Her eyes narrowed as she pondered the question herself. "They're the same size, same build, have the same aura of authority . . ." Annabel went on excitedly, not seeing the look of worry on Jeremy's face. "They are! Tremaine's the Falcon! He does things with his voice to disguise it and wears that scary mask, but underneath all that, the Falcon is really your stepbrother."

Jeremy thought of Tremaine's warning about revealing their secrets to the American girl and heeded it. Though he himself thought Tremaine's suspicions were unfounded, Jeremy's loyalty was first and foremost to his stepbrother. "That's probably what the men in Parliament, including Newton Fenmore, would like everyone to believe. They've considered the Sheffields too powerful in their influence for a long time and would love the chance to bring this latest heir to ruin."

"So you really don't think they're one and the same?" The romantic in Annabel's soul sighed in disappointment.

"I know they're not. You see, I've been to several of the meetings and twice saw my brother in the crowd. Another time, I saw him coming home from dinner at the Fenmores' not twenty minutes after the Falcon had finished his speech." Jeremy was lying, but he had every intention of making the circumstances he described part of the near future. Tremaine was in too much danger, not from Isobel, but from those who shared her suspicion.

"Hmm. Well, I know you wouldn't lie to me, dear Jeremy, so I shall do my best to forget my silly little ideas and continue working at making myself more palatable to your stepbrother."

Jeremy kissed her on the nose, laughing. "If you make yourself as palatable as that vegetable dish you showed Maude how to make for last night's dinner, we shall all be gorged and roll down the stairs. Now, put on that riding outfit I had made for you and let's give those fat horses something to do rather than graze all day."

"I'd love it." Annabel was out of bed in a flash. She had always loved riding, though she had not had access to the sport since graduate school. What fun it would be to gallop over the green countryside around the manor!

After donning the snug-fitting riding habit in hunter green with a dashing hat and snug boots to match, Annabel paused at the mirror on her way out. She snapped a smart salute with her riding crop to the image in the glass. "Frankly, my dear, I don't give a damn about Lord Sheffield's opinion—you're totally ravishing!"

And oh so modest, she had to add with a grin. Still, she showed herself well on horseback and hoped Tremaine was around to notice.

On their ride along the river path, Jeremy and Annabel encountered the Fenmores, who hailed them with enthusiasm, especially Newton. "I say, Simmons, this is my lucky day. I've called and left my card several times, but Miss Isobel is always resting or engaged."

Annabel sent a grateful look Jeremy's way, knowing he'd been the buffer between her and "the Pink Man." "I'm sorry, Mr. Fenmore,

143

but my days have been incredibly busy. How anyone can call living in the country dull is beyond me." At the little sound from Felicia, Annabel included her in the conversation. "My dear Lady Fenmore, what on earth happened to your face?"

Newton hastily explained the still swollen look of his sister's mouth. "Poor Felicia tripped over a rug the morning after your delightful soiree and is just now being seen out and about. May I accompany you on your ride, Miss Isobel? I'll send back to our kitchen for refreshments if you'd care to have a bite to eat and drink on the banks . . ."

Jeremy rescued her. "Afraid not, Fenmore. Isobel's afternoon is fully taken. We're getting ready for a trip to London to buy her some new frocks . . ."

"And have tea with Keats before he leaves on his journey," Annabel added wickedly, knowing that tidbit would drive Newton insane with jealousy.

"Oh, I'm planning to be in London during the next few days myself, and Felicia says she will join me. Perhaps we could all get together at my apartment, maybe have dinner one night . . ."

"I thought I heard you'd given up your London digs," Jeremy said with an innocent look. *I'm not the only wicked person in this family*, Annabel thought with a secret grin.

"A good friend of Felicia's has a place we use when we're in town," Newton said, his face going even pinker at Isobel learning of his financial straits.

"Well, we won't be staying but one night, thank you." Jeremy tipped his hat to Felicia, who had not yet opened her mouth, being pea-green with jealousy at the way Isobel looked on horseback.

"I say," Felicia said. "Is that the riding fashion in America, straddling one's horse like a man?" Actually, Felicia was thinking of talking to her dressmaker about fashioning a skirt like Isobel's, with cleverly disguised folds and pleats that allowed the wearer to straddle one's horse both gracefully and comfortably.

"It's much more fun than riding sidesaddle, Felicia. You ought to try it." Annabel's horse whinnied impatiently, ready for the pelting race that her mistress always made along the river-bank. The girl whispered into the horse's ear, "Patience, L.G. You'll have your gallop, but I must not be rude. Not yet, anyway."

"Is that another American riding custom— telling secrets to one's horse?" Felicia's lilting laugh turned into a grimace when her sore mouth protested the movement.

Newton chided his sister, "Felicia, you're too sharp with Miss Isobel. I think she looks quite charming, not only in her riding habit but in her horsemanship."

"Ladies do not ride astride their mounts," Felicia said a bit shrilly.

"This one does. Perhaps you'd like a little race to the bridge?"

Felicia's small, sharp teeth showed in a contained snarl. "Oh, let's make it more interesting than that. Let's say the copse beside the brook, past the stone wall."

"Felicia, we know you've jumped in many shows, but Miss Isobel may not—"

"Miss Isobel will do whatever Lady Fenmore suggests. Apparently I must prove that America's style in everything from underwear to horseback riding is up to snuff." Annabel patted L.G., who was snorting at the bit to show Miss Proper Priss and her sissy-tailed horse what good riding was all about. "Jeremy, why don't you give us the countdown to start? And, Newton, perhaps you should go back to your house for more medical supplies, since your sister seems to be accident-prone this week."

Felicia's look was withering. Between clenched teeth, she hissed, "Perhaps we should make the bet even more interesting. She who returns to this spot first shall exact the penalty of her choice from the other, short of bodily harm."

"Fair enough," Annabel said coolly.

Felicia's smile became a real one. "I shall have a terrible time deciding whether to ask you to return to whence you came within twenty-four hours, or for the jewelry you were wearing the other night."

Annabel's heart constricted. Did the woman know the history of those ornaments? "And I shall have a dickens of a time deciding which body of water I'll ask you to jump into."

Newton said nervously, "I think I will go back to see about those medical supplies."

At Jeremy's signal, the two women were off.

For Annabel, it was the ride of her life, seeing the river flashing by on one side, the trees and grounds on the other. She had taken an early lead, and since the path was narrow, there was no way Felicia could pass her.

Annabel awaited the jump of the fence that lay ahead, excited about the challenge that would show her rival once and for all that Americans knew how to ride. Lady Godiva was reaching her stride by the time they reached the bridge and were out of sight of Jeremy. Annabel looked back to see that Felicia was several yards behind. So much for English riding superiority.

But, wait; Annabel realized that the woman behind her seemed to be in distress. She was sliding to the side, her voluminous riding habit dragging on the path. "Felicia! Are you all right?" Annabel wheeled Lady Godiva to a circling stop.

"It's my boot. It's caught in the stirrup." Felicia bent down to move her skirt.

"Here, let me help." Annabel cantered up and slid off her horse.

Before she could reach Felicia's side, the Englishwoman kicked her horse, and with a deprecating trill of laughter, she raced away. "Catch me if you can," she taunted her rival.

Annabel stood there for a moment, her fury mounting. Then quietly she said to Lady Godiva, "L.G., that woman just got my dander up. How do you feel about a little detour?"

The horse felt just fine, and her rider guided her up the grassy knoll above the path. There were a few scary stumbles and a leap or two over unexpected ditches, but Lady Godiva was a country-bred horse who would not be deterred by such things.

They reached the fence seconds before their competitors on the smoother path, and Lady Godiva's arching leap was a picture to behold. Annabel felt her seat leave the saddle briefly, felt her hat with its feathers take off like a bird in flight. From the side of her eye, she saw Felicia sailing off the back of her steed, like the girl on the flying trapeze, as her horse leaped over the fence.

"Well, so much for riding sidesaddle," Annabel murmured as she and L.G. trotted back to the starting line.

Penalty time, she reminded herself with a grin as she ambled up to where Jeremy and Newton were waiting. "Evel Knevil has landed," she told them, getting looks of total bewilderment. "Don't mind me. Newton, I hope you have an ice pack in your bag there. Your sister is going to need one. And if you happen to have brandy with you, I could certainly use a shot of that."

She sipped brandy while Felicia Fenmore limped back, leading her horse. Instinctively, Annabel looked up at the knoll along which she had made her victorious ride and was shocked to see a still, dark figure on a black horse. "The Falcon!"

Chapter Nine

At Annabel's cry, everyone's eyes turned to the knoll. Then Jeremy laughed. "It's only Tremaine. He's holding up your hat, Isobel. Apparently you ladies had an audience for your entire race."

Felicia did not look very happy about that. "My stupid horse balked at the fence for some ungodly reason or I would have won easily. Well, Isobel, I suppose I must live up to the bargain. What ghastly penalty are you subjecting me to?"

Annabel lifted her brandy in salute. "Not a ghastly one at all. As penalty, you must be pleasant to me for the remainder of my stay and never again speak about the inferiority of Americans."

"By Jove, now there's a good sport," Newton said enthusiastically. "Felicia, you must admit Miss Copeland is being more than generous. I'm sure had you won you would have been much harsher."

Felicia looked at Annabel with sheer loathing. "Miss Copeland will probably wish I had won before her visit is over. I'm a notoriously poor loser."

With relief Jeremy hailed his stepbrother, who had cantered down the knoll to join them. "Do you think we'll start a new Ascot right here at Sheffield? You saw our little race. Isn't Isobel a splendid horsewoman? And Lady Fenmore, too, of course," he added hastily.

"Well, I could have won if I had thrown dignity to the wind and ridden astride like some country wench." At Annabel's wagging finger reminding her of the pact, Felicia conceded sulkily, "She does jump rather well, for an Amer—Tremaine, for heaven's sake, let's have a ride, a civilized one, and talk about London, or something interesting."

Tremaine said with a tinge of amusement, "I'd say you've had enough riding for one day, Felicia. And whatever did you do to your face?"

"Oh!" Felicia looked at Annabel in fury, and mounted her horse. "I'll have a ride on my own since Medea here is better company at the moment than any of you." Kicking her mare, the Englishwoman was off in a cloud of billowing skirts.

What a perfect name for a hellion's horse, Annabel told herself. But her satisfaction at having bested Felicia was fast evaporating. The woman struck her as being someone who would not soon forget a humiliating defeat at the hands of another woman. "I'm sorry. I seem to have gotten off on the wrong foot with your sister, Lord Fenmore."

Newton shook his head as he watched his sister pelting away. "It's I who should apologize to you for my sister's poor manners, Miss Isobel. She's not been herself since we moved to the country, not a bit of it. I suppose she's bored and misses London and her friends there. Well, perhaps our little trip to the city will cheer her up."

Annabel doubted that anything short of a personality transplant would make Felicia Fenmore more pleasant to be around. "Perhaps so." She turned to catch Tremaine Sheffield eyeing her with new speculation. Dared she think there was a glint of admiration in his eyes? "Lord Sheffield, I can't thank you enough for rescuing my hat. Poor Jeremy went all over the village looking for just the trim for it." Her hand touched his as he handed her the chapeau, and she felt the tingle of electricity that jarred a memory, one that eluded her as quickly as it came.

"Not at all. I'm glad I decided to go riding or I would have missed the show. But there is a penalty of sorts attached to the return of your pretty little hat."

Annabel braced herself. "Not so fierce a one as Lady Fenmore had in mind, I hope."

"I hope you won't think so. I want you to call me 'Tremaine' and allow me to show you about in London. My brother will certainly not feel he has the right to monopolize all your time there as he has here."

Annabel's mouth dropped open and she looked at Jeremy, whose smug expression said clearly, *See, I told you he really likes you.* "Why . . . why . . . I suppose that depends on how much time we have. We'll be visiting with Jeremy's friend Keats, you know" (She saw Newton's pained look at this reminder) "and going shopping and . . ." Annabel looked hopelessly at her cousin, imploring him silently to come to her rescue.

He did the contrary. "Oh, Isobel, could you take Tremaine up on his offer? Not that I shouldn't enjoy spending every moment with you, but there are some friends I must see on business that would be dull for you. And besides, you will be good for Tremaine. He never takes time to have fun whilst he's in the city." Jeremy turned to his stepbrother. "I'm delighted you're accompanying us, Trey. What on earth made you decide to do so?"

"I decided it was time I got to know Isobel better," Tremaine said quietly, his eyes on hers. "I'm very sorry, Fenmore," he said without looking at the man, "that there won't be room in our carriage for you and your sister, but I'm sure Felicia will be carrying enough boxes for you to require your own coach."

"You are right about that. Well, Miss Isobel, if you're sure you won't reconsider having a spot to eat with me, I'll be taking my leave."

Annabel opened her mouth and closed it when Tremaine answered for her, "She's lunching with me. I made arrangements for a picnic before I came out to ride. Ready, Annabel? Jeremy, we'll see you after lunch to set out on our trip. I've already had my bag put below, and Todd is seeing to the horses for the journey."

Jeremy winked at Annabel, who was in a semidaze at the sudden turnaround in her host. "You've got it, old bean." He gave Annabel a boost up onto Lady Godiva and winked again. "Don't try to race his lordship there, love. He won't be beaten."

"True," Tremaine said as Annabel moved up to his side. "And not only at jumping fences."

They rode off together, and Jeremy said admiringly to Fenmore, "Have you ever seen a more magnificently matched pair?"

"Well, they came from the same sire, after all," Newton said musingly.

"What?" Jeremy looked astonished and then burst out laughing. "I was referring to the people, old chap, not the horses!"

"He's a bit too swarthy for Miss Isobel," the other man said with a sniff. "And she would never have a man with a hideous scar like that."

Jeremy looked at Newton Fenmore and thought pityingly, *She's more likely to overlook Trey's scar than pink nose hairs, you egotistical dolt.*

"You're full of surprises," Annabel said as she looked around her surroundings for the picnic.

"No more than you are. I would never have expected you to be able to jump fences like that."

"It wasn't I who jumped it, my horse did." Annabel took a dainty bite of the crusted pâté, and then had to restrain herself from gobbling it up. If she ever did go back to where she came from, she planned to take half of Maude's recipes with her.

"You're very far away, Isobel. You do that often. I've watched you more than you know during the time you've been here. I think you're as full of surprising twists and turns as this maze."

"Well, I hope not." Annabel looked around the hedged enclosure where the picnic had been awaiting them when she and Tremaine reached the center. "There are at least six ways to turn from every corridor in this thing. I was totally confused after the first turn."

Tremaine poured them more wine. "Jeremy told me you've been wanting to come in here and that he forbade you to do so alone. Could you find your way out if I left you?"

Annabel stared at him. "Are you crazy? Of course I couldn't."

"Then this apparently doesn't belong to you." Tremaine held out his hand in which two mother-of-pearl chips lay. "Or this." The tortoiseshell comb was similar to the ones Annabel wore in her hair, but she shook her head.

"No. I have two like that one but they're in my hair. See?" Annabel pulled out the combs in question, not seeing that Tremaine was looking more at the shining mass of curls tumbling to her shoulders than at hair ornaments. "And I don't even know what those little chips are."

"They're part of the marked trail someone left for someone else to this center of the maze, apparently overlooked when they went back."

Annabel looked at him in bewilderment, then his meaning sank in. It was so ridiculous, she laughed. "Tremaine, how would I find my way here in the first place, much less be able to map the way for someone to follow?"

"Todd has a map secreted in the pantry so he can do things like this when the occasion arises. You spend a good deal of time in the kitchen giving cooking lessons. If you'd seen the map, you'd know that if you keep following the left-hand wall of the maze you'll reach the center eventually."

She was angry now. "You're insulting. Now I see why you brought me here—it wasn't because you decided maybe I'm not some kind of villain after all, but because you wanted to trap me into admitting I am! Well, I've had enough of this." Annabel jumped to her feet, scattering the crumbs of her pâté.

Tremaine laughed softly. "If you don't find your way out, shall I tell Jeremy we're leaving without you?"

Annabel turned back to him, her anger becoming disappointment. They had been having such a lovely time! "Why? Why do you treat me like this? What have I done to make you think I'm a spy or worse?" Tears started rolling down her cheeks. "Don't you know I could never do anything to hurt

Jeremy? I already love him as much as you do. And though the Falcon doesn't trust me, either, I would never lead anyone to him, even if he were meaner to me than you are."

Annabel turned away, her shoulders shaking as she sobbed.

Then there were muscled arms around her and strong hands pulling her head gently against a hard chest. Tremaine stroked her hair, and Annabel felt his lips kissing the top of her head. Then the fingers tenderly lifted her chin so that her tear-soaked face was turned up toward his. Annabel caught her breath at the closeness of his lips; then they were closer, and she shut her eyes while her tears were kissed away.

"I'm sorry, my darling. I couldn't bear to think it was you, either. But there are those trying to trap me, and they'll use anything and anybody to accomplish their rotten ends."

"They aren't using me," Annabel whispered, her eyes welling with tears again.

With a soft groan, Tremaine bent his mouth to hers. "You taste like salt," he said a moment later, with a crooked little smile.

And you taste like divinity, Annabel thought weakly. The Falcon's rough kisses had been like hailstones, battering at her vulnerability. This man's kisses were like soft dew on the moonflower, inviting it to open itself to the night. "Jeremy says that you're practically my cousin, too."

"The hell with Jeremy. The only blood between you and me is that which is boiling in my veins right now as I think about what your kiss makes me want to do." His mouth captured hers again, and Isobel melted in his embrace, sure the earth would open beneath her weak knees.

She almost fell against him when he let her go suddenly. "No. No, that's how it would happen if you were an impostor. You'd have us all in your spell and we'd lose all our caution. Jeremy says you've already been with the Falcon. What if it had been him just now instead of me? You'd have him under your spell as you almost did me."

She didn't know whether to laugh or cry. Then an idea struck her. If she could come up with a plausible reason for not disembarking from the packet she was supposed to have been on, maybe Tremaine would believe she really was who she was taken to be. "Look, I guess it is time for me to be completely truthful. No, I'm not going to tell you I'm an impostor, but I am going to make a confession." Annabel took a deep breath. "I made up the story about the ship being too crowded and taking another one and then missing you at the dock because I was too ashamed to tell you the truth when I saw you."

"I can hardly wait to hear the truth for a change," Tremaine said dryly. "By all means, tell me."

"Well, I was a stowaway aboard the *Fugitive* instead of a paying passenger, and I sneaked off it with the freight so the captain wouldn't see me and have me thrown in jail."

"What happened to the money I sent you for the passage? Why didn't you buy a ticket as you were supposed to?"

Annabel's mind raced. What to tell him? How could she add the right touch of pathos that wouldn't leave her immersed in guilt over more lies? But Tremaine was capable of leaving her to spend the rest of her life in the maze if she didn't come up with something. "I . . . uh, lost the money you sent me and was too embarrassed to let anybody know."

Tremaine said gruffly, "So you decided to be a stowaway. My God, do you realize the kind of things that could happen to a young woman like you on a ship with all those rough men having the advantage of you?"

Annabel had the grace to feel slightly guilty. "Well, since neither the captain nor anyone else ever saw me, it turned out all right." They hadn't seen Annabel, she justified, happy to be truthful about at least one thing with this suspicious man.

Tremaine Sheffield patted the miniature of Isobel in his pocket. The girl's story held a ring of sincerity, but he still was going to ask more questions of the captain and perhaps this time a few shipmates, some of whom had to have spotted the "stowaway" at some time or other.

He had checked with his London shipping office about the whereabouts of the *Fugitive* and learned it would be in dock for the next two days before heading to Calais. Before it left, he would find out once and for all if Isobel had really been on that ship.

The miniature Isobel burned in his pocket as the full-sized one was beginning to do in his mind and heart.

The mood of the three travelers was extraordinarily gay. Annabel could not believe as she rode with her two handsome escorts that she was really on her way to 1818 London, booked in the Charing Cross Hotel on the Strand, and invited for tea with John Keats in Hampstead.

The banter between Jeremy and Tremaine was unending. Annabel gave up trying to compete and just looked out the window, drinking in the sights of the small villages they went through. Wrotham, Seven Oaks, West Wickham . . . it was increasingly hard to believe that all of this was real.

The feeling of unreality persisted through the late supper they shared in Jeremy's suite. She was planning to tour with Tremaine the next morning, have lunch with him and Jeremy at a tiny inn overlooking the Thames, be out-fitted for her new wardrobe in her room at the Charing Cross, then join Jeremy for tea in Hampstead.

Tremaine was the perfect tour guide, not giving the driver his head but telling him exactly which back streets to take, which old coach roads to use, and which to avoid because of disrepair or congestion. His crisp history of each place they visited, from the gateway to the "city," the old Temple Bar, to Fleet Street where Tremaine said Jeremy was meeting with a publisher, was concise and interesting. The driver finally sucked in his ale-reddened cheeks and just pointed.

Breakfast at Lincoln Inn left Annabel quiet and subdued. She was still thinking about her glimpse of the Traitor's Gate at the Tower and how prisoners such as Sir Thomas More had been accompanied through it, with the fatal sign of the "Ax of Office" telling what their sentence was even before they began the final walk to the Tower.

Annabel was hard put to describe what she felt as she moved about the city in Tremaine's company. "I think it has held up better than Los Angeles will," she murmured as they passed over London Bridge.

"What?" Tremaine was growing more used to his companion's strange sayings, though he was still having trouble with how he felt when she jostled against him in the occasionally rough bounces on cobbled streets. "Isobel, Bedlam is full of people who talk to themselves."

"Well, they get intelligent answers back, I'll bet. When's lunch? It's been at least three hours since I've consumed large quantities of food."

"You really do have an unusual way of stating things." But Tremaine leaned forward and instructed the driver, "Staple Inn." He sat back, his shoulder touching hers as he explained, not knowing that he was almost paraphrasing Charles Dickens, who would write about the "stillness of London" much later, "It's one of those little nooks one finds in the city, an island of cotton and velvet where we'll be away from the clash and crush of London."

Annabel knew only that the day was fast turning into one of total magic, one which she would never forget. After a bowl of soup at the inn, they moved on to meet Jeremy.

They had chops in the George & Vulture Tavern, along with large mugs of ale which Annabel hoped would not dull her excited observation of everything and everybody she saw in this most colorful era of England's history.

She sighed, and both men turned to her, one noticing how enchanting she looked in her dove-gray travel suit with black piping and smart feathered hat and the other concerned that she was getting overtired.

"Oh, no," she assured Jeremy. "To the contrary, I just hate the idea of spending the afternoon in my suite trying on clothes, when I could be out seeing everything."

"Well, it's not as though you will never get to London again," Jeremy said with amusement.

Annabel fought a sudden feeling of sadness. "I know you plan to see more writing friends, Jeremy, before we have tea with Keats. What about you, Tremaine? Will you be gadding about while I'm having my waist nipped in and tucked and heavens knows what else?"

Tremaine thought of the miniature in his pocket. "I have some important business to attend to involving shipping problems. And, I say, it's time we all got on with it. I'll see you two for sherry back at the hotel, then?"

Jeremy left, too, with a kiss on Annabel's cheek. "You'll love the pretty clothes, dearest. And if half of them look as fetching as what you're wearing, you'll set London on its ear. I'll have a carriage waiting for you outside to take you back to the Charing Cross."

Annabel had to admit it was fun having the proprietress of a high-toned ladies salon call upon her in her suite, with box after box of wonderful fashions, boots, and accessories. Tremaine had arranged for champagne to be sent up to accompany the trying-on of gown after gown. Annabel noticed with amusement that after about the first three gowns, Madame Heloise was well on her way to being inebriated, and she decided to quickly sort through the collection on her own. "This, and this, and oh, I could not live without this burgundy riding coat and the gray skirt . . . and this . . ."

By the time Annabel closed the door behind the dressmaker, she was exhausted—and the owner of a very modish new wardrobe. Exhausted, she decided against a nap. She still had two hours before the long-awaited tea. What should she do till then?

In Lord Lunsford's office Felicia Fenmore sat fanning herself and wishing that Lord Royalston, Lunsford's associate and a loud advocate of the current Corn Law and tax legislation in the House, would stop trying to look down her bosom.

But the news he had brought to his colleague and which Felicia was hearing now was more distressing than she cared to let on. "So the Falcon and his friends suspect that they're being watched and that not everyone in their scabby little audiences is on their side." Felicia shrugged. "What's that got to do with me?"

Lunsford leaned forward. "More than you think. It's a matter of time till someone identifies you and then your connection to me is discovered and then . . ." He looked at Royalston and waved his hand. "Tell her, Royalston, what you have in mind."

The other man had something quite different in mind but he hastily dragged his concentration away from Lady Fenmore's décolletage and forced it upon the issue at hand. "We've been watching that pack now, that Sheffield crowd, and know most of their comings and goings. There's an American girl that we think we could put to good use . . ."

"Don't trust that little snake for one minute!"

Derek Lunsford looked interested for the first time since the meeting had begun. He was growing bored with Felicia Fenmore and her prima donna vanity and was thinking seriously of having Royalston take her off his hands as soon as this Falcon affair was resolved. "I think you're letting your emotions rule, love. Tell her, Royalston, about your little plan."

"Very well. It will require your help, Derek, since the leak connects you with the mystery woman that the Falcon's aides are trying to uncover. But after you take a look at this picture that we, ah, borrowed from Jeremy Simmons's apartment, perhaps you won't be reluctant to play your little part in shifting suspicion from Lady Fenmore."

Lord Lunsford took the miniature laconically, then sat up very straight, adjusting his monocle which had fallen to his cheek. "Damn, the girl's a beauty."

Felicia said icily, "If you like women who take the sun on their skin and ride like Indian savages."

"Oh, come now, love, this is all business, a plan to keep you from falling under suspicion. And I certainly have no plans for a long-term seduction," he added untruthfully, looking more closely at Annabel's likeness and wondering how this plum had fallen into Sheffield's lap and if he were already bedding her . . .

"Your Lordship! We haven't much time!" Royalston insisted on regaining his colleague's wandering attention. "The young lady in question is alone in her suite at the Charing Cross Hotel as we speak. I have sent a note begging her to allow you to call on her in the receiving room to offer condolences on the death of her mother."

"Her mother? What's her mother got to do with any of this?"

"She was an actress briefly at Drury Lane before she left for America, when you were still a young man and quite impressed by the lovely Miss Miranda Fell." He stopped Lunsford's protest with an upraised hand. "While you're reminiscing with the young lady, who will come in for tea but young Jeremy, who'll be in Lady Fenmore's hands and very subtly guided to witness the supposedly clandestine meeting of his cousin with one of his family's and the Falcon's deadliest enemies."

"I never met Miranda Fell, nor do I have the slightest idea who she was!"

"She was small and blond and very pretty, and I'm sure that anything you say about her to her daughter will be welcomed. The main thing is that you'll be seen in cozy intimacy with her, and that fact will be reported back to Sheffield, and through him, to the Falcon. Our dear Lady Fenmore will be free to continue acting as our liaison with the insurgents, and attention will be diverted from her to the American."

Derek Lunsford's jaded eyes perused the face of the young woman smiling up at him from the duplicate of the picture that Tremaine Sheffield was at that moment showing to a young seaman.

Tremaine had spotted the *Fugitive,* a three-masted schooner, from London Bridge and could see the hands loading on supplies. He had hurried down and first spoken to the captain as protocol demanded.

The captain, whose eyes shifted from the picture he was shown very quickly, barked an order to the men scurrying below deck. "Watch those bales, you idiot. If they start swinging, they'll put the whole lot off balance." To Tremaine he said, "I told you, Sheffield, the girl wasn't on my ship. You think I don't know my passenger list? I'm one of the few Brits'll take on passengers with freight from Florida. A lot of us haven't forgotten New Orleans and those bloody pirates that dragged our troops through the swamps."

"She wasn't officially a passenger." Tremaine repeated Isobel's story about sneaking passage.

The captain laughed, but his eyes stayed cold and dangerous. "I'd like to see the slip of a girl who could pull off a bloody trick like that on Captain Pollack! Forget the girl. If she said she came in on my boat, she's lying. Whoever this vixen is, she's pulling something over on you."

He turned his back on Tremaine, obviously through with the interview and barking commands to the men loading the hold.

Tremaine stopped a young seaman who was carrying a bag of flour aboard. "You were on the trip over from America two weeks ago?" At the boy's nod, Tremaine showed him Isobel's picture. He saw the boy's mouth working painfully and then looked up to where the boy's eyes, suddenly frightened, had gone.

The captain was looking straight at the two of them, his face grim and menacing. The young seaman licked his lips nervously. "No sir, I never seen that girl on the boat or nowhere else. Now, the cap'n be hollering at me if I don't get on my way."

Tremaine's shoulders slumped. He had hoped against hope that he could prove once and for all that Isobel was who she claimed to be. "Well, I'll be in that pub over there for the next hour. If anybody you know saw the girl, I'd like to hear about it. And your captain will be none the wiser."

The sailor, seeing the captain's glaring face above, pretended not to hear and scurried down the plank toward the galley.

Tremaine waited alone in the dark pub. It was filled with sailors, but none was from the *Fugitive*, the barmaid informed him. "Wot's a chap like you doing here?" she asked him. "You could get a knife between your shoulders if you're being nosy about these sea fellows. They all have their secrets and they like them to stay secret."

Tremaine gave her an extra coin when he saw behind her the young seaman he'd asked about Isobel. "This is for keeping those secrets and bringing another ale for my young friend here."

The boy was sweating as he slipped into the chair at Tremaine's table. He drank down the draft of ale in one swallow. "Another."

Tremaine nodded to the barmaid, and she brought back two more mugs. "You saw that girl on board, didn't you?"

"If the cap'n finds out I'm talking to you, he'll have my throat slit." The boy looked around nervously.

"There's no one from your packet in here. I already checked. Why would he slit your throat for talking to me?"

"Because," the seaman began and downed his ale. "Because he said we didn't need to talk about what happened, that it was an accident and that some of us would be blamed and the boat held up. He's a bad man, the cap'n, and he's been known to cut a man before just for not speaking to 'im right."

"What happened? Dammit, man, I'll do worse to you than your captain would if you don't tell me. What happened to the girl?"

The boy licked his lips. "She was so pretty, and she talked to me real nice. She'd talk about how she didn't have nobody back home, but once she got to England, she'd have a real family again. I didn't think it was right, what he done, that's why I come here to see you."

Tremaine wanted to shake the man, to get out the rest of the story, but he restrained himself. "Your captain forced his advances on her, is that it? And then when she wouldn't have it, he put her off somewhere and that's why he's claiming he never saw her."

The boy shook his head, and to his amazement, Tremaine saw tears welling up in the dark eyes. "It was worse than that. I had night watch and I saw her crying out when the captain was trying to kiss her. Then the cap'n saw me and made me go below."

"Go on."

"Next morning she was gone. I looked in her cabin and there wasn't nothing left of hers. It was like she'd never been there. We'd been out to open sea for two days, warn't no land in sight. Besides we didn't stop nowhere. I finally got up the nerve to ask Cap'n Pollack where she was. He said . . . he said . . ." The boy wiped his eyes with a dirty sleeve and the final words came out in a whisper. "Cap'n said he tried to stop her, but she jumped off and drowned."

Tremaine stared at him, not believing what he'd heard. "Drowned?" He put his head down into his hands, knowing that what he had dreaded was true. The woman he was falling deeply in love with was an impostor, and the real Isobel was dead.

But how could the fake Isobel know that? Tremaine struggled with all the unanswered questions. Well, at least the captain would have a few to answer!

He lifted his head and saw the empty chair next to him only a moment before he heard the harbormaster signaling the all-clear for ships bound out to sea.

Chapter Ten

Felicia Fenmore was waiting for Jeremy when he came in the entrance to the Charing Cross. "Darling! I'm so glad to see you. Do buy me a spot of tea in the Fountain Room and let's catch up on the gossip." She put her arm through his and pulled him with her, not taking no for an answer, though Jeremy protested that he had to go up and change shortly for his tea engagement and his drive out to Hampstead.

"Oh, pooh, you have a few minutes. It's barely three o'clock and no respectable Englishman would serve tea till four. Come along, I've spotted a perfect table for two."

It was far back in a corner where they had a perfect view of the room but couldn't be easily seen. As Jeremy gave the order, tea and scones for the lady, whiskey for himself, Felicia peered over his shoulder, watching for the twosome she knew would be appearing at any minute. When they did so and were led to a table, she was annoyed at how charming Isobel looked in a voile and lace ensemble whose Empire lines showed off her figure becomingly. Lord Lunsford's fawning attention did not escape Felicia's notice, either.

"These scones are quite dry, waiter, and the tea practically cold," she snapped when she and Jeremy were served. "Please bring fresh."

Jeremy sipped his whiskey, looking at her wonderingly. "My, your mood is changeable. The scones looked fine to me, and I could swear I saw steam rising from the teapot."

Felicia restrained her anger. "Oh, these upstart waiters must be kept in their place, darling, I'm simply doing the hotel a favor." She chatted busily about the latest London gossip and fashion and which friends she had cut for being too busy to come to the country to visit, and then, seeing Lord Lunsford take Isobel's hand to kiss, she stopped in midsentence. "Oh, my dear, it can't be! But it is! Jeremy, there's Lord Derek Lunsford across the room, and you'll never in a thousand years guess who he's with."

Jeremy's whiskey glass was frozen at his lips at the mention of the corrupt, powerful enemy of the Sheffields. Slowly he turned in his chair, just in time to see his cousin's hand at the lips of a man who Tremaine had said was singly responsible for most of the destructive legislation of the past twenty years. "What the . . . ? How on earth would Isobel know that blackguard? And what the devil is she doing keeping company with him?" Jeremy threw down his napkin and scraped back his chair, but Felicia restrained him.

"Darling, it's obvious she doesn't want to be discovered. Let the girl have her little secrets. After all, you're her cousin, not her keeper. This is London, city of rendezvous and assignation. Let your little country mouse sniff the air of the cosmopolitan life."

Jeremy sank back down, though he glowered at the pair, who had still not seen him. "It's rotten air that she'll be sniffing around him," he muttered. "What the devil? He's passing her money!" Jeremy stared in bewilderment as he saw Lunsford press several pound notes into his cousin's hand.

"Perhaps your little Isobel is employing that so-called American free enterprise and charging him for her company."

Jeremy flung out his chair and threw down money for their service. "Dammit, Felicia, that's not funny. Please excuse me, but I've had enough of watching my cousin being taken in by that bastard manipulator." He strode from the room, not looking back.

Felicia was not far behind, though she lingered long enough at the entrance to catch Lunsford's eye and nod.

It had gone perfectly as planned. The seeds of distrust were firmly planted in young Jeremy's mind. Lily-white Isobel was for all practical purposes compromised, Felicia thought gleefully. And dear Derek would pay for drooling over her far beyond the call of duty.

"Lord Lunsford, I cannot accept money from you. This so-called Aspiring Actors Fund sounds quite worthwhile, but I cannot consent to starting such a foundation in my mother's name." It had been all Annabel could do to manage not to look surprised to find out that Isobel's mother had been an actress in her youth. And her instincts about this man who claimed ties to her were unflattering, to say the least.

He took with feigned disappointment the pound notes she handed back to him. "But I tell you, people like your mother—whom I saw only once in her brief stage career—bring pleasure to others far beyond their compensation. Why, I was only a small boy when I saw Miranda Fell, but I shall never, ever forget her grace and charm."

Annabel knew she had to steer the conversation away from this dangerous ground. She had absolutely no knowledge of Isobel's mother and her acting career. "Lord Lunsford, it's painful for me to talk about my mother. Do you mind . . . ?"

"Well, of course." Lunsford changed the subject hastily, keeping his gaze averted from the table across the room. He could feel Felicia's glares burning into his skull. "Will you do me the honor of dining with me some evening when next you visit London?"

"As I said, I'm not sure if I'll be in England much longer." Annabel took up her wrap and stood, holding out her hand for a farewell shake. "Thank you for the reminiscences about my late mother. It was kind of you to look me up."

"Well, when Jeremy let it out that his cousin was coming from America, I was excited at the prospect of meeting the daughter of the lady on whom I had a huge crush from the age of six." He held her hand lingeringly, then put it up to his lips. "An infatuation which can easily be transferred."

Annabel withdrew her hand abruptly. "I must go. Jeremy will be wondering what happened to me."

Indeed he will, thought Lunsford as he watched Annabel make her way across the room. Indeed he will.

Meanwhile, Jeremy was pacing up and down in Tremaine's room, waiting for his step-brother's arrival. Should he tell him about the meeting, feed his already deep suspicions about Isobel? "But, no, she could be none other than my cousin!" he said, thinking of the miniature, the warm memories of their parents they'd shared. "There's some reasonable explanation. Isobel herself will probably tell me about it, how the arrogant bloke sat down without an invitation and immediately began flirting with her. He's notorious for that."

Tremaine came in the door and at the grim look on his face, Jeremy knew something was dreadfully wrong. "Trey! My God, what's happened? Not another arrest of one of our London contacts!"

"No. I thought you and Isobel would be gone already." All the way back to the hotel, Tremaine had dreaded telling his stepbrother the truth. The younger man was so enamored of the girl and had taken her into his heart so totally that Tremaine was afraid this final indictment of Isobel's sincerity would break his heart. *I won't tell him yet. I'll let her play out her game, see what she's up to, find out who's behind it; then I'll pack her off to America on the next boat. Jeremy need never know.*

At the same time, Jeremy was deciding on a similar plan. His news would turn Trey completely against her, and perhaps it was just a coincidence, her being with Lunsford. *I'll wait to see what she says on the way out to Hampstead. Maybe I won't have to say anything to Trey at all.* "No, she got through with her fitting early and was down in the Fountain Room having an ice. I . . . glimpsed her in there on my way in."

"Well, you caught me reeling from the news of a very bad price fall in the wool market. My Calais office had to sell at losses for the month."

"Oh, so that accounts for the grimness. Look, old bean, are you sure you won't ride out with Isobel and me? I'm sure Keats would love to meet you, I've talked about you often enough."

Tremaine shook his head. He was considering finding the closest pub and drinking himself into a stupor. To think he had started caring about the vixen! That innocent look, those heart-melting smiles, they were all sham. "No, thanks. I'm not feeling very poetic at the moment."

"Well, we shan't be late for dinner."

"Oh, that reminds me of a thought I had on the way back from my . . . office. I've heard rumors and more rumors about the Falcon. It seems that even after our little ruse the other night, Lord Sheffield still thinks me the leader of the insurgents. Perhaps as you mentioned the other night, it's time to dispel that rumor. I could be arrested and interrogated at any moment if the bastards get to rumbling any louder."

He explained his plan, and Jeremy agreed to it enthusiastically.

Annabel would not have traded anything in the world for the wonderful afternoon she spent in the company of one of the greatest poets of English literature.

She was filled with awe upon entering the small house, whose interior was exactly as she would have pictured it: books and prints everywhere, small mementoes of his tramps all over the country, worn but comfortable furniture placed without much thought to decor, but every attention to sensory gratification. Annabel thought she might faint when John Keats, not as tall as she but still well formed and compact before the illness that would waste his body, held out his hand. She looked with hidden emotion at the clear-cut features, into the large, meditative dark eyes, and saw him to be the open, kindly, manly person that literary history had portrayed him to be. That he was sensuous to a fault, a character trait that critics had deemed weakening to his poetry and deleterious to his health, lay in Annabel's mind as she listened to the sweet melody of his voice.

Jeremy was excitedly telling his friend about his newest poem and, in the midst of it, showed concern for his friend's state of health. "I say, I heard when I went by Blackwood's that you'd been sent home from Inverness. You and Brown really made an ambitious tramp."

Keats laughed, his eyes soft with the images of all he'd seen on his trek through the Lake District and part of Scotland with his friend Armitage Brown. "Yes, but I apparently overdid as usual. The physician at Inverness ordered me back here." Keats's face saddened as he added, "Poor Tom. I got home in time to nurse him through this damnable consumption of his. My brother amazes me, though. He's loud and boisterous and always joking, even when he's so sick he can't hold his head up. But enough of that! Miss Isobel, will you do the honors while I see to my brother? I heard him coughing just now and should see if he needs a drink."

"He's wonderful," Annabel said, her eyes full of tears, knowing that Keats's own health was failing and that he was less than three years away from his own death. "Cousin, I'm so very glad that you got over your pique with me. I could swear on the ride over that you were angry with me. . . . That is, until I told you about my strange encounter with an obnoxious stranger who turned out to be a man you despise."

Jeremy had been overjoyed when Isobel had volunteered her story of being accosted by a man who claimed to know her "mother." He pointed out the weakness in Lunsford's claim: Miranda Fell had never used her real name in her career.

"He was using you to try to get at us, I'm sure," Jeremy had said, cheered by Isobel's explanation. He could now mention the incident to Trey without fearing its negative effect on his feelings toward Isobel. "Avoid Lunsford and the other muckety-mucks he runs with, Cousin."

"That won't be hard," Annabel had muttered, remembering her repulsion at having the man's lips at her flesh.

Now Jeremy said, just before his friend came back into the room, "Angry with you? Whatever gave you that idea! Keats, old soul, my cousin is much too polite to make the request herself so I'll make it for her. Please read one of your poems. Of course, I shall plug up my ears since I don't enjoy such things." They all laughed at that.

"I shall shock your cousin with my grisly little story poem whose title bears a resemblance to her own name."

Jeremy clapped his hands. " 'Isabella, or The Pot of Basil.' Oh, Isobel, prepare to weep."

"Or laugh at its absurdity, as people sometimes did at Boccaccio." The poet cleared his throat and read the poem about a young woman whose love for a young man of whom her brothers disapproved went far beyond the grave. When Keats got to the part about Isabella planting the severed head of her murdered sweetheart in a pot and daily combing the basil that sprouted, Annabel felt delicious shivers go up her spine. She and Jeremy sat in rapt attention before applauding at the end.

"That should show your critics who called 'Hyperion' the work of a 'poor man's Milton.' By George, you are going to be the greatest poet alive, my friend."

Or dead, Annabel added to herself, the old sadness creeping back in. And when the poet deflected their praise with typical modesty, she thought about how erroneous the epitaph that would appear on his tombstone turned out to be: "Here lies one whose name was writ on water.—Feb. 23, 1821."

In her emotion, Annabel came close to making a real blunder. "You should write a poem in honor of Miss Fanny Brawne."

At the stares that that brought her, Annabel suddenly realized the reason for Keats's perplexed expression. He would not meet and fall in love with Fanny Brawne until the approaching fall. "I beg your pardon?" Keats said. "Is this an English personage with whom I should be familiar?"

Oh, dear. What if she had just stuck her finger in the future of this man and caused it to shift somewhat?

"I . . . it's just a name I saw somewhere in a romance novel. Oh, Jeremy, I do so hate to be the one to say this, but we really must be leaving if we're to be on time for dinner with your brother."

Jeremy thought of the plan he and Tremaine meant to put in force that night. "My dear, in the excitement, I failed to tell you. I shall have to leave you in the hands of my stepbrother. I've been asked to dinner at Joseph Severn's to see some of his paintings—"

"Which are absolutely stunning," Keats interjected. "We shall all be gathering in his honor, just a motley group of frustrated artists such as myself—"

"And Charles Dilke and Armitage Brown." To Annabel he added, "Don't let him fool you, Cousin. In spite of some of the nasty remarks by jealous critics, Keats is held in the highest regard by his old friends."

"Add to that by his new friends and pray that he will count me among those." Annabel was a little disappointed that she could not be a part of such a distinguished evening, but the thought of having another interlude with Tremaine Sheffield was almost as exciting. "Will you be leaving with us for Sheffield in the morning, Jeremy?"

"No, in fact, I'll just have to make my own arrangements to go home, perhaps tomorrow afternoon or the next."

Annabel kissed Jeremy. "I'll miss you, dear. Please see to it that he doesn't keep you up all night talking, Mr. Keats."

"John, please. And I'll take one of those cousinly kisses, if you don't mind."

Alone in the carriage on the way back to the hotel, Annabel held her finger to her cheek where Keats had kissed her and wished she could preserve the precious spot as she would always preserve her memory of actually meeting the greatest English Romantic poet.

Tremaine's heart lurched when he saw Annabel coming down the stairs to meet him in the Charing Cross Hotel lobby. Her dark hair was caught up on one side with a glittery ornament and cascaded charmingly across the other shoulder. The white dress with its off-the-shoulder style nipped in at her tiny waist, then clung to slender hips before falling to a flounce at the knees. A suggestion of glitter at the daring split drew stares from all over the lobby. Tremaine caught envious looks when Annabel glided toward him and put her arm through his.

"You look ravishing. Let's be on our way before I have to fight a duel over you."

Annabel noticed that not a few women in the room were apparently smitten with her escort's looks. Tremaine was indeed striking in black and white formal attire. He never showed the slightest sign that he knew the whispers behind the fans concerned the vivid scar on his face.

"Where are we going?" Annabel was helped into the open carriage and Tremaine squeezed in next to her, making it hard for her to concentrate on the sights of a darkening London.

"Oh, you'll find out soon enough." Tremaine leaned forward and whispered an address to the driver. Annabel was too busy observing the teeming life of the Strand to notice the surprised expression on the man's face.

She thought about the grim sights that had met those who passed through the old Temple Bar, as the Strand met with the city proper. Severed heads and limbs of persons executed for high treason had served as reminders to the living about the folly of betrayal. Daniel Defoe had once been pilloried there for his "treasonous" writings. His admirers had pelted him with flowers instead of the usual rotten fruit and dead cats and had strewn the arch with flowers.

"I'm sorry, Tremaine. You were saying . . . ?"

"You certainly seem entranced with our city." Annabel didn't know it, but he had been watching her face as she'd craned her neck to see everything. Perhaps her mother had been a mediocre actress, the man thought cynically, but the daughter was a past mistress at dissembling. "I said, I am very sorry Jeremy couldn't be with us, on one hand. On the other, I haven't been alone with you, really alone, since we've been in London."

The way he was looking at her made Annabel's insides quiver. "It's difficult to be alone anywhere in this city. There are so many people, so much going on. Do Londoners ever sleep?"

"They generally make time for the normal activities, such as . . . sleeping."

Annabel was puzzled by the new tone in his voice. It was, well, insulting almost. Maybe Tremaine's recent improved attitude toward her had been for Jeremy's benefit alone. "Oh, how beautiful!"

They'd pulled up in front of one of the fine old residences on Mansion House Street. As Tremaine helped her from the carriage, she looked up to see a curtain flutter at an upstairs window. "The finest private dining in London. Madame Charlotte Eames prepares individual dinners for the elite who don't wish to jostle with the public."

Upstairs, Lord Derek Lunsford pressed fifty pounds into the plump, beringed hand of the proprietess of Number 52. "They're here. Now remember, Charley, you must be subtle. Sheffield knows your reputation for discretion. If you tell right out that you've seen the girl here with me many times, he'll be suspicious. Let something drop, and then pretend you're devastated at what you have done."

The money went into the safekeeping of Madame Charlotte's ample bosom. "Leave it to me, love. Not even the girl will be aware of what's going on."

The man left by the back stairs as Tremaine and Annabel were entering the front door. Madame Charlotte made a big fuss over her guests, raving to Tremaine about his beautiful companion. To Annabel she whispered, though loud enough that Tremaine could hear as he was meant to do, "The white dress is ever so much more becoming than the red one you wore last time. And this one," she hooked her head indicating Tremaine who was idly examining a whatnot in the foyer but really listening to every word, "is much handsomer."

"I'm sorry?" Annabel said, not whispering. "You must have me confused with someone else."

In the mirror Tremaine could see the broad conspiratorial wink that accompanied Madame's innocent, "Oh, of course I do. Will you have the brocade or the jade silk room, Your Lordship?"

"The brocade will do nicely. And we'll have champagne to start, with strawberries if you have them."

"For you, anything. Follow me, love."

Annabel was sure she had never dined in a more opulent room. The rich brocade was draped over an ornate gold table set for two in front of a deep-cushioned settee. Everywhere were richly fringed pillows. A scent of lilac permeated the room, which was lit by candles. "It's . . . unique." Annabel didn't know what else to say.

They were alone with the champagne and strawberries that had been brought immediately. Annabel hesitated about where to sit, but Tremaine decided that for her, leading her to the settee. "Now for the champagne." He poured glasses of the bubbling liquid and sat beside her. "Cozy, isn't it?" He picked up a strawberry and took a bite from it, looking at the creamy swell of Annabel's bosom as he did so. "Delicious," he murmured. He reached over and pressed the remaining half of the strawberry between Annabel's lips.

She chewed numbly, wishing Tremaine would stop looking at her as if she were next on the menu. "Oh, I do wish Jeremy could have come along, though I'm sure he much prefers being with his artist friends. Tremaine, please, not another. I don't want to spoil dinner. Won't it be coming any moment?"

Tremaine laughed at that. The little vixen knew from previous visits here that the meals were served at midnight if at all. "One more won't hurt. Just for me." He put the plump strawberry to her lips, letting his fingers slide into the moisture behind it, and murmured, "Save half for me," before pulling his portion out lingeringly and popping it in his mouth.

Annabel's nervousness was increasing by the minute. "Do you know, Tremaine, maybe we should just go back to the hotel since we're leaving early in the morning. I'm not really hungry, anyway."

"But I've already ordered for us." Tremaine poured them more champagne. "Relax, Isobel. You keep looking at me as if you think I'm going to bite you."

That was exactly what she'd been thinking, Annabel thought. She almost jumped straight up when Tremaine suddenly stretched out and put his head in her lap. "Here, come and get it and you win." He put a strawberry between his teeth and pulled her head down toward his.

"Tremaine, what if someone walked in right now and saw us doing this silly strawberry thing?"

"They won't, believe me. If there's another good thing about this place beside the strawberries, it's the privacy. Now, come on, be a good sport. You've accused me of being stiff and formal with you and here I'm trying to be playful and you act like you're trapped with Genghis Khan."

Reluctantly, Annabel lowered her lips to the waiting strawberry. As her teeth got a purchase on the fruit, Tremaine swallowed it and captured lips already moist and sweet.

The kiss went on for a very long time, though Annabel tried hard to free herself. She had enjoyed the embrace in the maze, but this time she felt that Tremaine was distancing himself from the lovemaking.

When he started pulling her off-shoulder gown down further and buried his face in the cleavage revealed, she struggled to sit back up. The settee was a soft trap, and Tremaine was taking advantage of her helplessness. "Please don't do this. I was just beginning to really like you and feel safe with you. You're a gentleman, not someone like the Falcon, who forced himself on me."

"I thought you had the notion, or so Jeremy says, that I really am the Falcon."

"Jeremy said you couldn't be, and he would never lie to me."

Tremaine sat up, looking at the girl with an expression close to pity. He was beginning to think the girl was not as manipulative as she was naïve. "Isobel, take my advice and remember that everybody lies when there's no other way out. I'm not talking about my stepbrother, he's as honest a soul as you could meet, but I am talking about most men." She looked so adorable with her hair mussed and her dress askew that he had to fight his baser instincts which had led him to bring her here.

Why hadn't he followed through with the seduction? The girl, whoever she was, intrigued him and set his pulses racing every time he was around her. It wasn't as if he would be ruining an innocent young woman like the real Isobel, who'd drowned, no doubt protecting her chastity from that bastard captain. This woman was a spy for the most infamous fornicator in London and no doubt had been passed around to his friends.

Still, he couldn't bring himself to make love to this girl as he'd vowed to do before they left Madame Charley's. "You know, you're right about the service being slow here. We'll go back to the hotel and have the cook send you up a pork pie and ale. And I'll have the same, only double, in my room."

The look of relief on the girl's face really shocked Tremaine and made him wonder if she truly did look on him as some kind of predator. *Was I that bad?* he thought with a tinge of amusement. She didn't seem to mind the Falcon's embrace all that much.

He had thought the strawberries added a creative touch. Once her lips had met his over them, he'd stopped thinking about anything except how very much he wanted to make love to this girl and have her make love back.

The first news that greeted the travelers when they got to Sheffield Hall was that the Falcon had held a meeting the night before in a field outside Leeds. Tremaine had smiled secretly at Annabel's transparent expression of astonishment.

When Jeremy came up two hours later, still in his travel clothes, he and Tremaine exchanged looks that carried mutual self-congratulation: it had worked!

Actually, as Jeremy told his stepbrother later when they met privately to discuss the previous night's rally, he had enjoyed taking Tremaine's place as the Falcon. "I could get used to having people cheer at everything I say, have them look at me like I'm some kind of hero."

"Well, maybe I can remind you of your eagerness to fill the Falcon's mask when he catches a bullet or is hauled off to Newgate."

Jeremy didn't laugh very hard at Tremaine's little joke. He knew that someday his stepbrother would be called to task for the unrest he'd raised among thousands of people. And when that time came, Jeremy vowed to himself, he would be right there by the Falcon's side.

Chapter Eleven

Annabel's London adventures were enough to make her content to enjoy the serenity of Sheffield Hall for the next few days. She resumed the pleasant routine of morning coffee with Jeremy, a ride before lunch, a stroll or ride by the river in the afternoon. Sometimes she had tea with Jeremy in the tower, while he read his newest poetry aloud.

How she longed to be able to share with him some of the famous odes that marked Keats's declining years and finest period of genius. But she had a responsibility, she knew, to refrain from revealing the secrets that only she knew.

Tremaine kept his distance, though every

time she came near, he watched her. The evening at Madame Charley's might have been a dream. Now that the Falcon had made his appearance at a time when Tremaine Sheffield had been visible in London, the talk about him died down. Sometimes Annabel dreamed about the Falcon, about his strong arms around her, about the strange feelings she'd had in his embrace, as though he were her protector.

"He's an outlaw," she would remind herself and go to one of her favorite idling places, the garden off the kitchen yard, where bountiful colorful flowers vied for space with the herbs and vegetables.

One morning she was out with her basket, a beribboned hat shading her from the sun, an occasional breeze lifting the soft skirts of her summery morning gown, when she looked over to see Jeremy standing in the tower watching her.

She waved at him and he waved back. Picking up her skirts and holding on to her hat like a schoolgirl, she ran across the grounds to the tower and, out of breath by the time she reached the top, panted, "I picked these for you." She held out the basket of peonies, roses, and snapdragons.

"And I wrote this for you."

Jeremy held up a sheet of paper and read the title. "To Isobel, in Her Garden."

Annabel was dumbstruck when she read the poem that had started the whole adventure.

"Oh, Jeremy, that's beautiful. I hope you'll show it to your friend Keats."

"I did. Right after you left that night. He teased me about imitating him in some spots, but I could tell he liked it. He made some notes, see? And while I usually don't affix my name to my poems for superstitious reasons, I signed this one just for you."

Annabel held her breath as she saw the spidery handwriting that would endure two centuries. "Will you let me have it?"

"Oh, no, I must revise it and make you a neat copy; then you can have it."

Mustn't tamper with the future, Annabel reminded herself, as much as she longed to have the original. If events were to follow as they must, the manuscript with notes from Keats must be placed beneath the stone . . . she wondered when. "I'm more touched than you know, to have you write a poem just for me."

"Trey was up here just now. We watched you as you cavorted in the garden, and I must say, a pretty picture it was. When I said as much, my stepbrother didn't even hear me. I think he's entranced by you, darling."

"That's not the word I would use. Has he talked to you about our evening in London?"

"About taking you to dinner at Madame Charley's? Indeed, he did and I must tell you, I was shocked that he would expose you to that level of London society."

"Oh, so then it was not a respectable place, after all." Annabel said to herself grimly, *I thought as much.*

"Respectable?" Jeremy laughed. "Ha! Far from it. That's where married men take their mistresses or less-than-acceptable liaisons to have private rendezvous. I gave my stepbrother a hefty piece of my mind for taking you there, but he said he thought you might enjoy seeing that side of London."

"I think he took me there to . . ." She couldn't bring herself to say it, to put Jeremy in the middle of the bizarre relationship between her and his stepbrother. "To shock the naïve little American. But no harm came of it."

"I say, you didn't by chance run across Lunsford while you were there? The Charing Cross proprietor told me when I checked out that someone had snooped around and found where you two were dining that evening. I thought perhaps that snake might have been behind it and planned to barge in on you again as he did in the Fountain Room."

"No, I didn't see anyone I knew, although . . ." Annabel thought back to the proprietress of 52 Mansion House Road and how she had acted as though Annabel were a familiar visitor. Well,

Jeremy didn't need to have that to worry about, she decided. "Although I must say I was far too busy ogling the place to pay any attention to other guests. Jeremy, was that all Tremaine had to say about our evening?"

"Well . . . he acted a little reluctant to talk about it. But then, he's been acting peculiar about you ever since we returned from London. When I told him about the absurd interview you had with Lunsford, he didn't say a word, though I thought he'd be angry about the man's insufferable nerve, as I was. He just looked grimmer than ever."

In fact, Jeremy recalled, Trey had said several words about Lunsford. That was why he had stormed out of the tower when he'd seen Annabel heading up to the tower with her basket. "Lunsford would never give a shilling to some ridiculous cause like the Aspiring Actors Fund and we both know it," Trey had told Jeremy. "He wouldn't dare approach your cousin in public, either, unless he had good reason to know she was amenable."

"Trey, what on earth are you getting at?" Jeremy had said. "Isobel couldn't have met Lunsford previously! Besides, she volunteered the information about the meeting and seemed just as puzzled as I am by your suspicions."

"Of course, she would tell you about seeing Lunsford. She knew you would think it odd that she'd met with one of our family's deadliest opponents." Trey had murmured mysteriously, "When I know everything for certain, I won't be suspicious anymore."

Annabel was resting in her room when a frightening thought struck her. What if Lunsford had sought her out with a more menacing purpose than any of them had guessed? What if someone had seen her wearing his wife's stolen jewels the night of the gala and reported to him?

"Of course, I don't really know that they were stolen," she thought. "Tremaine might have said that just to frighten me." She walked over to take the necklace and earrings from the drawer where she'd secreted them. The garnets gleamed up at her like evil ruby eyes. "What must I do? Why would the Falcon give these to me if they were indeed stolen? Only he has the answer." She would not take them to the constable until she was sure that they were indeed the property of Lady Lunsford.

"Even then, it'll get the Falcon into deeper trouble, since I'll have to reveal how I came to have the jewels." Annabel sat down on the bed, worrying.

"There's only thing I can do, without getting everybody into trouble, including me. I have to give them back to the Falcon."

But how would she find him? The leader of the Corn Laws revolution had not been active since the night she and Tremaine were in London.

"Greymalkin. That old woman knows everything that goes on." The cat who'd been sleeping at the foot of Isobel's bed raised her head and looked at her mistress with wide cat-eyes. "Yes, I'll ask Greymalkin if she can get a message to the Falcon that I want to meet him."

She put the jewels back in their hidingplace and, with a final stroke of the cat, went downstairs to find Jeremy's old nanny.

Annabel had never been inside Greymalkin's room before and was a little nervous about going in it without an invitation. Jeremy had told her how the old woman had moved into a closed-off wing of the old servants' quarters that was no longer used. The stairs down off the pantry that led to the abandoned cellar floor were dusty and cobwebby. Annabel felt her way gingerly, glad she'd brought her candle.

When she reached the foot of the stairs, her light flickered over musty old wine racks and trunks that were rusted with disuse. Maude had told her that Greymalkin's room was right off the cellar, and Annabel made her way along the wall toward a door that showed a dim light beneath it.

Her hand slid over a cold, slippery surface and she let out a little yip when a bat flew off, squeaking shrilly.

"Mary Shelley, where are you now? This would be the perfect setting for the sequel to your *Frankenstein*."

She knocked on the door to the old woman's room, surprised when it eased open at her first touch. "Oh, dear. I don't like this." She held her candle up to augment the one that was sputtering on a table in a corner of the sparsely furnished room. "Jeremy, you should be ashamed of yourself, letting your poor old faithful nanny live like this." The room was bare except for a crudely made wooden bed, the table, and an ancient trunk. "Greymalkin?" Annabel called uncertainly. Then she jumped and yipped again when something warm wrapped around her ankle. "Oh, Moonbeam, will you please stop doing that to me?"

The voice that spoke from a dark corner followed a low chuckle. "Cats like to sneak up on people. You should know that by now."

"Greymalkin, you scared me more than the cat did. What are you doing sitting there in the dark not saying anything?"

"I long ago found that people don't want to hear what I have to say."

Greymalkin came into the light, her yellow-green eyes catching the light of Annabel's candle. "Be careful of that dripping wax. Everything's dried up like the grave down here and a spark could burn us all down."

"I'm going to speak to Jeremy about this," Annabel said, indignant that the old woman who'd cared for him from childhood should be living like a vagrant.

"I like it. He's tried to put me in one of those fancy rooms like you stay in, but I'm like a mushroom. I thrive on mustiness and dark. What you be coming to me for, girl? Wanting a few newts' eyes and mandrake roots to put a spell on somebody?" The woman cackled. "In my day, I could've accommodated you, but I gave that hocus-pocus up a long time ago."

"No, I'm not here to get a hoodoo to put on anybody." Annabel's nose wrinkled up. "Lord, what is that awful smell?"

Greymalkin cackled again. "I'm stirring me up some witch's brew. Isn't that what witches are supposed to do? No, come on, girl, I know you aren't here to smell my soup. What is it that's brought you down to see old Greymalkin in the second floor up from Hades?"

Annabel decided not to beat about the bush. "I need to meet with the Falcon and I know that you're probably the only one who will tell me where I can find him."

"And what makes you think I would tell you, even if I could?" The bright eyes, so incongruously alive in the wrinkled flesh and humped form, didn't stray from Annabel's.

"Because you know that I'm here for reasons that not even you understand and that I have to be given enough time to do what I came to do."

They stared unflinchingly at each other, the old woman and the young one, both aware that of all the people at Sheffield Hall, they were the only two aware that anything unusual had transpired with Annabel's arrival.

"I'm an old worn-out cat, I can't outstare you," Greymalkin said finally with a snaggle-toothed grin. "But if you'd been around in my younger days . . . all right, you want to meet with the Falcon. It's not a smart thing to do, Missy. People in these parts are protective of him and what he's doing. They won't take kindly to finding out you're here to show him up."

"That's not what I want, I just have to see him. It's . . . it's a matter of great importance, one that could affect him as well as me."

The old woman narrowed her eyes and took a drag from a clay pipe that had been smoldering in a bowl by the soup. "Jeremy said I wasn't to be talking to anyone about the Falcon, not nobody."

"I'm not just anyone. I'm a member of this family."

"Well, I'm not convinced about that," Greymalkin said, holding out the elderly pipe. "Want a puff?"

Why not? She hadn't had a cigarette in . . . Annabel took a long drag off the pipe and blew the smoke out her nostrils, impressing Greymalkin greatly.

"How'd you do that?" The old woman looked at the smoke curling up to the aged ceiling and back at the younger woman. "I'll make you a covenant, Missy. You teach me how to do that and I'll tell you where you can find the Falcon."

"Deal. And I promise I won't ever bring you into it if something goes awry."

"I know you won't."

Greymalkin finally got the hang of French-inhaling, and the first time she sucked smoke up her nostrils, she gave a whoop and cackle that Annabel was sure would bring down the crumbling masonry of the old woman's tomb-like quarters.

Annabel had made friends with the stable-boy, Perkins, and had ridden at odd hours on enough occasions that he didn't think anything about her asking him to saddle up Lady Godiva an hour after dinner, when everyone had retired to his or her own bedroom.

"Well, Miss, I just hope you'll watch out for sinkholes on the path along the river. That can throw a horse, even the most surefooted, and hurt a body for sure."

"I'll be very careful." Annabel fastened the black cape she'd put on over her riding outfit, wanting to blend with the velvet night as much as possible. "Perkins, if anyone asks about me, just say I've gone out for a ride to be by myself. Mister Jeremy especially might worry. Please try to set his mind at ease. You've seen how I ride."

"Yes, Mum, I have," the man said admiringly. "Nobody don't need to worry about you on horseback, that's for sure."

"Thanks." Lady Godiva, as though knowing they were on another adventure, was pacing to be off and Annabel let her have her head, though she reined her in at the turnoff from the main road that Greymalkin had told her to watch for.

From there she would seek the woodcutter's cottage that Greymalkin had told her would be the place where she could find the Falcon.

Annabel's heart pounded along with Lady

Godiva's hooves as she sped through the dark night, the garnet necklace and earrings in her cape pocket weighing heavily on her hip and conscience.

Chapter Twelve

When Annabel dismounted at the deserted-looking cottage, the enormity of what she was letting herself in for struck her and she almost climbed back on Lady Godiva and lit out for home.

But the weight of the garnets in her pockets reminded her that she had a good reason to seek out the Falcon. She refused to admit that perhaps the jewels were an excuse to see the Falcon again.

"Hello?" she called softly as she opened the door. "Is anyone here?" A woodmouse ran across her foot and she let out a little scream.

There was no one in the tiny cottage. Annabel could see that when her eyes adjusted to the dark. In fact, there was very little to see. "Surely no one could live here," she said, her nose wrinkling at the unkempt straw mattress and broken wooden table that provided the only furnishings of the miserable cottage. The Falcon was too proud a creature to roost in these poor quarters.

Disappointed, she went back and remounted Lady Godiva for the ride home. As she passed the clump of trees before rounding the last bend near the main road, a dark shape suddenly appeared at her side.

A hand went out to stifle the scream in her throat. "Shh. You've already alerted everyone within a mile's hearing with that little show of hysterics in my humble abode."

It was the Falcon on his black horse. "Will you stay quiet now if I remove my hand?" he asked.

Annabel nodded enthusiastically, and the Falcon lowered his hand to the reins of her horse. "Why weren't you in the house where I was told to meet you?" she queried.

"I wanted to make sure you didn't have someone waiting to surprise us. Besides, falcons don't like to be caged up."

"I can see why. That's a dreadful place. Surely you could manage a nicer hideout."

The Falcon drew closer, looking at her with those glittering eyes that seemed all the more mysterious for their slitted holes. "You're a funny little creature, worrying about the Falcon's nest. Last time we met, you could hardly wait to escape my clutches."

"I . . . have important business. Where can we talk?" She didn't relish the idea of going back to the depressing little house, but it was dangerous out here in the open.

"Well, I can't take you to my real 'hideout' as you oddly call it, though I think you would love it. You're still an unknown, Miss Isobel Copeland-or-whoever-you-really-are, and I can't take the chance of your leading my enemies to my eyrie."

"Eagles have eyries, not falcons," she blurted out.

"I have a place where we'll be safe and I can have my moonlight swim while we talk. Maybe you would even be interested in joining me." The glint of devilish amusement in the slitted eye slots made her sniff with disdain.

"I don't go swimming at night with my friends, much less strangers."

"But, Isobel, you know as well as I do that you and I are not strangers to each other." The mesmerizing whisper froze her blood, and she knew the Falcon spoke the truth. Her feelings for him were as confusing as those she felt for Tremaine. How much simpler to explain that confusion had the two turned out to be one and the same!

"I . . . will watch from the bank. If anyone comes, you can swim away and I'll say I just got lost on my moonlight ride."

"You'd cover for me?" He was leading the horses deep into the copse, through thick shrubs and overgrown thickets which seemed almost to open up for them to pass through. When they reached a seemingly impassable hedge, the Falcon dismounted and opened up a disguised gate. "Enter my private retreat, Your Ladyship. This is not my real 'hideout,' but it's a place where I often relax by myself."

She gave a little exclamation of pleased surprise when Lady Godiva poked her nose through the last leafy barrier and a little fairyland opened up before their eyes. A stream cascaded over rocks, water merrily gurgling. Grassy banks ringed with sheltering low-growing trees were dotted with wildflowers. Frogs and small wood creatures made their night calls.

Annabel caught her breath when a doe, her delicate nose sniffing for the source of the new human scent, came gingerly to the opposite edge to drink. "Oh, how beautiful," she whispered.

"You don't have to whisper. That's Guinevere. I saved her from a pack of the King's hunting dogs and she's been a pet ever since. Watch this."

The Falcon gave a soft whistle between his teeth and the doe lifted her head, then bounded across the stream's shallows to poke her nose into the man's outstretched hand. "She loves sweetmeats," he said, scratching the deer behind her ears.

Annabel watched the spectacle, not believing that this could be the same man feared by powerful politicians, revered by landowners and working people alike.

She was seeing the man behind the mask.

When Guinevere had left, the Falcon stripped to his waist. "I don't usually swim in my disguise, but since you're here, I suppose I have no choice."

"I'll close my eyes if you want to swim without it."

He laughed and waded into the water. His muscles rippled under the glistening water that he splashed onto his arms and shoulders. "Never trust a beautiful woman until you've bedded her, my father always told me."

"How chauvinistic!"

"There's that word again." The Falcon stood up, his wet trousers outlining his powerful thighs and legs. "I suppose it means when men act and talk like asses about women."

She was surprised that he'd gleaned the meaning of a word that wasn't used much

215

until the twentieth century. "Exactly right. I've met a lot of those men since I've been in England."

"You don't have chauvinistic men in America?"

She laughed. "You've got me there. Men rule their women there, too. But I don't think that's how things between men and women were meant to be."

The Falcon splashed his chin, letting the water dribble down his neck. "And how do you think they should be?"

"I think . . . that men and women should be partners, maybe not equal in their given talents, but both sexes devoted to making the world better without giving one gender control over the other."

"This Sheffield. Do you think he's chauvinistic?" He stood quietly while she searched for an answer.

"I think he wouldn't be if he met the right woman."

The Falcon looked up at the sky. "Sailor's moon. Aren't you afraid, being out here in the wilds, in the moonlight, with a half-naked man who probably hasn't had a woman in longer than he could count?"

"I should be, I suppose. But I came in good faith and I think you'll treat me likewise."

"And what was this business you came about?"

"The garnets you sent to me when I first arrived. Tremaine said they belonged to Lord Lunsford's wife."

The Falcon picked up a rock and angrily skimmed it across the stream. "The bastard stole the jewels from my family. They'd been a gift to my mother from my father, not long before she died. Though they were a present to my father from the old royal regime for favors rendered, Lord Lunsford had them confiscated as part of the new king's treasures. No need to guess who wound up having them to give to his wife to wear around her skinny neck."

"Then you did steal them. You put me in terrible danger! If someone had recognized the garnets that night at the Sheffields' party, I could have been charged!"

"Sheffield would not invite any of Lunsford's mob to his house, I can guarantee you that. No, Isobel, keep the jewels safe until all of this is over. Then you can return them to me or wear them around your pretty neck."

She stood there, uncertain what to do next. If she insisted on making him keep the jewels, he could be charged with the theft if they were found with him. If she kept them, she might be the one charged with theft. "I . . .

217

thought I might turn them in to the constable at Maidstone, saying I found them in the woods."

"The constable is a poor cousin of Lord Lunsford's. How he would love locking you up and throwing away the key. He would find some way to involve Jeremy and Tremaine, I promise you." He strode up to the bank and shook the water off. "I wish you'd come for a swim with me."

"I can't. I'd drown in these clothes."

"Then take them off," the Falcon whispered. "I won't tell anybody."

"My daddy told me a few things, too, like a nice girl doesn't go skinny-dipping with a man in a mask—unless she's wearing one, too."

The Falcon put his head back and laughed. "Touché. 'Skinny-dipping.' I shall have a whole new repertoire of phrases when we're done, Isobel-whoever-you-are."

"Please stop calling me that," she said, on the verge of tears. She knew who she was and she knew she wasn't Isobel. "Oh, damn you, I'm coming in. Turn your back. I swear if you peek, I'll turn your name in to that constable tomorrow."

Laughing softly, the Falcon turned his back while Annabel stripped down to her chemise.

He didn't peek, but when she splashed into the water and he saw the way the wet chemise clung to her body, he wasted no time looking his fill.

"You're quite a woman," he told her admiringly. "I already knew what a beautiful body you have, but I didn't think you'd be this sporting."

To be truthful, Annabel didn't understand it either. A sailor's moon did strange things to people, she guessed.

It wasn't until she was in her nightgown and taking a last look at the moon that Annabel remembered she had failed to ask the Falcon one other question: How had Tremaine Sheffield gotten his scar?

The man who bore that scar walked out onto the balcony just as the question crossed her mind. "Isobel? Up so late?" He yawned and leaned on the balcony rail next to her. "I was asleep when I heard you coming up the stairs. Perkins told me when I came in from a late ride that you were still out on Lady Godiva."

"I like riding at night. I hope Jeremy wasn't worried about me."

"He was working in his tower and wasn't worried about anybody or anything. When that brother of mine gets started on his writing, he's in another world."

Annabel pulled her robe about her tightly and looked at Tremaine as directly as the moonlight would allow. "I hope you aren't turning my cousin against me. Unlike you, he trusts me."

"That's one of Jeremy's nicest traits. He never distrusts a soul until that person gives him ample cause, like your friend Lunsford."

Annabel gave a little cry of protest. "My friend? I never laid eyes on that man before in my life until he railroaded me into sitting with him in the Fountain Room."

"'Railroaded?' You Americans do use odd expressions. Isobel, I don't want to keep fighting with you. I know things about you that make trusting you impossible, but at the same time, I'm attracted to you. Like right now." He moved closer to her, his shoulder nudging hers on the railing. "I think about that kiss in the maze, about the way your lips looked so moist from the strawberries, and I think that I want . . . to . . . do . . . this . . ."

He pulled her into his arms and tangled her loose hair in his hands, dragging her head back to make her mouth vulnerable to his. She could hardly breathe as he took all the air from her body, as well as all of her strength to resist.

"I didn't come out here for this," she finally managed, pulling away. "Not after the way you treated me that night in London."

"I thought parts of it were rather nice," Tremaine murmured, lifting a lock of her still-damp hair from her cheek and smoothing it back with a touch that made her shiver.

"I never know how you're going to treat me from one day to the next. One day it's as if I'm your long-lost friend, the next it's as if I'm some sort of pariah who might contaminate you if you get close. Dammit, Tremaine, how did you get that scar?"

He stared at her, dumbfounded. Then he laughed. "You do have a way of getting a man's attention. Why are you so interested in my disfigurement?"

She had a quick image of another scar in another time on another man. "Because it's important to me for some reason."

He looked at her long and hard. Then, "I don't know."

She stared at him, not believing what he was saying. "You don't know? You have a scar reaching from your temple to the bottom of your cheek and you don't know how you got it?"

Tremaine passed a finger along the line she had described. "All I remember is that I fell from my horse when I was trying to train him and I had a strange vision of men rushing toward me, piling on top of me. I was in a vast field with no trees and there were people leaning over me when I awakened. I don't remember anything after that, but I knew it wasn't my horse who had maimed me."

"They said you wouldn't let him be destroyed."

"A fine piece of horseflesh like my Mordred? I would sooner put an arrow through your gentle Lady Godiva."

It was an odd story, one which Annabel felt she knew the answer to deep within her being, but had not the stamina to deal with. It had been a very long night.

"I must be off to bed. The ride tired me. How can I expect you to act toward me tomorrow—as friend or foe?"

Tremaine laughed. "Be adventurous. Have breakfast with me in the maze and find out."

"In the maze? Won't the eggs be cold by the time they get there?"

"There's only one way to find out, isn't there, Isobel?" He kissed her hand lightly. "Good night. I'd tuck you in but I have the feeling you've had enough of me for one night."

Annabel went to bed with confused feelings that would have been severely complicated by Tremaine's tucking her in after she had swum practically naked with the Falcon.

It had been quite a night, and breakfast in the maze was coming up. Annabel hoped somebody was keeping notes.

*   *   *

Two things awakened Annabel the next morning: Moonbeam's soft paw touching her cheek and the delicious aroma of hot coffee on the tray beside her bed. She sat up sleepily and was surprised to see that the bearer of her morning tray was none other than Greymalkin.

"Greymalkin!" Annabel rubbed her eyes, wondering if she were still asleep and dreaming. Jeremy's old nanny hadn't been in her bedroom since the day she'd helped arrange her hair. "What are you doing here?"

"Bringing you coffee, Missy. Jeremy says you can't get out of bed without that first cuppa, and I just thought I'd come along with it."

Annabel poured a little of the rich cream into her saucer for the cat, who immediately went to work on it, purring all the while. "You shouldn't be hauling heavy trays up these stairs. Maude has some young kitchen-maids who can do that."

"I may be humped over, but I don't have one foot in the grave yet," the crone said sharply. "Well, did you meet with the Falcon? Was he where I said he'd be?"

"Not exactly, but I did meet with him. What's this, a note from Jeremy? I wondered why he wasn't up here for our usual coffee-time." The note was not from Jeremy; it was from Tremaine.

My dear lady, I am very sorry but I've been called to my London office to handle some shipping problems and shan't be back till tomorrow. We'll still have that breakfast, just another day. T. S.

Annabel felt the disappointment with a sense of shock. Was it possible she was falling in love with a man who treated her one day like a loose woman with hidden motives and the next like a discovered treasure? And how could she feel the way she did about him at the same time that she enjoyed the embrace of the Falcon? She sighed, looking up to see Greymalkin eyeing her with a speculative look.

"Ah, it's just as well, I suppose," Annabel decided. She put the note down on the tray and retrieved the saucer Moonbeam had licked clean. "Greymalkin, how does Tremaine feel about me? You know everything, I know you do. Why does he pull away from me just when I think we're getting to be friends?"

"I wasn't his nanny; I was brought in for Jeremy when the late Lord Sheffield married my boy's mother. Tremaine has always been an odd one. I knew he was destined for something great from the time I laid eyes on him."

"Where did you come from, anyway?"

Greymalkin looked startled, then cackled. "There's some would say I come from under a rock, others from Hades. In fact, I come from the country, from a poor village where the seventh child, which I was—from a seventh child—was considered a curse and was turned out soon as she was old enough."

"How horrible! You were turned out of your own family's house?"

Greymalkin shrugged. "I was more than ready to go. You may not believe it, looking at me now, but I was pretty then, real pretty. I figured I could make a better life for myself, and I did." She cackled again. "Look at this mansion I live in, at the people who take care of me and leave me alone. How many old hags do you know who have this when they get to my age?"

Annabel had a sudden vision of old women pushing grocery carts along cluttered alleys, scavenging for garbage and discards. The old woman had a point. She changed the subject. "You know who the Falcon really is, don't you?"

"I know a lot of things, but I don't go around telling 'em. But I do read tea leaves, so if you want to leave off that poison you're drinking and have a spot of that tea I put on your tray, I'll tell you what I see."

Annabel wasn't sure she wanted her fortune read. But curiosity was a permanent part of her makeup so she poured a cup of tea and drank it down.

The old woman came over and took the cup

Annabel held out. "I don't tell folks what they want to hear, girl, so if you don't want to know your fortune, you'd better say so right now before I read your leaves."

"I may not believe what you say, but go ahead."

"That's your choice, Missy. . . . Well, well, I thought as much." The old woman, looking down into the cup, chuckled to herself. "I saw it in my own leaves a long time back, and wondered if I'd read 'em wrong."

"What? What do you see?"

"I see you in a man's arms, but he ain't no man I've ever seen the like of. And I see you crying, and there are some bad dark spots like a shadow from the gallows and pain and sorrow. But there's a bright moonlike circle around you through it all, like you've got some kind of talisman protecting and saving you . . ."

Annabel's breath was coming in short gasps as she listened to the woman's hypnotic drone. When Greymalkin gasped and turned pale, Annabel urged her to tell her what else she'd seen.

"Nothing that I want to put into words, for fear that'll make it more likely to come true." Greymalkin put the teacup down with shaking hands. "I'll send someone up for your tray. And you'd better be getting dressed. That cow-turd from next door has been waiting down in the parlor for an hour and swears he won't leave till he has a word with 'Miss Isobel.'"

Annabel forgot for the moment the reaction her fortune-teller had shown. "Newton Fenmore? Oh, my Lord. Please have Todd get rid of him."

"He's already tried. The man refuses to leave. See him, girl. The man's a fool, but he could tell you things about goings-on in that idiot asylum they call government that I can't tell you. You may be able to keep Jeremy from getting in too deep."

"Help Jeremy?" But by the time Annabel was on her feet, bent on preventing Greymalkin from leaving before she'd explained that cryptic statement, the old woman was gone.

Annabel was left with the prospect of dressing and going down to see her persistent suitor. She chose a pink dress that matched his nostrils and ears and, sighing that the anticipated breakfast with Tremaine had degenerated into a distressing session with Greymalkin and now a forced encounter with Newton, went downstairs.

"Dear Miss Isobel, how charming you look!" Newton rose from his chair in the parlor and grabbed Annabel's hand to kiss it. "You're wearing my favorite color and look like the rose I picked on my way over."

227

He held out a pink tea rose that was drooping on its stem, and Annabel took it with a half-hearted murmur of thanks. "Lord Fenmore, I'm shocked that you called at such an ungodly hour. I'm sure you have more important things to do than sitting around waiting for me."

"Not at all. I told my sister that I was not taking no for an answer, that I would pay my suit today or die trying."

"Lord Fenmore, I've tried very hard to discourage you from your suit as gently as possible . . ."

"I won't be discouraged." The man fell to his knees and put his head in Annabel's lap, clutching her legs. "I'm in love with you, Isobel, and I want you to consent to be my wife."

She stared down at the wispy hair in disbelief. "Newton, I've given you absolutely no encouragement. Please get up from that ridiculous position!"

"Not until you consent to hear the poem I've written to you," he said, his voice muffled against her skirt.

"If I hear your poem will you promise to leave without another word? As for marrying you, I certainly will not. I hardly know you and, quite frankly, am quite satisfied with that."

"So cruel, so beautiful, oh beautiful lady without mercy."

"I think that line has been taken," Annabel

said crisply. Keats would not love to hear his ballad's title on this buffoon's lips, she was sure. "Now read your poem and read it quickly, before I lose patience and have my cousin escort you to the door."

Quick as a jack-in-the-box, Newton was on his feet, and Annabel was treated to the dramatic reading of one of the most awful poems she had ever heard. In the middle of the recitation of 'My Leaping Heart,' she looked over the poet's shoulder to see Jeremy standing in the doorway listening, his shoulders shaking with silent laughter. It was almost all she could do to keep from giggling.

When Newton had trailed off on the last line, touching his eyes with a pink handkerchief as he did so, Jeremy applauded from the door. "Why, Fenmore, I do believe my cousin has inspired you to your best work. 'Take my heart, but wound it not.' Why, that's almost Byronic."

Annabel's portly suitor did not miss the underlying ridicule in his uninvited critic's voice. "Sir, I don't recall having asked you to join Miss Isobel as audience."

"But since this is not your house, I was quite comfortable in doing so. Has your lovely sister recovered from her injuries?"

"Felicia has been sulking in her room since we returned from London, though I will certainly pass along your concerns," Newton said sarcastically. "Miss Isobel, I entreat you to join me for a ride and then lunch at my house."

"My cousin is already engaged for both morning and afternoon. Fenmore, when do you take care of the country's business? Or are all of our members of Parliament so much at leisure?"

The look Newton gave the other man would have killed had it been a bullet. Annabel, watching this exchange with, at first, amusement, and then some concern, saw Newton Fenmore's face pale under its long chop whiskers, and she had a sudden ominous feeling. This man was a ridiculous, pleasure-loving clown, but he was dangerous all the same. "Jeremy, perhaps you and I can call on Lord Fenmore's sister one day soon to help her out of her vapors."

She quickly herded her unwanted caller to the door before Jeremy could spur him further. When she returned, she and her cousin had a good laugh over Newton's delusions of being a poet, but Annabel ended the conversation on a serious note.

"The man does not take kindly to being reminded of his inadequacies, Jeremy, either as a man or as a poet. We must be more careful. The fellow has friends in high places who would probably not hesitate to make use of his pique against you and Tremaine."

Jeremy poured them each a glass of sherry from a decanter on the highboy. "Fenmore is a fool who has squandered his family's holdings, and any reputation he might have had, through gambling and womanizing. He doesn't have the courage to come up against my brother and me."

"Jeremy, he might not do that, but he wouldn't be above coming at you from behind. Cowards, and I'm sure Newton is one, do that."

"You worry too much," Jeremy said, putting his hand on her cheek. "Let's have that ride before lunch and then I want you to come help me plan our trip to visit Byron."

The mention of Byron put thoughts of the insipid Lord Fenmore to rest for the day. Annabel went up to change into her riding habit floating on a cloud of happy dreams.

Chapter Thirteen

"The rick-burnings in the villages have gone beyond control, and while there has been no real violence, it will come. In the meantime, the Falcon has been seen everywhere and is becoming some kind of god to his followers, invincible, all-powerful, beloved. And all the while that damned rag, *Legal Watch,* is finding its way into the hands of every poor devil from Cornwall to Kent. We've got to put a stop to it!"

Lord Lunsford beat his fist on the table of the Butcher's Table pub outside Maidstone while his minions Royalston and Boynton cringed. "Derek, we know the paper's coming from this county. We know the Falcon makes this his

233

seat of operation. Why not take the offensive and search every suspect house in the district until we locate the evidence we need to put these radicals in jail for good?"

"Because," Lunsford said between his teeth. "We're already under criticism for all our rotten boroughs and bought government posts. We have to trap these people at their own game, show them up to be just as corrupt as we're thought to be, and hang them in public. Make somebody like the Falcon a martyr and you'd better pack your bag for your old post in far-off York."

Lady Fenmore spoke up from the dark side of the table where she was sipping her mug of ale. "I've been to the last three rallies. The Falcon is gaining momentum. If he lasts until Cobbett returns to revive the Radical movement, I'd say all of you would do well to think of moving to the north country. Or perhaps even farther."

Lunsford stuck his monocle in his eye to peer at his mistress. "Have you discovered anything that might work against these people? You must at least know who's writing that infamous newspaper. The last issue not only mentioned my name as a supporter of the new Poor Laws but said that I was using the taxes to feather a luxurious new 'nest.'"

All eyes turned to him, then away. Everyone was thinking about the monstrously large house Lunsford had built recently not far from the royal palace. After a brief, uncomfortable silence, Royalston cleared his throat and said, "I think it's time to move, to discredit either the Falcon or his mouthpiece. If we don't do something soon, they'll have this whole district in their pockets."

"Well, we'll meet back in London to discuss that." Lord Lunsford half-rose, signaling an end to the clandestine meeting.

"May I see you back to your home, Lady Fenmore?" Geoffrey Royalston offered. "I have my carriage outside, and Mr. Boynton is staying the night with friends."

Derek Lunsford let his monocle drop menacingly as he fixed a cold eye on his underling. "Lady Fenmore will be driving with me, Geoffrey. I do hope you'll give your wife my best when you return to London tonight."

Felicia Fenmore giggled all the way back. "He's such an old fool, the way he looks at me every time he thinks you're not watching." She tickled her companion in the ribs, sidling up to him and cooing, "Did my Lunsie miss his little Leesie?"

"Very much," Derek said with a pat on her backside. "Have you seen the Sheffield girl?"

"She's not really a Sheffield," Felicia said, miffed. "I'm not sure what that little slut is, but she's certainly not worth wasting our time talking about before you have to leave." She stroked his thigh and guided his hand to her breast. "Don't you have a little time for me before you go back?"

Lunsford hid his impatience. Felicia Fenmore was becoming increasingly irritating, but she was the closest tie they had to Sheffield, and thus the closest connection to the Falcon. "Love, it can only be a very little time. Living in the country as you do, you forget the demands of the city on a man of my position."

He leaned forward and whispered to his coachman. "Not the maze tonight, darling?" Felicia whispered as they turned into the road that led to the river.

"No, not tonight. That place spooked me the last time."

When they reached the river, Lunsford helped Felicia from the carriage and led her to a secluded bank, putting his cloak down for her to lie down upon and immediately shedding his trousers.

"My, we're in a hurry tonight, aren't we," Felicia said in a deceptively sweet voice.

"I told you I hadn't much time. Enjoy what we have, love." Lunsford fell upon her with a loud grunt, and soon the two were rolling in the grass, off the cloak, their moans increasing in volume till the driver of the carriage discreetly plugged his ears with his fingers.

"Who's that?" Lunsford sat up, his lust quelled by the sound of hoofbeats on the riverbank, coming toward them. "Oh, my God, I can't be caught with you." He hastily grabbed up his pants and cloak, flinging a half-clothed Felicia aside like so much baggage, and dashed for his carriage.

Felicia sat there, disheveled, her bodice ripped so that one milky breast spilled out. "Bastard," she said, her breath still coming hard as she shook her fist in fury at the receding coach. "I'll get you for this someday, you coward."

She stumbled to her feet just as Tremaine Sheffield came thundering up on Mordred. He reined in the horse just before running over the woman.

Jumping down, he cried, "My God, what's happened to you, Felicia? What on earth . . ."

She started crying piteously and went into his arms, holding her scraps of gown up just enough to cover her nipples. "Oh, thank goodness, you came along! Some peasant caught me on one of my walks and tried to . . . tried to . . ." Felicia grabbed him tightly. "Oh, Tremaine, it was so awful. Thank heaven you came along when you did."

Tremaine looked at the red marks on her breasts and throat. "The brute. I'll go after him."

237

"No, no, he was frightened off. I know he won't come back now. He didn't . . . he didn't . . . oh, Tremaine, I feel so safe in your arms."

"What did this man look like? I swear I'll find him and beat him within an inch of his life."

"I . . . couldn't see his face," Felicia said, her voice muffled against his chest. She turned her head slightly and caught sight of a cloaked figure coming toward them on the path. "He was big and burly and had a bushy mustache and these terrible rough hands and . . . Tremaine, please hold me tight!"

She put her face up to his and before the man knew what was happening, pressed her lips against his, moving his hand meanwhile to cover her breast.

"Felicia, don't . . ." Tremaine looked over then to see the last person he wanted to encounter at that moment. "Isobel!" He dropped his arms and then, seeing how nearly naked Felicia was, quickly pulled off his own cloak and wrapped it around the woman. "What are you doing out here?"

"I don't have to ask you that question," Annabel said in a choked voice. "Nor Lady Fenmore." She wheeled away and started running back toward the Hall.

"Wait! It's not what you . . . Isobel, dammit,

stop and let me explain what happened!"

But Felicia was still holding on tight, and Tremaine watched helplessly as the other woman disappeared up the slope to the house. "Damn! Well, I'll explain it to her after I get you safely home."

"Tremaine, please, please don't tell anyone about this incident. You know this county and how they gossip. I don't want all the village busybodies hearing about my humiliation, even though you stopped him just in time. My name would be ruined. News of it would reach London and I'd be cut by everybody!"

"Felicia, I can't have Isobel thinking that you and I . . ."

"Well, I can't have all those busybodies around here knowing that I was almost raped by a dirty peasant. It would ruin me! I swear, Tremaine, if word gets out about this, I'll kill myself. I will! I'll kill myself!"

Tremaine pulled her hands from his face and tried to calm her. "Don't talk that way. We'll catch the man and he'll be punished and no one will think any less of you."

"They will, they will," Felicia cried, sobbing hysterically, as she gauged how convinced Tremaine looked by her histrionics. "You know how all those biddies are always talking about me anyway. If they hear I've been attacked by . . . by some haymaker, my name will be ruined."

Tremaine looked down at the shaking head and shoulders pressed into his chest. "Do you mean it would have been acceptable if it had been some high-blooded bastard who'd done this?"

"Now you're making fun of me!" Felicia wailed. "I want to die. Just leave me here and go to your Isobel."

"I'm not going to do any such thing. I'm taking you home where you should've been instead of roaming around out here."

Felicia touched her sleeve to her cheeks. "I was lonely. You haven't had much time for me lately since that . . . that cousin of Jeremy's came." She sniffed and dried her eyes. "Tremaine, please don't say anything about this. You frightened the man off, he'll never dare try anything like that again. Please leave me with my dignity."

"I won't say anything till you've had a chance to pull yourself together. But before Isobel leaves for Italy with Jeremy, I intend to tell her. I can't have her thinking that I'm some kind of philandering brute." But Tremaine was thinking to himself bitterly that he really shouldn't be concerned about what Isobel might think about the scene she'd witnessed. He'd heard about Lunsford's infamous sexual excesses, and no doubt Isobel, for all her feigned shock, had experienced more than one rough-and-tumble roll in the grass.

"Please promise me, Tremaine, that you'll keep this to yourself," Felicia pleaded.

"What makes you think Isobel won't spread stories about you and me?"

Felicia looked up at him innocently. "Well, if she does, you'll just have to make an honest woman of me, won't you?"

Tremaine jerked away from her, his face turning grim at that idea. He had long ago decided that Felicia Fenmore was not the woman he wanted to be his wife. "Let's get you home and make sure you aren't badly hurt."

"You haven't promised me yet."

"All right. I promise not to say anything—yet."

When he had escorted Felicia into her house, Tremaine left with a heavy heart. For all his suspicions about Isobel and his doubts that she was not the person she pretended to be, the thought of her thinking badly of him hurt deeply.

He would never forget the look on her face when he'd turned to see her standing in the path, visibly shocked and disbelieving. A little anger crept in to reside with the hurt. "Well, if she thinks I'm that kind of animal, she doesn't deserve any kind of explanation."

He turned his thoughts to Felicia's ordeal and the man who'd caused it. Who would have dared come up on Sheffield property, knowing that every man jack in the county was loyal to the old families?

Well, he would worry about finding the man later. People talked and men bragged. He would keep his ears open.

Newton Fenmore, in his bathrobe and slippers, came into the salon where Felicia was assessing the damage to her newest gown. "My God, Felicia! What happened this time? I'm beginning to wonder if you will ever come home looking like anything but an alley cat that met up with more than one tomcat!"

"Shut up, Newton," his sister said between her teeth. "At least he doesn't pinch when he's making love like some men I've heard about."

Fenmore blushed. "Who told you that?"

"Never mind. Get me a brandy, will you?"

When her brother left, Felicia looked at herself in the mirror and cringed at how awful she looked, hair stringy and bedraggled, dress torn, lip and eye paint smudged. Damn Lunsford's eyes, he would pay, not just for the dress and the bruises, but for his cowardice in leaving her like that.

On the other hand . . . by the time Newton came back and handed her the brandy, she was feeling triumphant. That little slut would have something to think about now! She smiled maliciously at the memory of the shock on the girl's face and the disbelief when Tremaine had turned around to reveal himself as the man in Felicia's embrace.

The little twit had probably never even kissed a man, much less satisfied him. "Newton, darling, I really would like it if you'd read to me a bit. Nothing lengthy, mind you, I'm near-dead for bed, but one of your sweet little poems."

"You mean it?" Newton's face lit up like a child offered an unexpected candy stick. "Oh, I have the nicest new ballad. Short," he added quickly, "but it will bring tears to your eyes."

Felicia leaned her head back and dreamily thought about what had happened and Isobel's reaction as she half-heard her brother's dreadful poem about a milkmaid whose cow stomped her to death while she was mooning over an unfaithful lover.

When he'd finished, she tardily clapped and called out, "Wonderful! Absolutely wonderful."

Her adjective did not apply to the ghastly poem but to her fantasy about the misery Isobel must be feeling at that moment.

In fact, Annabel was still numb from what she'd seen. For all Tremaine's alternate coldness and seeming attraction toward her, she had always considered him a blooded gentle-man who would never, never do what he'd apparently done to Felicia Fenmore.

"Well, I know now how our little strawberry festival would have ended had I not discouraged him," she said, brushing her hair over and over again with brutal strokes as she relived the scene she'd witnessed. "Even that awful man Lunsford would never treat a woman like that, I'd warrant."

A tap at her balcony door interrupted her disturbing thoughts. She pulled her peignoir close about her and went to the door.

"Isobel, please let me talk to you. Please."

"Go away." She leaned her back against the door. "I swear, if you don't leave, I'll scream for Todd."

"And if you don't open this door, I'll tell Jeremy what I've learned about you, that you're no more his Cousin Isobel than I'm his Aunt Agnes."

Annabel closed her eyes, then braced her shoulders and opened the door. When Tremaine would have come into her room, she said, "Oh, no. I don't need to be compromised by you on top of everything else. I'll come out on the balcony. I'll thank you to remember that you have a very short time to say what you want to say to me."

"I just want to say that what you saw on the

river path, between Felicia and me, was not what it seemed. I can't tell you more than that, but please believe me when I say that I have no feelings for Lady Fenmore."

"That was obvious," Annabel said icily. "From the state she was in, I would say that anything you felt was entirely in the realm of animal lust."

"Isobel, just hear me out." Tremaine's anger at being falsely judged was split between the woman he'd just left and this one, whose big, hurt eyes were accusing him of a crime he had not committed. "There's a part of the story that I'm honor bound to keep quiet, but please believe me when I tell you that I would never treat a woman with that kind of disrespect."

"You took me to one of the most disreputable places in London and would have seduced me if I hadn't resisted."

"That was . . . something else entirely." Tremaine realized how hollow his explanation was. He'd treated the woman before him the way Lunsford would have done, and now he was asking her to accept the fact that he had not subjected Felicia to the same kind of male insensitivity. "I hope you won't say anything to Jeremy about this. It would upset him terribly."

"To discover that his stepbrother, whom he idolizes, is in fact a lascivious libertine. Do you know, Lady Fenmore is not my favorite person, but I hardly think she deserved to have her dress ripped half off for your pleasure. She looked frightened, to tell you the truth."

"She was, because she'd been . . . oh, hell, Isobel, I'm not a beast. When I saw you looking at me like that, my heart went stone-cold. We haven't been truthful with each other, you and I, but I swear this is the truth. I did not make love to Felicia Fenmore tonight as you think."

"No, I'd say you didn't. Lord Sheffield, I am very tired. I promised Jeremy I'd spend the day in Maidstone with him tomorrow helping him pick out gifts to take to Italy when we go to visit his friend Lord Byron. If you will excuse me, I'll say good night."

"One favor before you go." The scar on Tremaine's temple caught the light from the moon and Annabel felt a twinge. Why did she trust him so much in her heart of hearts when she couldn't be around him for more than five minutes without having some kind of terrible argument?

"Only one. And I make no promises."

"I'm not demanding any. I just want you to think about doing me a favor that would mean a great deal to me. I know that you have strong feelings for the Falcon. Jeremy thinks that your intimacy with him is inevitable." He put up his hand at Annabel's gasp and demurral. "Don't

246

deny it. I'm asking that when you are in his arms and reach the ultimate closeness that you mention my name."

He left, and Annabel stood there, frozen to the floor, feelings rushing over her that she could neither explain nor deny.

She hadn't given him an answer, but she knew that when the time came—as she knew that it would—Tremaine's name would be in her heart if not on her lips.

It was impossible. She was in love with two men simultaneously.

Maybe three, something inside her suggested.

Chapter Fourteen

Jeremy Harker knew his brother well and was beginning to know his cousin equally well. "Something has happened," he told Greymalkin when she was cleaning his tower as he worked on a new poem. "I don't know what Trey has said or done, but I know that those two are acting very peculiarly around each other. Have you noticed?"

Greymalkin noticed everything but usually kept her observations to herself. She had learned that lesson halfway through her life-time when her gift of sight had gotten her into trouble. "Aye, but it's none of my business, nor yours, Jeremy. You'll do well to stay out of bad currents that can sweep you right into the deep."

Jeremy laughed at her. "You're a cheerful old puss, you are. Well, I've tried and tried to get it out of both of them, separately. I know Trey has this funny idea about Isobel not being trustworthy, but surely he's seen by now that my cousin is a dear, wonderful person, albeit complex and often a bit mysterious." He looked off into space, nibbling at his quill tip. "She often says strange things, as though she's someone different, and then laughs it off and is our darling Isobel again."

Greymalkin scrubbed at the floor, carefully avoiding the loose stone that she knew secreted papers that Jeremy did not want seen. She'd watched him hide papers there but naturally had kept his secret. Her Jeremy was her heart, and any harm that came to him would hurt her, too. "She's not an ordinary girl, that one, I can vouch for that. There's some deep layers to her, all right, layers that you might do well to leave buried."

"Oh, you are an old soul, Malkie, but I love you like I did my own mother." Jeremy perused his page of lines. "If only the words could come as easily for me as they do for my colleagues." He made a face. "But at least I'm not as bad as poor Fenmore. If he only knew how hopeless he is as a poet. And the wretch keeps insisting on coming by to read his miserable doggerel and listen to mine."

"He's a dangerous man, Jeremy, I keep telling you. These whining fools who act like they've got noodles for spines are the ones to watch. They'll hurt you when you're not looking, because they're too cowardly to do otherwise."

Jeremy pooh-poohed the notion of Newton Fenmore being a threat, "Except with his horrible poems, which may be the death of me yet. But, here, the man is coming any moment for tea and writer's talk. I managed to warn Isobel of his visit and I'm giving you the warning so you can finish up quickly."

Greymalkin put away her scrub brush and pail and slipped out the door.

Newton Fenmore was standing on the landing outside. From the enhanced red of his cheeks, the old woman correctly surmised that he had been eavesdropping. "Good day, Lord Fenmore. You're expected."

The man ignored her, obviously too puffed up about what he'd overheard to be polite as he usually was to the old nanny. *Watch your step, Jeremy, he's a snake with shoulders.*

But Newton's cheerful greeting to his host revealed no evidence of his anger at being

251

made of fun of. "Ah, Harker, I'm so glad you allowed me to drop in. I've despaired of ever catching your cousin unengaged, but I'm glad to see you before your trip to Italy."

Jeremy's greeting was as insincerely warm. "I'm sorry about having to turn you down again about going along, but Byron especially is very peculiar about visitors he's not acquainted with." *And allergic to bad poets like you,* Jeremy added to himself. "Have a seat. I was just finishing a line I was having trouble with."

The other man sat on the window seat and picked up a paper lying there. It was Jeremy's poem to Isobel. "Oh, let me have that," Jeremy said. "It's still in the rough and I've got to copy it for my cousin."

Newton held on to the poem long enough to see that it had notes from Keats on the margins. His heart nearly exploded with jealousy, and at the moment he hated Jeremy with a vitriol that came partly from envy and partly from the ridicule he'd overheard. "Perhaps you will read it to me sometime."

"Perhaps. But I'm sure you have your own poem that you want me to hear." Jeremy sat in a polite listening attitude as the other hemmed and hawed, obviously wishing to be persuaded.

This was done, and Jeremy was treated to the "Milkmaid's Lament" that Felicia Fenmore had fraudulently lauded. "What do you think?" the plump poet asked anxiously after he'd finished.

Jeremy was at a loss for words. He knew of no kind way to encourage or discourage the man. To falsely praise such atrocious writing went against his scholar's nature, but to give Fenmore his honest criticism would infuriate a neighbor who, for all his shortcomings, was a political influence in London. "Well . . . the pastoral setting is an appealing one. The lines need work; maybe you need to tone down the pathos so your audience will cry and not laugh."

Newton pretended to be grateful for the advice, though inwardly he was seething. Had Jeremy said outright that the poem was awful instead of acting like a patronizing know-it-all, he might have felt different. "Well, I've taken enough of your time. I hope you will give Miss Isobel my regards."

He got up to leave, and Jeremy rose, too, saying politely, "And please convey my regards to Lady Fenmore. I haven't seen her out riding lately. I hope she's well."

Newton thought about the state his sister had been in two nights previously. "She's been a bit under the weather lately but I'm sure she'll appreciate your thinking about her."

On the bottom stair of the tower, Newton Fenmore stopped and viciously tore his poem into shreds. "We'll see which one of us is remembered, Harker. You may have the gift of words, but I've got connections."

He stopped at the bottom of the stairs, calming down and thinking about how he could alter his position. Derek Lunsford may have paid some of Newton's debts but he still owed Felicia's brother a great deal. Newton had kept his mouth shut about a lot more indiscretions than Lunsford's whoring, some of which had potential political repercussions that would put Lunsford away in the London Tower for good—if not land him on the gallows.

On instinct, Newton pretended to go out, closing the door audibly but actually remaining inside the tower. He had already gotten one earful; maybe he'd catch something else on the sly. Very quietly for a fat man, he made his way up to the opening to the turret. He saw Jeremy on his knees and at first thought the man was praying.

But then he saw him lift a stone and remove a box full of papers. On the top, clearly visible, was a copy of *Legal Watch*. *So Jeremy is the Falcon's mouthpiece*, Newton crowed silently. *Probably he hides his poems there, too, so no one will steal them.*

An idea was born. Fenmore and Lunsford could both benefit from Jeremy being exposed as the underground heir to Cobbett's radical writing mission. If Jeremy were arrested, condemned for treason among other civil crimes that Newton was sure Lunsford would be able to come up with, his estate would be up for grabs.

And the part of that estate that most interested Newton Fenmore was the stack of unpublished poems. He and Lunsford could work out a quid pro quo arrangement, he was sure. Newton would inherit the traitor's literary works (and the rest of his estate) and Lunsford would be given the head of the Falcon, for if Jeremy were caught, the renegade hero would not be far behind. In addition to that, the senior politician would win the gratitude of the stockjobbers and bankers, not to mention the King.

But Newton must be very careful. Derek Lunsford was as slippery a snake as had ever held a seat in London's highest government offices. If Newton were not careful, he could wind up in Newgate, instead of Jeremy and the Falcon.

"Maybe I could even persuade Miss Isobel to marry me, in exchange for intervening on her cousin's behalf at some point." That was a delicious thought, but one which he cleverly decided he would not mention to Lunsford.

*   *   *

"Fenmore, I told you not to come to me groveling for any more money. I've paid your debts over and over again and I shan't dip into my coffers for you again anytime soon."

Derek Lunsford was irritated to receive his caller. Newton Fenmore was a man he thoroughly despised. "I'm not here for money, Your Lordship. I've had some lucky streaks of late, and, besides, it's much cheaper living out in the country."

"Then what are you here to see me about? On your sister's behalf, no doubt? Well, please inform Lady Fenmore that if she sends one more dressmaking bill to my office, I shall cut off her credit for good. The woman is insatiable." He smiled at his little double entendre. "Which, of course, is sometimes one of her more appealing qualities."

Newton Fenmore hid his anger at the insult to his sister. Felicia could look out for herself, the way she always did. "I just wanted to make sure we have an understanding, one that you've hinted at before, but which has not been put into plain English. If I succeed in exposing the man who's been writing and publishing that treasonous underground newspaper and help bring the Falcon to justice, will I still be given whatever lands are forfeited?"

Lunsford made an impatient sound. "Dammit, man, I've told you that already, but I certainly haven't seen any progress since you've been out there."

"Well, that may change. I'm on the trail of the traitors, and it won't be long before I'll be turning over the evidence that will put them behind prison walls, or in the noose."

Lunsford looked at the plump pink dormouse who appeared on the verge of bursting with his self-importance. "Well, man, tell me what you have. Out with it!"

"Oh, no, not yet, not until I have the proof." Newton had no doubt that Lunsford would take his hard-gained information and act on his own, collecting the glory for himself along the way. "It would be premature to act now, or to say too much. But I will let you know when the rat is on the edge of the trap—and then we'll snap it."

Lunsford settled back, looking at his visitor with a new gleam of speculation. "What do you really want out of this, Fenmore? I know the estate's value is important so you can keep on with your infernal gambling and whoring, but there's something else."

Newton Fenmore thought about his vision of having his poems published, of seeing his name in print, and having people in awe of him as they were of Byron and Keats. He was not a good poet, he knew deep within his soul, but he knew enough to recognize that Jeremy's work would be recognized. "I don't suppose you'll believe me when I say that I'm loyal to England and the King and think the unlawful insurgents should be brought to justice."

Lunsford's smile was slow and terrible. "Next, you'll be singing 'God Save the Queen' with bowed head. No, Fenmore, I don't believe you. You don't have a patriotic bone in your over-indulged body, and we both know it. I don't know what you're after, but since your moti-vation seems to be goading you to exposing the bastards I'm after, I'll leave that alone for now. Just make sure that you don't cross me. I've played along with your petty ambitions and propped up your sorry finances, but I won't have an iota of mercy if you foul up this thing with your own private maneuverings."

"Your Lordship, I would not dream of being disloyal to you or our Majesty and the Govern-ment."

"Forget the last two," Lunsford said with a menacing look. "If you cross me, it'll be your worst nightmare, one from which you'll never wake up."

Newton left the office with sweat pouring down his face. When he stopped at the nearest pub to have a cooling ale, the barmaid said saucily, "Might be I should pour this over you, darlin'. You look like you've been wrung hard and hung up wet."

"Just give me another brew, wench, and shut your slutty mouth."

The barmaid gave him a dirty look but left him alone to wonder if he'd just set in motion a plan of triumph over the man he envied the most in the world—or dug a trap for himself, with a hungry lion waiting for him to take a misstep and fall in.

Tremaine's private vow to set the record straight between him and Isobel about what had happened between him and Felicia was not carried out. Every time he tried to get the girl alone, she ran away from him, until he began to feel like a pariah. He finally approached Jeremy.

"I know you are excited about this trip to Italy, but I wish you would delay it. The old coach roads are still not all that safe. I hear tales of highwaymen everywhere between here and Calais. Can't you delay your visit till I can arrange to accompany you and Isobel?"

Jeremy knew there was more behind his step-brother's entreaty than fear for their safety. "I say, old bean, what is it between you and my cousin? Every time I ask her what's wrong, she puts me off, and I haven't been able to get a straight answer from you, either.

What the devil has happened between you two?"

"I can't get into that. It's a misunderstanding, but one that I'm not at liberty to explain at this point." Tremaine had never felt so frustrated. He had called on Felicia Fenmore and been met with a minor replication of the hysterics she'd displayed the night of her "attack." "It's not just the thing with Isobel and me, there's something in the air, something that makes me uneasy about your being away right now."

Jeremy was packing his bag while they talked and he paused with a packet of papers in his hand. "It's not as if we'll be gone that long. The Falcon has gone into hiding for a while, we agreed upon that, since there were new rustlings in London about a stepped-up aggression against outspoken opponents. When I get back, we'll work up new strategies, new plans for attack."

"Well, at least plan your route to circumvent Paris. I never trusted that place, for some reason."

Jeremy hooted. "Now I'm beginning to get the picture. You're jealous, because you're stuck here and Isobel and I are headed for exotic adventures outside stodgy old England! Well, not to worry, dear brother. We will stay well out of harm's way."

"Well, if you must go, have a safe trip."

Jeremy put his arms around his stepbrother. "I will. We will. And don't try to perform any heroics without me around to pick up the pieces."

"I'm learning not to make promises I might not be able to keep." But Tremaine hugged Jeremy back with sincere affection. "Since Isobel has avoided saying good-bye to me, say it for me."

"Not good-bye, 'au revoir.'" Jeremy saluted his stepbrother. "Greymalkin has my instructions to protect you from Lady Fenmore until we get back."

"Great," Tremaine muttered, watching Jeremy go down to the carriage where Annabel sat waiting. "Where was she the other night?"

Annabel's excitement had softened the dismal feeling she still had about the strain between her and Tremaine. She still couldn't believe that she was setting out on a journey that would bring her into contact with two of the greatest literary figures in England.

She would also meet Mary Shelley's sister Claire, whose daughter Allegra was being taken to join her famous father.

The flying coach that would take her and Jeremy to their connection to Calais was sure to create excitement in itself. Annabel knew that every step from Calais, to Rheims and

261

Dijon, through the highest part of the Alps to Milan and thence to Este near Venice, would be fascinating.

She was not disappointed.

Nor was she disappointed in Jeremy's store of anecdotes about Byron. "He entertained Shelley and his bride and her sister at this most wonderful place on the lake, and, I tell you, Cousin, literary history was made during that brief spell. I shan't shock you with stories of my colleagues' excesses with . . . ah, mind-enhancers, but I will say that they didn't outdo pretty Mary when it came to dreaming up fantasy. That delicate little eighteen-year-old concocted a story about the most horrendous monster that anyone could ever conceive of. Byron told me privately that after reading about Herr Frankenstein he shivered in his bed every night for a week."

"Boris Karloff has made a fortune off that movie."

"I'm sorry?"

Annabel realized the slip that had occurred in her excitement. "I said, barring carts, these coaches could make a fortune off moving."

Jeremy shook his head. "You worry me sometimes, Cousin. Look, I do believe that's Shelley himself standing outside the villa. Oh, doesn't he look well? I thought he was a girl the first time I saw him, he was so fair and slender, but a less effeminate man you'll never meet."

Annabel's heart stopped when she saw the very youthful man whose dark blue eyes, when she drew close enough to see, were full of artless wonder.

Then Lord Byron appeared and the melting of Annabel was complete.

Chapter Fifteen

Venice, the "greenest of all islands" as Byron described it, was a magical place for Annabel. So was La Mira, on the road to Padua, where Byron had kept quarters since the previous summer.

It was soon apparent, however, that things would get increasingly unpleasant between Byron and Claire Clairmont, whose relentless pursuit of Byron before her pregnancy with their love-child, Allegra, had bordered on mania. "It has turned mere tolerance of the woman into loathing," Shelley confided unhappily after one of the stormy quarrels that abounded in the Byron household.

The short boat trips and walks in between,

though, were delightful, and Annabel heard the three poets reading their magical works as though in a dream.

She was surprised on one such occasion to discover that of the three men, only one was able to swim. Byron had used the sport therapeutically to help strengthen his deformed foot and weakened leg, but Shelley often joked to Byron that he must not try to save him should he fall overboard.

Jeremy just laughed when Annabel expressed her worry to him privately about his being a nonswimmer. "I can think of no nobler burial ground than the sea or one of the beautiful lakes we've boated on."

But Annabel's image of a gray sea and a floating body made the issue much more important to her mind.

She even made halfhearted attempts to teach her cousin how to stay afloat in water, but he was so lackadaisical, she finally gave up on the project. Shelley, too, just laughed, whenever she broached the matter of his learning to swim since he loved the water so much.

"I shall always have a sturdy vessel to hold me afloat, sweet Isobel. It's unnatural for a man, especially a poet, to grow fins like a fish."

Only she knew the irony of that statement, since she had secret knowledge of the watery death that would take Shelley only four years later. His body would wash ashore on Via Reggio and there be cremated, though the heart would not burn.

Her helplessness in changing this bit of history was, she knew, providential. Shelley's death must come, as, she was becoming more and more sure, must Jeremy's. That led her to abandon her attempts to change the future course and to concentrate instead on long talks with Byron and Shelley, quite often about politics, which, she was surprised to learn, interested them both.

"Lord Byron was on the side of Cobbett, too," she announced to her cousin one evening when they had gone off by themselves to escape the growing tensions inside the house. "I didn't realize he'd had a seat in the House of Lords."

"Oh, yes. Byron, born to the blue as he is, has deep convictions that the strength of a country lies in its people instead of its legislators. Don't get him started on that."

In fact, Annabel had been very careful around the brooding, handsome poet, whose loveline, a string of broken hearts, stretched from England to Venice. His affair with his half-sister had been dangerous, but not nearly as threatening as his future alliances with young boys.

She could certainly understand why women sought him out almost obsessively. The man was, like both Shelley and Keats and, yes,

Jeremy, so attuned to the sensitive underside of humankind and nature that one felt almost raw, yet sweetly understood, in their presence.

Byron said lovely, complimentary things to Annabel, but because of his friendship with Jeremy, never once put her in the kind of situation that would have made her uncomfortable.

Thus the magic days stretched out, until an ugly scene occurred between Byron and Claire about his insistence on rearing their child in a fashion that she called "stifling." Jeremy's opinion was called upon, and Annabel's, but neither succeeded in influencing the warring factions.

The visitors did their best to serve as peacemakers, along with Shelley, but there was no hope. The tranquil time the poets needed for their work was gone. Jeremy reluctantly broached this to his cousin and suggested that it might be best to leave Byron and his problems and return to England.

Annabel, though enchanted with living through her favorite part of literary history, was enthusiastic about the notion of returning to Kent. The two weeks had left indelible memories, but she was quite sure that another week of the temperamental Claire and moody Byron would be too much. Jeremy agreed.

"I've had a chance to talk with Byron and Shelley about my newest works, and they both thought they were my best to date." Jeremy laughed. "One exception—they made gentle fun of my Isobel poem, saying it was sweet Keats all over, but I really do feel good about their criticisms and suggestions."

Byron's arrogance vanished when they were taking their farewell of him, of Shelley, of Italy. "I'm sorry about the unpleasantness about Claire and Allegra," he told them, not pleading that they extend their stay. "You do realize, Isobel, that your cousin will someday be considered a fine poet."

"I intend to see to that," she replied enigmatically.

"Take care of your beautiful cousin, Jeremy. Don't let her be swept off her feet by some wispy poet friend of yours. She needs a rugged, strong-willed protector."

Byron's lips pressed a kiss to her cheek where Keats's lips had pressed, and she almost cried. She did cry when she was hugged enthusiastically by boyish Shelley, who, she had decided privately, was completely adorable.

"Good-bye. Au revoir! Arrivederci!"

Annabel closed her eyes after imprinting on her mind irrevocably the picture of the famous men whose lives would be tragically but eternally chronicled in literature and history.

She slept almost all the way back to Calais. They sailed to Dover, where they again boarded a flying coach. Suddenly awake again after the wearying journey, she was excited. England felt like home, she decided, and she was glad to be back on its shores.

The road between Dover and Canterbury was dark and deserted, and Annabel found herself wishing that Jeremy hadn't fallen asleep. She had an uneasy feeling about the driver, who'd appeared at the dock and pressed his services upon them almost as if he'd been expecting them.

"Jeremy, are you asleep?" she whispered. She took her cramped feet off the box of papers, his entire collection of poems, which he'd taken with him to Italy and was bringing back full of precious notes and suggestions. "Jeremy, we're coming to a stop and I don't know why. Did you want to spend the night at an inn this close to home?"

Jeremy groaned and muttered, then reluctantly came awake. "Wha . . . at? Why are we stopping?"

"That's what I want to know. Jeremy, there's something funny going on. I knew the driver seemed suspicious. I mean, don't you remember how he barged ahead of that other fellow with the horse wearing a daisy hat?"

"Shh. Let me listen. I hear voices. I don't like the sound of this, Isobel. You stay quiet, now, no matter what. I'm getting out."

She tugged at his shoulder. "No, no, don't! Jeremy, if it's highwaymen, let's just let them have what we've got. It's not that much, and at least we can escape with our lives."

"Damned if I'll give up anything to such scum." Jeremy leaned halfway out of the coach and called up to the driver, "I say, why are you stopping here in the middle of nowhere? If it's nature's call, you can wait—"

He stopped suddenly and pulled his head back into the coach, his face grim. "The bastard's taken off. You sit tight and let me handle the bounders."

The voice that called out from the road ahead was crude. "You, there, we've got you stopped, and if you don't do what we tell you, you'll be meat for the morning vultures. Give us your valuables, and if you have a pistol, you'd better throw it out too, because we've got you covered from three sides. We'll shoot the girl first, if you make a move."

Annabel saw another black-hooded, horsed figure on her side and shrank back against the seat and closer to Jeremy. She was thanking heaven that she had not brought the garnets as she'd been tempted to do, being afraid to leave them unguarded. "Jeremy, please don't do anything. There are three of them and I think they mean to hurt us if we don't do what they say."

"Don't worry. I'm not going to do something foolish like going up against a bunch of rogues that would as soon shoot me as not."

"I've got very little to offer, but you've got money with you which should appease them. Here." Annabel unfastened the simple pearl earrings Jeremy had bought her in Italy. "And here's the ring Shelley gave me as a keepsake. Not valuable, but at least it looks as if it is." It was valuable to her, but Annabel wanted to survive this attack.

The rogues hardly looked at the trifles and money bag that Jeremy passed out to them. "There's a box of papers. We want that."

"What? It's a box of scraps and pieces of my writing, not something you can sell."

The leader of the group of outlaws came closer and waved his gun menacingly under Jeremy's nose. "I said, give me the box of papers. I'll decide if it's worth anything or not."

Jeremy paled at the thought of the notes on those pages that would mean nothing to these renegades but meant everything to him. "Please give them back after you've seen there's nothing there worth your while."

"I told you we'd be the judge of that. All right, we'll untie your driver now and let him take you folks on your way." The leader showed a wide, snaggle-toothed grin and lifted his shabby hat. "Have a real good trip home. Ma'am? Sorry I didn't get to spend some special time with a pretty lady like you, but maybe we can meet again sometime."

"I certainly hope not," Annabel said with asperity.

The man laughed and with a whistle to his accomplices, was off into the dark night.

The driver came out of the woods looking sheepish and guilty. Jeremy took one look at him and said between his teeth, "You treacherous bastard, I hope you have a sturdy pair of boots on you because you're not getting back on this coach. And I can promise you that the company will hear about this."

The man whined and pleaded, but Jeremy ignored him and took the whip and reins on the driver's seat. They left the man who'd deceived them cursing in the middle of the deserted road.

"I'd like to sit up there with you," Annabel called out the window. Jeremy stopped, and Annabel climbed up beside him, her mind probing the circumstances of the senseless robbery. "Why would they want your papers? How would they know about them?"

Jeremy looked grimmer than ever. "Lunsford's behind it, of course. He thought I might have taken some . . . important papers with me, not wanting to leave them behind."

"What kind of papers, Jeremy?"

"I can't tell you right now," her cousin said, giving another crack of the whip just above the horses' heads. "Don't ask any more questions, Isobel. We need to get home and find out what's happening with Tremaine and the Falcon and the movement. I have a bad feeling."

So did Annabel.

Tremaine met them when they came in, bedraggled and weary, and, after one look at them, sent a maid off to have Maude prepare a hearty stew and pudding. "You both look like you could do with a mug of strong spirits."

The ale Todd brought was indeed welcome. Annabel was turning into a beer drinker, she decided. There was something about the brew that put stamina back into one's limbs, color on one's cheeks. "Jeremy came close to being hurt tonight," she told Tremaine, who had hugged his stepbrother upon their arrival but had not attempted to do so with her. She was sorry, in a way. She needed a hug, even from the man she knew now to be Felicia Fenmore's lover. "We were held up by robbers on the road to Canterbury."

Jeremy told Tremaine how the highwaymen had seemed to be only after one thing, his box of papers.

"I can hardly believe a band of ruffians would have designs upon my poor literary drivel!"

Jeremy said, trying to make light of it.

But Annabel could tell from the look that passed between the two men that the box had been suspected to hold more than poetry. She was tired of being kept in the dark about so many things and decided to bring an end to it. "I'll go check to see if Maude needs help in the kitchen while you two catch up on county matters."

Outside the door she stopped to listen, and sure enough, Tremaine jumped right in. "My God, Jeremy, if you had your pages of the next issue of *Legal Watch*, they'll use them to arrest you. The ones I read contain libelous material about Lunsford and his cronies."

"Libel is an untrue accusation. I only tell the truth about his deals to get the machines into the hands of stockjobbers who sell them at exorbitant prices to the companies who make their own blood money at the expense of laborers. But rest at ease. My political papers are safe in their hiding place. The damned bastards only got the poems I'd taken to Italy with me."

"I'm sorry," Tremaine said, his voice full of sympathy. He knew how hard Jeremy had worked on the collection of poems, and how much the notes of his two mentors meant. "Maybe they'll turn up somewhere safe."

Annabel closed her eyes, wanting to cry in her secret knowledge that the precious works would not show up until much later—and then under another's name.

Her eyes flew open at a sudden thought. Could it be Newton Fenmore who had been behind the theft? Was it possible that the object of the robbery had been, not the political papers, but the poems themselves?

No. Fenmore would never have the gumption to instigate such a daring raid.

She listened more intensely as Jeremy asked Tremaine what had happened since he'd been gone.

The Falcon had not made another appearance, Tremaine said, but some unsettling pieces of mischief had been perpetrated on landowners in the area who were thought to be sympathetic with the fight against the Corn Laws. "Cattle and sheep have been killed, fields set afire. We weren't victimized, but only because after I heard about the first incident, I had our lands patrolled by men on horseback. I was right with them and chased off some trespassers the first night."

"Trey, Isobel is worried about me. I want to tell her everything, about the underground paper, the Falcon, everything."

"Not yet." Maybe not ever, Tremaine thought with the sadness that always accompanied the realization that he could not trust the woman he was falling in love with. "Jeremy, there are spies everywhere now. I'm not even sure we can trust the Falcon's own men. Lunsford has been putting his poisonous tentacles out into even the far reaches of the county."

"It's only a matter of time before we're caught," Jeremy said heavily.

"But perhaps by then the movement will be strong enough that it won't matter. Cobbett will be back, others will join the cause. Even Peel, they say, is talking about reform."

"I worry about you, brother," Jeremy said.

"And I you."

Annabel fought back a tear, hearing in their voices the resignation to their fate, which she was sure she was sent here to witness. She went to the kitchen with a heavy heart, feeling the rolling wheels of the future bearing down on her and the people she was beginning to love.

Her own fate was involved, too. Annabel knew it had to do with her relationship with the Falcon.

But even given the choice, she would not leave now, not until the future had unfolded.

Chapter Sixteen

Annabel left the two men up talking, her exhaustion overpowering her desire to learn more about their secret activities. Before she went to bed, she checked the hiding place of the worrisome jewels.

To her great relief, they were still there.

Her sleep that night was filled with strange combinations of people from Sheffield Hall, present and future. At one time, Greymalkin appeared to her shaking a bony finger and saying over and over, "It's time you went home, girl."

When she woke the next morning, she was surprised to find her usual tray at her bedside, but no Jeremy. When she dressed and went downstairs she learned from Maude that the men had gone off to Maidstone to take care of some estate matters. "They said they'd be back for dinner, Miss, but not to wait for 'em."

Annabel puttered about restlessly, the unsettled feeling that she'd had since leaving Italy still bothering her. It had to do with the Falcon. She knew that Tremaine and Jeremy were both treading on dangerous political ground, but the Falcon's danger was even more imminent.

He could be shot at one of his rallies and the killing justified by his enemies. At the very least, he could be arrested on some trumped-up charge at any minute.

"But they have to catch him first." And the man was as elusive as the bird whose name he had adopted.

The day dragged on. Without Jeremy to keep her company, even without the often-unwanted presence of Tremaine, she found herself getting bored. At every sound, she ran to the window to see if it was Jeremy and his stepbrother returning.

She sat alone in the great hall at the long table, feeling ridiculous for having the huge place and platters of food all to herself. When Todd came in bearing a small plain envelope, she pounced upon it. "Is it from Jeremy?"

"I don't know, Miss. It was left at the gate where the box for you was left when first you came here."

Annabel's heart trembled. A message from the Falcon! She hardly gave Todd time to leave the room before tearing into the missive.

Isobel [well, at least he had left off that annoying 'whoever-you-are' business!], *I must see you. Your cousin and his brother are in great danger and only you can help. Meet me in the maze tonight but don't tell anyone. Not anyone! Midnight, alone. Follow the markers I'll leave for you. F.*

Annabel's heart pounded. Was that why the two men had not come back from Maidstone when they'd planned? Were they even now being held in the jail over which Lunsford's cousin presided? And how would she be able to help them?

Well, the Falcon would know what to do. Annabel went to her room and paced, praying for the hours to pass until it was time to go to the maze.

It was scary at nighttime, tracing the little bits of mother-of-pearl to the center of the maze. At the sight of the first marker, Annabel remembered how Tremaine had asked her about the

281

bright chips. Now, of course, it was clear that it had been the Falcon who had used them to lead someone to a safe, secret meeting such as he was calling her to now.

When she neared the final gap in the hedge, the one opening to the core, she called softly, "Are you there?"

There was a muffled, "Yes, I'm right here."

She rounded the last barrier and saw the tall, dark figure in the now-familiar mask and gave a little cry of relief. "Thank God! What are we going to do? What's happened to my cousin, to Tremaine? Please, please, we must go to their aid."

He held her close when she ran into his arms for comfort. Then he was holding her in a way he'd never done. Annabel felt with a shock his hand moving to cover one breast and the tightening of his arm around her waist until she cried out, "You're hurting me!"

For answer, he pulled her even tighter, till she couldn't cry out for the painful grip. Then his mouth was on hers, ravaging it and swallowing her breath. She felt the shocking movement of his free hand pulling up her skirts and seeking her tenderest part.

Her mind could not grasp the meaning of the vicious embrace. Never would the Falcon treat her this way, not even knowing she was not the person she claimed to be.

It finally dawned on her.

This man was not the Falcon.

She waited until he'd moved his wet mouth down her throat and then she pretended to go limp and willing as though she welcomed the disgusting kisses. When he loosened his hold on her, obviously thinking he had her cooperation, she made a lightning move, ripping off the falcon mask and revealing the stunned countenance of Lord Derek Lunsford.

"So it's you." Annabel stepped away from him, putting the statue and bench between them.

"So you've uncovered the Falcon's identity," Lunsford blustered. "I hope you won't reveal my secret."

"You're not the real Falcon," Annabel said in utter loathing. "He's a gentleman behind the mask, and you . . . even posing as him, you're still the same despicable creature that you've been all along."

"Watch what you say, wench," Lunsford warned softly. "I planned to trick you into telling what you know, where to find the outlaw, but your beauty overwhelmed my plans."

"I can't tell you anything. Even if I could, I would die first."

"That may be a choice you have to make if you keep on befriending a known criminal." Lunsford started circling the bench, and Annabel moved away from him. "Come on, pretty little Annabel, you're not the sweet innocent you pretend to be. You've been bedded by the Falcon, no doubt, and Sheffield certainly wouldn't let a tasty little baggage like you escape his lust. I wouldn't be surprised if even that cousin of yours has had his go-round in bed."

That was too much. Annabel leapt across the bench and flailed at her despised tormentor, whose shock at the attack kept him from reacting. But when her nails tore his cheek, he grabbed her wrists and threw her across the little enclosure. Dabbing at the bloody marks on his face, he glared at the girl lying on the ground, struggling to catch the breath that had been knocked from her. "Bitch! I ought to kill you for that, but I won't because I still plan to have you in my bed before it's all over. And I'll see to it that you witness your damned Falcon swinging from the gallows, while your precious cousin and his stepbrother watch from a jail window, knowing they're next."

Annabel tried to get up, but she was still without breath. "What are you going to do?" she managed between gasps.

"I'm going to leave you in here to find your way out like a little trapped mouse." Lunsford started backing out of the maze, picking up the chips as he went. Annabel heard his laughter, that of a maniac, fading as he went through the corridors leading to the outside opening.

"Don't panic," she told herself, finally managing to get to her feet and to breathe normally. "You can remember the way you came if you just keep your head."

That was easier said than done. As Annabel felt her way along the first corridor, she tried hard to remember which opening she had taken. "It was the one on the right, no if it was on my right coming in, I have to reverse direction, so it'll be the one on the left . . ."

After an hour of trying, and taking one wrong turn after another, she finally slid down in an exhausted heap and began to cry.

"It's like Lunsford said, you're as helpless as a trapped mouse."

Mouse.

Annabel sat up, the memory of a half-forgotten conversation creeping into her mind. What had Tremaine told her about the key to the maze? Follow the left side to the center, he'd said.

She got up, her faith and energy revived, and put her hand on the right side of the corridor.

A few minutes later, she emerged from the maze and sank to the ground thankfully. And then she saw the light in Tremaine's room and heard excited voices on the balcony. Her name was at the center of the hubbub, and she stood up weakly and called, "Jeremy, Trey! I'm here, here at the maze."

Tremaine leapt over the balcony (a foolhardy thing to do, Annabel thought giddily, but oh-so-romantic). He ran up, and by the time Jeremy reached them, Annabel was being held in a warm, healing embrace that was the antithesis of the savage attack she'd been through in the maze. Through her haze of exhaustion, she heard Tremaine saying over and over as he cradled her tenderly, "Oh, my darling, if you only knew what terrible thoughts went through my mind when we got home to find you gone. Then when Todd told me about the note . . ." He kissed her cheeks, her eyes, her lips, and Annabel felt a smile coming on her lips. "You little idiot, going into the maze by yourself! We were just about to come search it when we heard your voice."

Jeremy's blue eyes were dark with concern. "Whatever possessed you to do such a thing at this hour?"

"It . . . was the note. I thought it was from the Falcon. He said something had happened to you two, that he needed my help."

Tremaine looked at Jeremy, his jaw hard and fist clenched. "That bastard Lunsford." To Annabel he said, "It was Lunsford who showed up there, wasn't it?"

Her eyes went wide at the thought of how that might look. "Oh, but Trey, I didn't know . . . I thought it was . . . oh, God, you don't think I

286

would scheme with Lunsford. Jeremy! Tell me that's not what you're thinking about me!"

"After seeing you like this, those bruises . . ." Jeremy's voice choked up. "No, Cousin, I'm sure whatever Trey had been thinking about you and Lunsford, he's changed his mind now."

"Where were you?" she asked. "I was so worried about you two, and then when I got that note . . ."

"We should be kicked for not sending you word," Tremaine said, "but there was a problem in Woltham with some overzealous radicals that could have ruined the whole movement in that territory. Oh, Annabel, I am so sorry!" He held her close as they went back to the house. "But that bastard Lunsford will pay for this. He has a lot to answer for already, but this is one mistake that will be his downfall."

Maude and Greymalkin both fussed over their charge while Tremaine and Jeremy discussed what had happened. "We can't let him get away with this." Tremaine's grim face was still streaked with soot from the fires he and his stepbrother had put out in a field near Woltham. "Lunsford has gone too far this time. Posing as the Falcon!" He hit his fist against the mantel so hard that Jeremy flinched. "And daring to force himself on a helpless woman. Wait." The image of Felicia's torn bodice and the marks on her throat and shoulders came into mind, and the realization dawned. Tremaine turned slowly to stare sightlessly at his stepbrother, his mind turning over clues that he had not noticed before. "It's not Annabel who's Lunsford's go-between."

"What are you talking about, Trey? How could you have ever thought that about my cousin?"

"It's a long story, Brother, and not a very pretty one. But now it all fits, and Lady Felicia Fenmore has some questions to answer. I'll be back in an hour. Keep an eye on Annabel and make sure she has everything she needs."

"But where are you going at this time of the morning?"

Not taking time to answer, Tremaine was out the door and off to saddle up Mordred.

"My God, man, do you realize what time it is?" Newton Fenmore stood at the door to his house which had nearly been broken down by his neighbor. "Sheffield, I don't appreciate your waking the household like this in the middle of the night."

"I don't give a rat's pellet for what you appreciate and don't appreciate, Fenmore. Where's your sister?"

"Where else but where most civilized people in the country are at this hour? In her bed."

"Well, get her up and down here. And tell her not to fiddle-faddle around with making herself beautiful. If she's not in this room in five minutes, I'm coming up after her."

Newton's indignation was overwhelmed by his fear of his visitor. "I'll go get her, but I'm reminding you, Sheffield, that this behavior is not acceptable and if you lay one hand on my sister, I'll have the constable out here."

"I'm not the one who's been laying a hand on Felicia," Tremaine said coldly. "But I know who has. Get . . . her . . . down . . . here."

Newton scurried like a rabbit, which indeed he resembled in his fuzzy nightshirt, cap, and slippers. If Tremaine had not been in the mood he was in, he would have laughed till his sides hurt at the ridiculous spectacle of Annabel's "pink man."

Felicia appeared not more than five minutes later, her eyes still heavy with sleep and her hair braided at her shoulder. "Just what is this all about, Tremaine?" Her offensive attitude was deliberate since her brother had hurriedly explained on the way down that he thought Sheffield's visit might have something to do with her doings with Lunsford.

"Don't put on airs with me, Felicia. I know about you and Lunsford. Why I didn't suspect before now, I can't imagine. You're two birds of a feather—both vultures."

"I don't have to stand here and be insulted," Felicia said, flouncing her peignoir a little looser around her full bosom so Tremaine could get a full view.

"Then sit down and be insulted." Tremaine pushed her down onto the sofa behind her, ignoring Newton's fluttery protests, and said between his teeth, "And don't bother flaunting your flesh. I'm immune."

She still blustered, trying to cover the very real fear she was feeling. "If your darling little American visitor has told you stories about me, I can match her lie for lie."

"Isobel hasn't told me anything about you that I don't already know—now. It wasn't a 'haymaker' who attacked you on the river path the other night. It was Lunsford, visiting his mistress after plotting with her to trap the Falcon and his friends."

"Oh, Tremaine, that's the most absurd—"

"And it was you who led him into the maze for one of your hellish rendezvous, giving him the map to the center so he could use it to lure Annabel there tonight."

Felicia's eyes widened at that and then narrowed in anger. "That bastard!" she screamed, throwing a pillow at a table and breaking a vase. "So he lied to me about not finding her or any other woman attractive. I'll kill him."

"Queue up, love, for your turn at that. That's not the only thing he's lied to you about. He told you that the money he used to bail your brother out was a gift, didn't he? Well, I heard your lover's kin in Maidstone talking about how he had some people in his pocket who were too stupid to know they were being used and then would be thrown away. Could that have referred to you and your brother?"

At a sound from across the room, Tremaine turned to see Newton Fenmore assuming a dangerous shade of purple. "He's lying, Felicia," the man squeaked. "Lunsford would never betray the people who are loyal to him."

Tremaine looked at Felicia as he asked softly, "Is your brother right, Felicia? Is Lunsford incapable of betraying the people who do his dirty work for him?"

She looked at him with sheer hatred. "None of this would ever have come about if your little American slut hadn't come in here and started stirring things up. I would have my house in town and fine clothes and jewels . . ." She stopped at that, and a crafty look replaced the anger. "Well, you've found out my little vice, which is, after all, born of boredom. Surely you can't think that I'm capable of spying on you miserable little country whiners, even if I found it amusing."

Tremaine looked at her long and hard. "Lady Fenmore, I'm beginning to think that you and your brother are capable of anything. But let this go down between your ears, both of you. So help me, if either one of you does anything from this point on to harm my family, including Isobel, or the people in this area who are trying to return England to its solid values, I will personally see to it that you are turned over to some very uncivilized riffraff who don't give a damn about your London 'connections.'"

"That's a nasty threat you're making, Sheffield," Newton said, moving back out of Tremaine's way as the taller man stalked to the door. "I shouldn't be making any threats if I were you."

"And I," Tremaine said, stopping and grabbing the lapel of the shorter man's robe, "shouldn't hang about here too long if I were *you*."

The slam of the front door behind him was like the portal to hell closing on two exposed sinners.

Chapter Seventeen

News came the next day that the Fenmores had packed up and left for unknown parts.

"Good riddance," Tremaine said when Jeremy brought the news. Annabel was propped in bed with her breakfast tray, which had been brought to her by a contrite Tremaine.

Jeremy helped himself to tea and buns and between munches speculated, "No doubt they've gone back to London and are with their friends. Trey, is what Isobel told me true, that you really suspected her of coming here to spy on us for our enemies?"

"It's true, all right," Annabel said, but her look in Tremaine's direction was not as stern as she would have liked. It was hard to be stern with the man who had held her in his arms and told her over and over again how dear she was to him.

Tremaine had the grace to look guilty over that, but he had his defense. "We still don't know who you really are, though I'm satisfied—now—that you have nothing to do with Lunsford and his mob."

"What do you mean, we don't know who she really is? She's Isobel, she's my cousin, and I'll thank you, Trey, to stop this ridiculous business of acting as if she's not."

Annabel and Tremaine exchanged long looks. "The real Isobel drowned, Jeremy." At the gasp from the girl lying on the bed, Tremaine looked startled. "You really didn't know?"

"No," Annabel whispered, her image of floating in the sea returning to her and confusing her beyond comprehension. The captain. The captain had pushed her over when she refused to submit to his advances. "I really didn't know."

Tremaine repeated the story that the young seaman had related to him. Annabel listened intently, strong emotion playing over her features for reasons she could not tell the others.

"Then how . . . ?" Jeremy's face was a wonder of astonishment. "Who are you, then?"

Annabel stammered, "I . . . don't know. I don't remember anything before arriving in your tower. All I knew was that I was thought of by everyone as being Isobel and I thought that's who I was."

Jeremy put his arms around her. "Poor girl, you were probably the victim of some awful tragedy and heard about the girl drowning on the boat from someone. Well, you're Isobel to me, and you always will be. I could not love the real one any more than I do you— Cousin."

Annabel burst into tears. "And I you, Jeremy. Dear heaven, if I knew how I came to be here and why, I'd tell you, I swear I would." In fact, had she thought that they would believe her story, she would have at that moment revealed everything.

"Well, what are we going to do about that bastard Lunsford? We can't let him get away with what he did." Jeremy's anger was returning as he noted the bruises on Annabel's mouth and throat.

"Jeremy, we can't do anything to put ourselves at risk right now. I expect the man did this deliberately to provoke us into a foolish act of vengeance. Then he'd have us." Tremaine shook his head, new steel coming into his voice when he said, "But I can promise two things. He'll never touch a hair on Isobel's head again, and he will pay someday for what he's done."

"Thank you," Annabel said in a soft voice. "Not just for defending me, but for calling me Isobel."

"Somehow that's who you are," Tremaine said quietly. "Somehow you came to us with her same fighting spirit. Remember the line from *Hamlet?* 'There are things in your philosophy, Horatio, that you have not dreamt of.'"

Annabel froze at the sound of the words that had been spoken by another very different voice. "What will you do now?" she asked. "The acts of aggression, the robbery, the attack on me, have shown they're getting bolder. Any day now, Lunsford and his mob will have one or both of you killed and claim himself a hero in the act."

"That is always a possibility, Isobel. But Jeremy and I decided long ago that our mortality was not an issue. We are patriots, first and last, who will not shun what we know to be our duty as Englishmen."

A lump rose in Annabel's throat as she looked at the two handsome men whose courage and fearlessness were unshakable. "I know that. And now that we are all agreed about my being on your side, whoever I might be, please let me help."

"You have helped already, more than you know. I must go now. There's much work to be done before that coward Fenmore starts causing trouble for us." Tremaine bent to kiss Annabel's forehead. "Take care of yourself, my dearest. I have someone at the gate and near the river with orders to shoot to kill if anyone tries to come up here without a good reason." His whisper was for her alone: "And don't forget your promise to me."

"Tremaine," she whispered back. When the man had gone, Annabel suddenly realized that his words had seemed like a permanent farewell. She turned to Jeremy, fear in her heart. "He . . . he sounded as if he's not coming back!"

Jeremy's face was grim. "He's not, Isobel. You will not look upon Tremaine Sheffield again."

Annabel stared at her cousin in horror.

But then a comforting thought came into her being, bringing calmness and certainty. *You will be with your love for always.*

Jeremy went back to his tower where he was preparing the most scathing sheet that he had printed yet. With him went the sense of getting closer and closer to his day of reckoning. When he reached his tower, he opened up his secret hiding place and took out the box of papers that would soon become the latest issue of the *Legal Watch*. He lingered over his one remaining original poem, the one to Isobel with notes from Keats. A copy of it had been stolen with all his other poems in the coach from Calais.

"It's all I have left, Isobel, and it belongs to you," he said to the empty room. He found an oilskin packet and put the poem inside. For extra safekeeping, he tucked the thin envelope into a crack along the hole where he stored his other papers. "There may be no more poetry, dear cousin, so someday you will have at least this one to remember me by."

He worked till his candle sputtered out, and then he wearily replaced his box of incriminating writings in its hiding place.

The next day Jeremy, too, bade his cousin farewell, but assured her he would be gone no more than two days. "The man who has always secretly done our printing for us was threatened and has gone to Ireland. I have to find a new press, not an easy task. People believe in what we're doing, but most don't want to put their personal safety on the line."

"You're not taking the papers with you," Annabel said, her voice full of alarm. From what Tremaine had said, Jeremy could be branded a traitor for some of his writings. "Remember how they robbed us and took your poems, thinking they had your political pieces."

Jeremy kissed her. "Not to worry, love. I'm leaving them in a safe place that only Greymalkin knows—and you have to admit that every torture rack in England would not suffice to make my old nanny reveal the secret."

Annabel had to laugh at that. "Do you know, you're absolutely right? But I can be trusted, too, Jeremy. If something should happen to you, God forbid, and Tremaine doesn't return as you said he won't, I could do the underground paper. Tell me where it is and I'll guard the secret with my life and limbs, just as Greymalkin would."

Jeremy's hand touched her chin tenderly. "It's not that I can't trust you, my darling cousin. Unlike Tremaine, I always have. But too much knowledge would be dangerous for you. We already have enemies seeking excuses to put us away for good. We don't want you caught in the middle." He grinned at her. "Hey, it's not your fight, remember? You licked us Brits once already. Leave it to me and Trey and some other stout hearts to win our fight this time."

She felt very much alone, standing on the stone buttress, watching Jeremy's horse and its rider fade into the distance. "God keep you safe," she whispered.

She felt a warm curling around her ankle and bent down to pick up the cat, holding her to her cheek and taking comfort from the cat's loud purring. "You're like the Falcon, you little creature. You come and go like the shadows, but you're always there when I really need someone."

She went inside to tell Maude and Todd that they could relax about meals for the next two days. She would do fine with cold meat, cheese, and bread.

Besides, she had little or no appetite without the two men whom she loved.

Sheffield Hall seemed very forlorn and abandoned when she went inside.

It did not remain that way. Three hours after Jeremy's departure, Annabel heard a shot from the direction of the gate and the sound of men shouting, then hoofbeats pounding up to the house. When she ran to the balcony, she saw Todd being held by two men, one of whom looked up and saw her.

"Stay where you are, Miss, and you won't get hurt. Tell your man here not to try to get to his weapon or we'll be obliged to shoot like we did at the gate. And have him call in your man from the river before we have to take care of him, too."

Annabel called down to Todd, "Don't try anything, Todd, until I find out who these men are and what they're doing here." To the leader she said frostily, "You've apparently injured one of our people already. Please allow Todd to go see about the poor man."

The man grinned up at her, showing a row of blackened teeth. "Ma'am, it'll be St. Peter's job to look after that bounder—or the other gatekeeper, depending on how good a man he was."

"He's dead?" Annabel's heart pounded. The danger was here, with no one left to protect her.

The man spat on the ground. "Dead as a doornail, like anybody else'll be who doesn't act in a lawful way to let me carry out the law's business."

"Who are you and why are you barging in on Lord Sheffield's private property?"

"I'm the constable, Ma'am, and these are my deputies, all on business for the King, so to speak. Now I'll be glad to tell Lord Sheffield to his face what we're here for if you'll be good enough to fetch him." The hateful grin came back. "From what I've heard tell, he's probably no further away than your bed up there."

Annabel restrained her fury. "Lord Sheffield is not here. I'm sure if he were, he'd throw you off his property."

"Might not be his property no more, Ma'am, soon's we make the search of the place like we've been authorized to do."

"What right do you have to intrude in a private household and search for anything?"

"If you'll come down here a little closer, I'll show you the papers giving me that right, papers signed by the Chief Magistrate."

301

Annabel thought about the stolen jewels with horror and made a move toward her door, but was stopped by the constable's menacing words. "And, Ma'am, I wouldn't be trying to hide anything, if I was you." He nodded to the man next to him, who was shimmying up the balcony in a flash to where Annabel stood, frozen in fear.

"I never shot a lady, Ma'am," the man told her, his smile not reaching his eyes. "Hope you won't give me cause to this time."

She heard them coming in and the sound of furniture being overturned, doors flung open. Maude and her help were herded into the pantry. Annabel could hear her shrieking from below and then she heard a sharp slap that quieted the screaming. She heard the constable, whose name she learned was Savage, ordering two of the men to go search the tower. He whispered something to one of them, which terrified Annabel even more. Maybe he was giving an order to kill Jeremy if he was found there.

But Jeremy was gone, safe from these animals. Tremaine, too, was safe, thank God. He would have fought them, she was sure, and been shot dead on the spot.

"Now, Ma'am, we've just about been through all the bedrooms except this 'un. This where you stay?"

Annabel nodded numbly. They would find the jewels. She realized from the way Savage was carefully looking behind doors, opening drawers, that he was playing with her, enjoying her torment. He knew what he was looking for and that he would find it in her room.

Someone had betrayed her, had told the constable where he could find Lady Lunsford's stolen jewelry. Annabel almost forgot her peril in straining to think who.

Felicia Fenmore. Of course. It could be no other than she. Looking back, Annabel could recall how the woman's eyes had widened that night at the sight of the jewels. Felicia needed to restore herself to Lunsford's good graces; what quicker way than to offer him the means to brand Jeremy's cousin as a criminal?

Then she would be their bait to lure the Falcon. Annabel could see it now. He would hear of her imprisonment and come to her rescue, wherever she was, and they would be waiting for him.

"Ah! What are these pretty baubles here?" Savage held up the garnets, even held the earrings to his ears and did a little mincing prance, making his cohorts laugh. "Now don't tell me these are real, Ma'am. From what I hear, you came to this place with not a dress to wear. How would a poor little relative like you come up with something like these?"

She would not involve the Falcon or Tremaine. "They were my mother's. She was a . . . famous actress, and men were always showering presents on her."

"Do tell. Well, funny thing is, these jewels look just like the ones my cousin—maybe you know the honorable Lord Lunsford? That's my kin—said was stole from his wife. My, my. You don't look like a thief."

Annabel said nothing. She knew there was no point. She just prayed that Tremaine or Jeremy wouldn't return and stumble into a death trap.

"We'll just take you into town for a little talk . . . oh, what's this?"

Annabel's heart sank when she saw what one of the men who'd been sent to search Jeremy's tower was holding out.

Savage dropped the jewels on top of the box of papers. He did a little jig and danced Annabel around in a stiff circle. "My, we are having ourselves a fine hunt, and it's not even the season yet. Might even get us one of them big, high-flying birds, if this keeps up."

He went over and picked up the paper on top. "Umm. Mister Jeremy, this here is what's called real serious libel. The person who wrote it could even be called a traitor."

"You filthy swine, you can't even read! I saw how you held that damned warrant upside

down when you were pretending to read it."
Annabel's venom made everyone's eyes turn
toward her, then to the no longer gleeful constable. His face was red with humiliation, and
Annabel knew that she had hit on a sore point. A
cousin of the aristocracy who was illiterate. . . .
She had gone too far, she could see that by his
face when he handed the box to one of the
deputies.

Then he came over slowly to Annabel and
looked down at her, his eyes full of pure vitriol.
"You better watch your mouth, slut, or you'll
be hard put to keep the teeth you got to eat jail
food. And the nights get real lonesome sometimes without anything but a few bugs—"

"And some big rats," one of the men shouted,
whereupon all the men laughed uproariously.
After a minute, Savage joined in.

"Yep, at least one I know specially likes tender young females."

Annabel turned away from his spittle that
was spewing out with the hateful words.

"Please don't harm them," she said as she
was led down to the great hall where Maude,
Todd, and the other servants stood helplessly.
"None of them has done anything."

"Well, as long as they keep that way, we'll
leave 'em be. Of course when this place is confiscated like it will be now, they'll be looking
for work." Savage tweaked Maude as he went

by her. "Come by to see me about cooking for the jail, pie-maker, and I'll see what I can do."

On the way out, Annabel wondered about Greymalkin. She hadn't seen or heard her since the raid had begun. She hoped that the old woman had heard and seen everything so she could keep Jeremy from walking back into a trap.

Annabel turned her head when she saw the man Tremaine had posted at the gate lying in his own blood. "At least have the decency to return his body to his family," she said.

The constable looked at her, apparently surprised that she wasn't in hysterics as most women would be by now. "Well, I guess I can spare a man to do that." He barked an order to a deputy who loaded the unfortunate sentinel up on a horse and set out to take him to the village Annabel named.

As they passed by the tower, Annabel looked up and saw Greymalkin looking down at her. She quickly lowered her gaze, knowing that if it was possible to get word to Jeremy about his imminent risk, the old woman would find a way.

The constable made sure that they were seen with their captive in tow, no doubt at Lunsford's orders. More of the villagers were secretly aligned with the Falcon's cause than not. Word would reach him, Annabel realized with anguish as they passed through Maidstone on the way to the stone jail. The Falcon would come for the bait, and Lunsford knew it.

"Please fly away. Soar to freedom and safety," she whispered.

As though in answer, a lone bird with broad strong wings circled above them, swooping into the skies with the grace of freedom. The constable noticed Annabel's fascination with the bird's flight.

"Look real good, wench, for the next bird you see will be a vulture circling your dead lover's carcass."

Only after she was in her cell, a terrible, dirty cubicle that stank of its previous occupants' misery, did she realize that Savage had implied that both Tremaine Sheffield and the Falcon were her lovers.

Did she love them both?

Incredibly, she found herself drifting off into exhausted slumber on a wretched pile of straw in a corner of her cell.

Annabel awakened not recalling where she was until she felt the filthy straw beneath her and saw the bars of her cell. From the tiny window above her head, she could tell it was dark.

Her throat was parched. "Constable, could I please have some water?"

Savage held up his jug. "Could give you something a lot better."

"Just water, please. What time is it?"

He brought her a mug of tepid water which she drank thirstily. "About suppertime. Don't expect no fancy dishes like you been eating at that mansion of Sheffield's."

"I'm not hungry." She went back to her straw bed, not liking the way Savage had looked at her when she was pressed against the bars.

The man sat back down and swigged his ale, wiping his mouth with his sleeve after every long gulp. "Well, now, we don't want our little rabbit to be unappealing when the Falcon swoops down on her."

Annabel ignored him until he finally gave up and went back to his jug.

Outside, the men who were under orders to stay hidden and watch for anything suspicious had their first excitement when someone appeared out of the shadows. "Stop! Who goes there?"

Greymalkin stepped into their view, and one of the men laughed. "It's the old hag. She won't hurt anybody, 'less it's with being so ugly." The man doubled up in laughter, and the others joined in the teasing.

"What did you bring in that basket, old witch? An ax to cut down the little bird's cage?"

"You don't really think you can go in there 'less we see what Grandma has under her arm, do you?" The man saying this snatched the cape open and saw the jug under the woman's arm. "Oh, so you were going to smuggle the girl some of your famous dandelion brew, eh, to take the place of that poison Savage gives his prisoners."

They opened the jug and started passing it around. When Greymalkin held her hand out for it and pleaded for its return, they laughed, and passed it just over her head, swigging as they did so.

"What's the pie you've got in that basket?" one asked.

"My special blood pudding." Greymalkin held on to the basket protectively.

"Oh, let her keep that for the girl. Go on in, old woman, and make sure you fatten up the wench so Savage will have something solid to keep him warm tonight."

Greymalkin knocked on the jail door and waited. When Savage, half-drunk, reeled over to peek out, she held up the basket for him to smell the aroma.

With his hand on his pistol, the constable let her in. "What's that you've got there, old hag? The girl's being fed well enough. We don't need you coming in here with your . . . umm. She says she's not hungry." He sniffed again and then took the pie from the basket and started wolfing it down.

"What else you got?" he asked with his mouth full. When Greymalkin pulled out one of the two loaves of fresh bread, he grabbed it. "Give the wench the other one. Maybe it'll make her appetite come back. But, wait, I'll give it to her. You might have some trick up your sleeve."

Greymalkin obediently handed him the other loaf, and Savage took it over to poke it under Annabel's nose. "Here's your bread, princess. You already had your water. Ain't that what they say prisoners are supposed to get—bread and water?" He laughed and hiccupped and went back to his pudding.

Greymalkin looked at Annabel and said softly, "Read your bread, girl. You'll need it where you're going."

Annabel wondered if she'd heard wrong. Read your bread? She went over to her corner with the loaf and, pretending to tear off a piece to eat, examined it carefully.

There was a small slit. Annabel slid her finger into the soft middle of the loaf and felt a paper. A note! She looked at Savage, making sure he wasn't watching, and popped a piece of bread in her mouth, pulling the paper out as she did so.

Quickly, while Greymalkin was distracting Savage, Annabel read the scrawled note:

*The guards will be asleep from Greymal-
kin's brew in another hour. The pudding is
one of her very special recipes. Don't go to
sleep but watch carefully.*

There was no signature and no initial, but
Annabel knew the handwriting.
The Falcon.

Chapter Eighteen

Annabel watched as Savage started nodding, once overturning the jug he'd been drinking from. She saw saliva mixed with pudding crumbs drooling from his open mouth and willed him to sleep.

She had torn the note into a thousand pieces and mixed them in with the straw of her pallet. The bread actually was delicious and gave her new strength. So much for the evidence. Now all she had to do was wait. The talking and laughing outside her window had died down completely. Annabel was sure Greymalkin's doctored wine had taken its toll on the guards. Now if only Savage would succumb as well. He still roused from time to time, looking over at her with bleary eyes. He was a big, strong man. She just hoped Jeremy's nanny had put in enough of the soporific to do the job.

Then he fell forward on his arms and began snoring loudly. As though that were the signal, the outside door opened quietly and a dark figure slipped inside. Annabel had seen Greymalkin slide the keys from the constable's table into her basket and had held her breath till the woman was safely gone.

"Isobel?" The whisper made her insides turn to water.

"Over here." She saw the Falcon's mask and wondered how she could have ever thought of the man beneath it as a predator and enemy. "Oh, thank God. But we must hurry. If they catch you, I know they'll shoot you."

The Falcon unlocked the cell door and held her in his arms for only a moment. He looked over at the prone figure at the table and said under his breath, "That bastard. If he laid a hand on you, I'll make sure he doesn't wake up from Greymalkin's potion."

"He didn't. Oh, please, I just want us to be gone from here. Don't do anything." Annabel saw the hunting knife her rescuer had pulled from his belt when he was cursing her captor. "Falcon, the important thing is that we get away and hide, the farther away the better."

He turned back to her, his eyes shimmering with emotion as he looked at her. "You may be headed into greater danger, my darling, fleeing with me to my 'hideout' as you named it. It'll just be us two for God knows how long. Jeremy's safe with friends and hard at work on a new paper and Greymalkin's with him by now."

"I can face that kind of danger," Annabel said softly. "As long as I'm with you, my protector, I can face anything."

"Well, try facing the business end of this pistol, wench, and have your lover do the same."

The constable stood unsteadily and Annabel muffled her scream as she saw him point his firearm at the Falcon and start to squeeze the trigger.

Then there was a gurgling noise and the man was staring at Annabel as though she were somebody from hell. "You . . . you . . ."

She saw the knife in his throat at the same moment that he slumped down to the floor, his pistol dropping beside him. The Falcon went quickly over and picked up the weapon, then put his finger to the side of the man's throat. The torrent of blood told the story, but the Falcon didn't want to take any chances. "No pulse. He's dead. Justice prevails for poor Rountree whom he had killed without any mercy."

Annabel stared at the lifeless hulk on the floor as she was led from the cell. "But now they'll be hunting you down for murder."

"They'll have the devil of a time finding me." He shushed her worrying as they left the jail, pointing to the snoring guards. "Look how their brilliant trap turned out."

Then they were flying through the night on the back of the black stallion, Annabel feeling safe in the arms of her rescuer, her fears dissipating as the distance between her and the dreaded jail grew.

She could not have retraced the path they took, nor did she care. When they cantered up a stream, she asked if it was the same one they'd swum in that night, and the Falcon laughed. "There are a hundred such streams and I know them all. From boyhood, I explored every inch of this countryside. I'm hiding our scent, for they'll probably use dogs to hunt us down."

She even found the night magical, with a bright moon making the ride seem almost dreamlike. When the dawn was breaking and they stopped to allow the overloaded steed a rest, she whispered, "I still can't believe that the Fenmores betrayed us like this."

"If only there had been time to retrieve Savage's booty," the Falcon said, referring to the jewels and Jeremy's papers. "But it was more important to save you from even one night in that hellhole."

"I shall always be grateful," Annabel said shyly.

"You will have an opportunity to show how grateful, my darling, before many hours have passed." He held her tight as he lifted her to the horse again and brushed his mouth oh-so-lightly over her face. "We're hunted outlaws now, you and I, and our only comfort shall be in knowing we have each other."

"I can think of no sweeter comfort," Annabel said, a catch in her voice.

They sped on, and when Annabel was sure they could not possibly go any deeper into the woods, they came upon yet another path.

Then they were at their destination—the Falcon's secret hideaway in a wood that no one but a falcon or his like would dare penetrate.

"I can't believe it. I simply can't believe it." Annabel turned to the Falcon, who was putting on a pot to boil over a fire. "When you said you lived in an eyrie, I never supposed you really meant it."

The structure he had built high in the trees hidden on a steep cliff had several rooms and was more comfortable than Annabel could have imagined a primitive treehouse to be. Though the furnishings were sparse and simple, there were touches in every room that delighted her. She put her nose to a huge basket of fragrant rushes and picked up an apple from a huge bowl of wild fruit. "You amaze me. How did you do all this?"

"I started building it years ago, knowing the day would come when my dreams for England would become nightmares and I would have to hide from my persecutors." He chuckled. "I've never been one for suffering, so I tried to provide the amenities. Which is why I stocked up on your favorite beverage when I saw this coming."

Annabel gave a little cry of delight when the Falcon handed her a steaming mug of . . . coffee. "Oh, how wonderful!" She gratefully sipped the delicious brew and closed her eyes. "Umm. If only Tremaine and Jeremy could be here with us."

She opened her eyes to see the Falcon looking at her solemnly. "You've become quite attached to those two, haven't you?"

"Jeremy's like a brother, and Trey . . . well, I can't quite put my finger on it. It's like he's always been a part of my life, only he's not free to express what he feels. Oh, Falcon, I can't help wondering what will happen to them. What will Lunsford and those other monsters do next?"

The Falcon put the pot back on to heat. "That's predictable. I shall be very surprised if we don't hear that the Fenmores have moved into Sheffield Hall by next week."

Annabel made a deprecating sound. "They wouldn't dare!"

"Oh, yes, they would. I'm sure Newton will be quivering in his boots every time he leaves the house for fear he'll be attacked by the people he betrayed, but I guarantee he'll satisfy his greedy little soul with playing the lord of the manor."

"That makes me sick." Annabel stirred her coffee viciously.

"Careful. We can't afford to break any dishes. We won't be leaving here for a pretty long time."

Annabel's heart contracted at the exciting implication of his words. "Is there food?"

"If you don't object to simple fare. I do have a nice supply of wine stashed away."

" 'It's not the necessities one needs, it's the luxuries,' " Annabel quoted some modern witticism.

"You do have the most unusual expressions sometimes," the Falcon murmured. "Now would you consider me 'chauvinistic' if I told you something that I'm not sure you've noticed in your tour of my modest household?"

"I'd better not say until you tell me."

The Falcon came up to her and took the cup from her hand, putting his mouth where hers had been and drinking deeply of the remaining coffee. "There's only one bed," he whispered.

319

"Mmm, that's not bad. Maybe I'll adopt some of your American habits, like drinking coffee."

Annabel did not react to that teasing statement. She was too busy reeling from the preceding one.

The day was magical. The Falcon caught three good-sized fish in the stream beneath the leafy lair while Annabel, clad in one of his shirts and trousers belted comically with a rope, washed her dress and her hair. "If you'll look under that middle bush over there, you'll probably find a couple of eggs. I've seen mama pheasant doing her best to hatch out a family."

Annabel did so, apologizing to the indignant mother as she stuck her hand in under the warm, feathery underside.

The breakfast was delicious, with Annabel's Southern hoecakes making a huge hit with the Englishman. "Just flour, salt, and water? I can't believe anything so simple could be so tasty."

"It's your fresh butter that does that."

The Falcon cleared the dishes and put out the fire. "We won't cook again today. Mustn't have any smoke leading our pursuers to our hideout."

Annabel smiled. "You really like that word, don't you?"

"Yes, I do. By the way, who is the Lone Ranger?"

"Oh, dear. You never forget anything, do you?" From the way the Falcon was looking at her, she knew he was remembering that first night, when he had kissed her and she had fought him, saying things that a man of his time would not know the meaning of. She was remembering it, too, but not for the same reason. "The Lone Ranger is a mythical hero in America, one who is never seen without his mask and who rides through the western part of our country helping the good guys against the bad guys."

She didn't tell him that as of that moment, the Lone Ranger was not yet a figment of the imagination of his creator—who hadn't even been born.

"Did a woman ever come into his life and unmask him?"

"No, I don't think so." She asked quietly, "Will you unmask yourself for me, Falcon?"

"When the time is right, I will." He got up from the bench on the little porch where they were sitting. "Come on. I know you're tired, but I have something to show you."

She followed him down the ladder and into a copse where she saw his black stallion in his stall.

Next to him, lifting her magnificent head in a whinny of welcome, was Lady Godiva. Annabel gave a cry of delight and ran to embrace her beloved mare. She looked at the Falcon grate-fully, tears rolling down her cheeks. "Oh, I'm so glad to have her here! I was so worried about what would happen to her, and with so much happening, I didn't want to ask for anything else. Oh, Lady G, I can't tell you how happy I am to see you."

"She's happy to see you, too," the Falcon said with a grin. "I'm a little jealous about all the kisses, though."

"Well, I'm sure Lady Godiva will kiss you, too, if you'll come over here," Annabel teased.

When the Falcon reached them, it wasn't the horse he kissed. Annabel thought she might faint when his strong arms encircled her and the Falcon's mouth closed over hers. When the kiss ended, she looked up into the face of the man she knew she was bound to forever. "Is it bedtime yet?"

With a groan the Falcon swooped her up and practically bounded up the ladder.

Morning, day, or night, it didn't matter. The time had come for their passion to be given its way and neither had any reservations about the union.

She felt like a wood sylph when he removed her clothes and traced her body from head to toe with a soft blue flower from the bowl near the bed. When it reached her lips again, she gently captured the hand holding the flower and drew a brown finger into the moistness of her mouth. "You are so strong and wonderful. You make me feel so safe when I'm with you."

"I hope that's not all I make you feel," he whispered, his lips going to the tiny dimple on her shoulder. "I'll take care of you, my darling, for the rest of your life, but I want to be more than your protector."

She let out her breath when he pulled off his shirt and she felt his muscled chest pressing against her breasts. "You are," she murmured against the dark hair that curled under his neck. "You are everything to me, now and always."

"I don't know about the 'always' but I do want to experience the 'now.'" Another maneuver and the Falcon was as naked as she, his body hard and warm against hers, causing sensations that she could hardly bear.

"I knew when I first saw you that you would be the woman for me, the one I'd love for the rest of my life." His hand was stroking her thighs, moving inward to the burning center that desired so much more.

"That night on the path? I knew, too, after I heard you speak, that you were going to be part of my life."

He murmured an endearment that was almost lost in the kisses rained upon every part of her body. He stopped to cherish her breasts, saying they were shaped by the gods.

Nothing could stop him from tasting the sweetness that she willingly offered him. She knew his need was even greater than hers at this point, and gently guided him to the soft entry to ecstasy.

At the moment he entered, she cried out, not even remembering that it had been promised, "Tremaine!"

He paused in his filling of her, the held-back passion arousing her the more. "Yes. Close your eyes, darling, and give yourself to me completely . . . yes, oh, yes. Yes!"

The scream of the Falcon when he possessed his mate in the deepest sense filled the air and was mingled with a softer cry.

When Annabel opened her eyes, she looked up into the unmasked face of Tremaine Sheffield. She drew it down to kiss the scar that was now naked and vulnerable in the soft light. "I loved you from the start, too. In my heart, I knew there could only be one such love."

He kissed her vehemently. "And I knew there could only be one Isobel—the one I fell in love with and could never hate no matter how hard I tried."

"So that's what Jeremy meant when he said, after you left, that we would never see Tremaine Sheffield again." Annabel traced the scar with a gentle finger, thinking of the story Trey had told her about how he'd gotten it. "You've given up your name, your home, your place in your country as one of its noblemen to run forever as the Falcon."

"My darling, I have you now. Even if we're together only for a short time, it will give me all the strength I need to outrun my enemies and continue my cause."

"What shall I call you?" she whispered with a smile.

" 'My love' will do fine," he said with a kiss. The kiss went on a little too long, and Annabel found herself responding to it in a way she would not have thought physically possible in her state of exhaustion. . . .

They lay together afterwards in a sweet glow, whispering endearments and long-pent-up expressions of their feelings for each other. Every bone in Annabel's body felt limp. If Lunsford and his men had chosen that moment to storm the stronghold of the Falcon, she would not have been able to move a muscle to escape.

"What now?" she whispered, turning her face toward Tremaine's. "As wonderful as it is, just being together, we can't stay here forever, my darling. Even if they don't find us, we have to get in touch with Jeremy and your friends, make plans."

"I'll think about that tomorrow," Tremaine said, kissing the rosy cheek of his lady love.

Annabel's head turned sharply at that unexpected plagiarism, but its utterer was quite innocently drifting off to a land of dreams.

"Are you sure you're really from this century?" she asked suspiciously.

A polite snore answered her question.

Annabel felt that she was living in a constant state of enchantment as she and the Falcon shared days and nights that seemed to melt into one another. She sometimes woke up in the middle of the night to the sound of a night creature and let the anxieties creep in. But after she was held close in Tremaine's arms, she would go back to her happy dream world in which there was no Lunsford, no danger, no dread of being found.

The animals that the Falcon had befriended, the deer Guinevere among them, made Annabel their friend, too. Lady Godiva often followed her and her lover to their favorite place, the stream with its cascade of water where Annabel regularly took her "shower."

Usually the shower turned into lovemaking, since Trey could never resist grabbing his wet nymph just when she was about to come out from under the falls.

He could not get enough of her. Though Annabel felt the urgency of their passion and shared it, she knew its cause better than he.

Their idyll would not last. Though she fought the sense of all of this nearing an end, she could not deny it. After a week had passed, every day a glorious tribute to their love, she started listening for the crack of a twig under a horse's hoof, the murmur of men's voices, the whistle of a bullet.

She jumped at every movement in the copse surrounding their trysting place, trembled in the night when some unfamiliar sound joined that of the night creatures.

One morning she woke to find the place next to her empty of the warm body she'd learned to snuggle up to even in her sleep. "Tremaine?" She leapt up, suddenly afraid. He was gone! Someone had found them! "Trey!"

"In here, my darling."

She found him looking out over the view of the countryside from the leafy porch. He handed her a mug of coffee and kissed her, but she could tell it was not the kind of kiss that they usually shared upon waking.

"Trey, what's the matter?"

"I can't let you go on being so afraid. I can't let you live with me like some hunted animal."

"Trey, it's been wonderful and I'm not always afraid, not when your arms are around me! And when I am frightened, it's for you, not for me."

"I know that." He looked at her, and his hand went out to grasp the long curl that had fallen over her cheek. "My beautiful darling, I know that. That's why I have to do something to make you safe again. This isn't your battle." He grinned at her. "It's my fight, not yours, and I brought you into harm's way when I gave you those damned jewels. Now I've got to get you out of it."

She grabbed him around the waist. "No! I don't care what they do to me, as long as I can be with you! Trey, please don't do anything foolish. Please! We can stay here until things quiet down, till they stop looking for us; then we can leave the country. We can go to Ireland or Scotland, or even America and start a new life."

"I can't do that," he said sadly, his hand stroking her cheek. "And you know it. My place is in England. She needs me now more than ever. If Lunsford brings down the Falcon, there'll just be others to take his place, and others after that. But if the Falcon flies away in defeat and cowardice, no one will believe in what he believed in enough to fight for it."

"I need you more than England does!"

He looked down at her and shook his head. "No, you don't. I still don't know who you are and where you came from, but your destiny is as strongly directed as mine. My darling, though I sense we may have to part for a while, I am convinced that our love will never die—no matter happens to either of us."

"It won't, I know it won't!"

They stood there in each other's arms as the sun came up and the singing and cooing of birds made them smile again.

"Jeremy will be here within the hour," Tremaine whispered to the woman in his arms.

Annabel lifted a tearstained face. "How did you get a message to Jeremy? You haven't left my side in over a week."

He brushed a tear off a dark eyelash. "We made our plans before I rescued you. I said I needed at least a week alone with you, and he had no objections whatsoever."

"This means that you're going to put yourself in danger again, doesn't it? You can't go out and appear in public as the Falcon! They'll arrest you—or kill you—on sight now that you've killed one of them."

"I'm just going to map out our strategies with Jeremy—who, by the way, I'm sure is very anxious to see for himself that his beloved cousin is truly well."

"I'll be glad to see him, too. But, Trey, you must promise me that you won't do something foolish . . ."

"I already have," he said softly, lifting her chin so that she looked up into his eyes. "I've fallen hopelessly in love with a woman who, if she isn't a witch, has certainly put me completely under her spell for now and always."

"Now and always." The "now" was almost gone, Annabel thought. That left only "always." She would settle for that.

Chapter Nineteen

Jeremy and Annabel hugged each other till they were sore, laughing and crying alternately and trying to make sure the other was all right, until Tremaine forced them both to sit down, a table between them, to talk calmly.

"You look wonderful, Cousin," Jeremy said, beaming at the girl across from him. "Doesn't she, Trey? Doesn't she look more beautiful than she's ever looked since she came here?"

Annabel reached out to grasp her lover's hand and looked at him with her heart in her eyes. "There's a good reason for that, Jeremy. I have never been happier in my life than I have been the past ten days."

"Nor have I," Tremaine said softly, pressing his kiss to her hand.

"Now who's being silly and sentimental?" Jeremy teased, but his own face showed how he felt about the two people he loved best being together in the ultimate sense. "Obviously, you two have been good for each other, but we need to put romance aside for the moment and talk about what's to be done."

"Well, one thing to be done is to get that fake theft charge lifted from Isobel's head so she can return to civilization and not be hunted down with me and you."

"I hate civilization! I want to stay here with you."

Jeremy's happy look faded. "Isobel, it's only a matter of days, maybe even hours, before they find this place. They're combing every copse, every weald, every hill. They've narrowed the search down to a few square miles. Using the dogs, they found a scent of the horses where you must have been riding together."

"What about you, and the people who've been hiding you and Greymalkin?"

"They're true-blue. Even though I had to leave, they promised to keep Malkie safe." Jeremy's smile was tender. "She's their 'old granny come to live with 'em from the Cotswold.' Greymalkin's fine. She was relieved when she learned that the escape was successful."

"Tell her when next you see her that I really do want her bread recipe," Annabel said with a grin.

But the thought of that escape brought back the memory of Constable Savage lying in his blood-soaked jail and the penalty that would surely come down on the Falcon when he was captured. "I just wish it had been I, not Trey, who killed that awful man."

Jeremy shook his head. "It would make no difference. Lunsford's got so many trumped-up charges against Trey for everything from pilfered sheep to flagrant treason that he wouldn't stand a chance of getting any kind of justice."

"What about the paper? Were you able to get it to the printer?"

Jeremy nodded. "I'm picking it up tonight and taking it to the distribution points right after that. Come tomorrow night, this whole part of the country will know what these political scoundrels are doing to ruin England. I'm naming names this time."

"I'm going with you," Trey said quickly.

"I am, too."

"No, Isobel. We're going to take you to the cottagers who're shielding Greymalkin. They can be trusted. As soon as your name is cleared in the theft of the jewels, you'll be kept at a gentlewoman friend's home until you return to America."

"I'm not going anywhere until you promise me that I'll see you again!"

Tremaine pulled her up into his arms. "I promise." To Jeremy, "Get the horses, little brother, and wait for us. I need a moment alone with your cousin."

When the younger man was gone, Tremaine kissed Annabel's damp eyelids and cheeks and trembling lips. "My darling, we've always known that we were meant to be together. Remember that and forget the times we're apart."

"But I can't bear to think what will happen to you—and to Jeremy." Annabel buried her head in his chest, inhaling the man-scent that she loved and feeling his protective arms as she would soon not be able to do.

"Whatever happens, you will know that you made these last few days the happiest of my life." He kissed her hungrily, holding her as though he could not let her go, ever.

But Jeremy's whistle from below reminded him that they must not be caught here. The treehouse had been a refuge of passion and love but could as easily become a cage for the Falcon.

Trey, holding his beloved's hand tightly, took a last stride around the place. "I have spent the best time of my life in this eyrie."

Annabel wanted to cry. "I just wish it had never had to end."

"But it must, as both of us knew it would." Tremaine stopped at the edge of the ladder leading down and put his hands on her face, turning it up to his. "My darling, if I come through this and foil Lunsford's plans for me, and I can come back to you a free man, will you be my wife?"

Her eyes filled with tears. "Oh, my darling—yes!"

"Then I have something to live for."

Their embrace lasted so long that Jeremy finally came up and reminded them that they would have to save their lingering kisses for their wedding day. It was time to leave.

Annabel was embraced by the Morgans, who made much over her after Jeremy and Tremaine left the girl in their care. "You're so much like our youngest, who just flew the nest, and so pretty and sweet."

She tried hard to match their cordiality but could only think about the two men who'd reassured her repeatedly that their mission was not as dangerous as it was vital.

Greymalkin came to her that night as Annabel sat stirring the soup pot over the fire, staring into the flames and dreaming about the week that had been such paradise. "Girl? Are you stirring that soup or letting it stick to the bottom? These people don't have food to spare, so don't

335

be letting your dreaming rob their stomachs of needed nourishment."

"Oh, I'm sorry, Greymalkin. I had my mind on Jeremy and Trey and wasn't thinking."

The old woman dished out two bowls of soup and took them into the kitchen for the Morgans, then came back to get her own and Annabel's. As they sat spooning their supper, they both had their own thoughts and were quiet.

Then Annabel put down her bowl and told the old woman, "I'll never forget what you did for me in the jail that night. You took a great risk and could have wound up in the cell with me."

"Jeremy loves you like a sister. Besides, I'm so old, it doesn't matter how or when I die."

"You love him more than anything, don't you?" Annabel looked at the profile of the ancient crone in the firelight. She could almost see the outline of her skeleton under the transparent, wrinkled skin. "Greymalkin, you're more to Jeremy than just his old nanny, aren't you?"

The woman turned to fix her cat-eyes on the other's face. "Yes. I'm really his grandnanny. When Jeremy's mother came to marry highfolk, she brought me along without telling 'im I was her first husband's mammy. Even Jeremy doesn't know."

"I think you should tell him."

"Maybe I will. It doesn't matter now. The boy's got enough to worry about without finding out I'm his grandmum."

Annabel got down on the floor, at the old woman's knee. "Greymalkin, I know you have . . . certain powers. Please tell me what's going to happen. I could see it in your eyes just now. You know the future."

"My eyes aren't as good as they used to be. What happens, happens. You came here from another place, didn't you, girl? I knew when I first laid eyes on you that you was from someplace else."

Annabel nodded. "From a very long way, and I don't mean just across the sea."

The crone closed her eyes. "I knew that, too. At first I was afraid, but when I saw that you weren't here to hurt my Jeremy, I started trusting you."

"Greymalkin, whatever happens, I want you to know that your grandson will be recognized one day as a very fine poet, along with the other great English poets."

"I never paid attention to that writing stuff, but since it made my boy happy, it made me happy to see him do it." Greymalkin looked at Annabel with her head cocked to one side like a cat sizing up another one of the same color. Then she cackled softly. "How're you going to get back?"

Annabel was startled. "What makes you think I will?"

"Because you aren't here to die in England, not now." She listened as voices from the kitchen got louder. "Shh. We mustn't ever let anyone hear this kind of talk from us. We'll be burned at the stake for witches."

The plump owners of the cottage came in, bustling about making up a pallet for Annabel and making sure she'd had enough to eat. When she assured them she was comfortable and very grateful for the attention, they went up to bed.

"I can't possibly go to sleep," Annabel said. "Not until I hear something from Jeremy and Trey."

"I'll keep watch and wake you at the first word," Greymalkin told her. "You need your rest."

She was tired, Annabel realized. She lay down on the fresh-smelling pallet that was a far cry from the filthy one she'd lain upon in the jail. "What about you?" she asked sleepily.

"Old women like me don't need much sleep. We've got the long one coming up too soon."

Annabel slept soundly as the old woman stared into the fire and occasionally got up to add a stick or two. It got chilly at night with the fall coming on, and her bones got cold easily nowadays.

* * *

"Isobel, Isobel, wake up! Come on, girl, we've just had someone come to warn us about what's happened. We'll have to leave here, or be in terrible danger."

Greymalkin's bony hands shook Annabel awake from a sound sleep in which she'd dreamed that she and the Falcon were pursued by hounds the size of horses. She let out a little cry, not only from the nightmare, but also from the fear in the old woman's voice. "Wh . . . what? Is it Trey? Jeremy? They're all right, aren't they?"

"No, they were captured at Leeds, at the secret printer's shop. The man betrayed them and has told everything, even about our hiding place here. We have to leave, and hurry. The Morgans have already left, fleeing to their children's home in the north."

Annabel hurriedly pulled on her clothes, feeling she was still in the middle of the nightmare with the giant hounds closing in. "They're not . . . Greymalkin, Jeremy and Trey aren't dead!"

"No, not yet," the old woman said grimly. "But they've been charged with serious crimes and will be taken to London tonight. Hurry, girl, the man said he couldn't wait for us, but horses are saddled out back."

They scurried from the cottage, Greymalkin

throwing water on the fire before they left. If the Morgans were able to return someday, it didn't need to be to a charred cottage.

"Where will we go?" Annabel's horse danced with the feeling of the danger all around them. Greymalkin's steadier mare waited patiently for the bag of bones that was scrabbling onto her back.

"To the last place they'll look for us. Jeremy's tower. It's been boarded up since his papers were confiscated, but I know a secret way into it that those bastards aren't aware of."

They sped through the night, stopping in dark shadows of copses when they imagined the sound of pursuit, picking their way silently through open spaces.

When they came up on the tower at Sheffield Hall, it was almost dawn. "What can we do with the horses?"

Greymalkin said, "We'll give them their heads. They'll head straight for the stalls and Perkins will hide them."

Annabel whispered an endearment to Lady Godiva as she got off and gave the sleek rump a gentle slap. She watched as the animals galloped for the stables. "How long do you think we have to stay here? I almost can't bear being so near to that bastard Fenmore and his sister. The thought of their living in Trey and Jeremy's home makes me sick."

"We won't stay here long, just till things die down." Greymalkin knelt at the foot of the tower, searching for the flap that proved to be a door of sorts. "Be careful. The stairs are steep and may have a few inhabitants that haven't been disturbed in a while."

Annabel crawled inside behind her and brushed thick cobwebs off her face and arms. The stairs were thick with dust but solid, and they were soon at the top, coming out in the turret through a trap door in the window seat. "This was built a long time ago, to help persecuted monks who often hid here before escaping by river."

Annabel sank to the bench in exhaustion. "I can't believe there was no sign of a search party after us." She saw the look on Greymalkin's face and said suspiciously, "If there was one at all. We're small potatoes; Lunsford wouldn't waste his men on capturing us, not when he's got the big prize, the Falcon, in his hands."

"I promised Jeremy I'd get you away from there if anything happened. He and Trey both knew you'd probably do something foolish and just get yourself caught or killed in the process."

Annabel closed her eyes. "They were trying to protect me, even when they were in terrible danger. Oh, Greymalkin, I can't just sit around here, waiting for news. We have to do

341

something." Her eyes flew open. "I could go to Newton Fenmore and beg him, in return for my favors, to use his influence to help Jeremy and Trey."

Greymalkin made a vulgar sound. "He's nothing but pig turd, his sister, too. No, we have to wait, girl, painful as it is." She pulled her shabby black cape around her and curled up on the window seat. "Now, I didn't get any sleep last night, so I'll just have myself a snooze while you look out the window and make sure nobody is creeping up on us. And make sure nobody sees you."

Annabel stared out at the ascending sun and the graceful swans on the river gliding around till their strong beaks dived for insects. This place had seen the beginning of the most adventurous part of her life.

Would it be the place for the end as well?

This time it was Annabel who awakened Greymalkin. "Perkins is here with a message from Jeremy. He managed to get word out to us about where they're holding him and Trey in London. There's a carriage waiting for us down the road. We can leave as soon as it turns dark."

The old woman's eyes widened as she was helped to her feet. "What, I've slept the day away? Why didn't you waken me, girl?"

Annabel held out the cup of tea she'd brewed over a surreptitious fire in the downstairs bedroom. "Because despite what you say about not needing sleep, you've had a pretty strenuous time for a woman your age."

"I can keep up with you young ones any day," Greymalkin grumbled, but she drank the hot tea greedily and ate the biscuits and cheese Annabel had discovered in Jeremy's larder. "Now what's this, Perkins? What have they done with Jeremy and where have they got him?"

"Lunsford's got him and Lord Sheffield locked up separately in Newgate Prison. A special court is being assembled quickly, one that's made up of Lord Lunsford's cronies, they say. A swift sentencing is expected, so that the Falcon's followers won't have a chance to organize and protest. Oh, Miss Annabel, 'tis a shameful day in England that two such fine men should be prosecuted on their names alone."

"Is there any chance at all that I could be allowed to see them?"

Perkins sadly shook his head. "Not likely, Miss. It's said that Lunsford has hired twenty head of extra guards to make sure that the Falcon does not elude his captors. He wasn't happy about that coup pulled at the Maidstone jail and won't see a repeat, he swears."

"Greymalkin, we have to see them. We have to help them somehow!" Of Perkins she asked,

"Didn't you say when you first came in that the Fenmores have packed up and gone to London?"

"Yes, or I shouldn't have felt easy about coming to you like this. They said they'd be at their friend Boynton's house, but, Miss, you mustn't trust those two. It was Lord Fenmore who turned in Master Jeremy to that scoundrel Savage, and it was Lady Fenmore who told him about the jewels."

"I know all that, Perkins, but I have a gun to hold to Newton Fenmore's head that will make him eager to help me gain access to Newgate." She had an idea or two on how to manage Felicia's cooperation, too. Annabel turned to Greymalkin. "Are you sure you're up to this trip to London? I'm sure Perkins will look after you here until I return."

"I'd like to see my Jeremy one last time," Greymalkin said, her eyes focused on something far away.

"Greymalkin, you mustn't talk like that!" Annabel's alarm was not only for the terrible prophecy of the words but at the resignation behind them. "We will do something to save them! We will!"

Perkins said in the little silence that fell between the two women, "I must see to the horses, make sure the man we're sending you with knows where to stop and where not to. I'd go myself, but someone has to be here to help with the place. Maude has gone to pieces since all of this happened, and Todd's not much good, either."

Annabel put her hand on the man's arm. "You're quite right, Perkins. The place must be protected, even though the Fenmores have already taken it for their own. Please tell Maude and Todd I'll let them know about their master as soon as I can."

"Yes, Miss. Please watch yourself. Though a paper was signed absolving you of the charges that Constable Savage brought against you, there's danger to anyone who's known to be associated with the Falcon." To Greymalkin: "And to Master Jeremy, kind folk though he's always been to all of us."

"We'll be careful, Perkins," Annabel said. "Thanks so much for all your help and especially for your loyalty. I know Lord Sheffield will be glad to know he has faithful people like you behind him."

Perkins's eyes filled with tears. "Lord Sheffield was the best a body could ask to work for, Miss. And knowing he's the Falcon has given all of us a pride that won't be moved by a few loudmouthed fools threatening this or the other."

"God bless you," Annabel said, her voice choked.

Nelle McFather

"And God bless you, Miss Isobel. We all have talked about how you're an angel sent to make our master and his brother happy again."

"I hope so, because I'll need wings to get into Newgate Prison," Annabel said on her way through the door. And maybe to get out of it.

Newton Fenmore's look of astonishment when he saw Annabel and Greymalkin in the formal parlor of the house where he and his sister were staying was almost comical. "Why . . . why, Miss Annabel. I can't believe . . . I heard you were . . ."

"In prison in Maidstone? I was, for a while. Thanks to your sister." Annabel picked up a small Shropshire vase and examined it as though that were her sole purpose for the visit. "Is Felicia here, by the way? I'd like for her to hear what I have to say."

Newton blustered about his sister being out and how he was certain there'd been some misunderstanding. In the middle of his babbling, Felicia waltzed into the room and said to her brother, "Newton, do shut up. Have you even offered these poor refugees tea or sherry or even some of that whiskey you've been sneaking from Boynton's decanter?"

Annabel looked the redhead dead in the eye. "I don't want a drink. Newton, please do sit down and stop fluttering. Greymalkin, please close the door. I don't want any servants eavesdropping on what I have to say."

Felicia smiled her meanest smile. "If it's about the little misunderstanding over those jewels, I hope you know it was all innocent on my part. I happened to mention to Lord Lunsford that I'd seen them on you at the Sheffield gala."

"Innocent is not an adjective that could ever be applied to anything you do, Felicia. I suppose the necklace and earrings are in your jewel case by now, as a token of your lover's gratitude for helping bring down the Falcon."

Felicia's gaze dropped guiltily. Annabel pursued relentlessly, "I have a note to that effect addressed to Lady Lunsford, telling her where she might have a deputy locate her stolen jewels." When the woman started, Annabel held up her hand. "There's more. This time for you, Newton. John Keats will in one hour be delivered a note expressing disgust that certain poetry manuscripts being considered for publication by a noted literary company are plagiarized. He will recognize my cousin's work, and you know that."

"Oh, Isobel, you wouldn't . . . !"

No, she thought with regret, she wouldn't. Couldn't. It was destined that Jeremy's collection of poetry be published in 1821, after Keats's death, under Fenmore's name. She could not change history even in this despicable situation.

It would change too many other things. "I will, unless you two help me see my cousin and his stepbrother."

"Derek won't let anyone near them," Felicia cried shrilly. "He's promised that anyone who allows his prisoners to escape will be hanged along with them."

"You'll think of something," Annabel said calmly. "Greymalkin and I are going to the prison where we shall wait outside for exactly thirty minutes before dispatching the letters I mentioned. Please don't be late, Felicia." She turned at the door. "Although you could use a bit of touch-up on that hair. I've heard that Lord Lunsford likes his mistresses quite young."

Greymalkin chuckled evilly as she followed Annabel down to their carriage. "You're a bit of a devil, Missy."

Chapter Twenty

The man who had just been thrown in the cell next to Jeremy's was cursing his captors and vowing that no landlocked jail could hold a man of the sea for long. Jeremy waited till the man calmed down before calling to him. "Shut up with your whining, fellow. It's bad enough in here without having some jackal braying. What are you in here for anyway?"

The man said in a hoarse whisper so no one but Jeremy would hear, "I was a cap'n on a boat bound for America. When it went down I was picked up by the pirate ship that attacked and scuttled us. Those bastards turned me in to one of our own ships, saying I had been the one who let them on board my ship for a cut of the swag."

Jeremy laughed. So there was honor among thieves! "Well, did you?"

The fellow cursed Jeremy until the guard came and got him. "Here, you troublemaking loudmouth. We'll put you in the dungeon where you can yell till your tongue dries out and no one will hear you."

Thus was Captain Pollack, lately of the English vessel *Fugitive*, shackled and led away down to the dank level where the most dangerous criminals were kept. He did not know it, but six cells down the narrow corridor Tremaine Sheffield, alias the Falcon, awaited his fate.

Outside the prison gates, Annabel waited nervously. If her bluff with the Fenmores had failed, she might never see the Falcon alive again.

She heard activity just inside the gate, but it was only a guard leaving his shift. She knew from English-history books that Newgate prison had been a debtors' prison for almost six hundred years. It had been completely rebuilt in 1782 and upon its completion, its builder proclaimed it the most secure prison ever built.

Its cells had no windows. Annabel's heart ached to think of her beloved Falcon unable even to look out upon the world of freedom in which he had always soared.

Again she heard voices, one familiar to her.

It was not the Fenmores who had driven up in a fancy coach. Annabel's hand squeezed Greymalkin's arm hard, unaware that she was leaving bruises. But she did not move an inch when Derek Lunsford came right up to her, so close she could smell the remembered scent that evoked unpleasant images.

"So, you really wish to visit your doomed cousin and lover. Well, I'm sure you made some sort of deal with my scurrilous colleagues the Fenmores, but that won't suffice. And the old woman's not to be in on the deal I wish to propose. I have a pretty good idea she might have been involved in that pretty little trick you and your lover pulled on poor Savage."

"What kind of deal are you thinking of? I have no money, no property."

Annabel did not flinch as his gaze traveled from her throat to her ankles, lingeringly, deliberately, insultingly. "Oh, I don't think that's all you have to trade."

"If you're thinking about my giving myself to you, you must be out of your mind. I would never go to my beloved with your filthy stench on me."

Lunsford's nostrils flared in anger, but then he smiled and Annabel remembered how he had enjoyed her fighting him. "But my beautiful Annabel, that wasn't what I had in mind

351

at all. I was thinking of afterward, when your Falcon is . . . not around to remind you of your passion for him."

"Exactly what are you proposing, Lord Lunsford?"

He examined his nails one by one before answering. "Why, one night with me in exchange for one last night with your precious jailbird," he snickered at his little pun, "before his final flight."

Annabel's skin crawled as she looked into the jaded face of the one person who could arrange for her to say good-bye to her beloved. She knew she had no other choice. And what did her body matter to her after the one man who'd brought it truly to life was dead? "If I say no?"

"Then your darling Falcon will be executed tonight at a secret place instead of in the morning as scheduled. I have total authority to order the change in time and place, since all I have to say is that some of the Falcon's followers are planning to break him out of Newgate."

"That's a lie. There's only Greymalkin and myself and you know it."

Lunsford smiled. "But the Falcon in his cage makes three, and that's what it took the last time."

"All right, you win. You can have me for one night, but for one night only, at the place of my choosing."

"I'm not concerned about how long you'll want to stay with me. After one night, I shan't have to bargain with you for your favors. But I can make that promise and let you be the one to break it."

She steeled herself against his insufferable conceit. "And the other condition, that our . . . union be at a place of my choosing?"

"If it's not a hayfield or that primitive place your lover took you to."

"I choose Jeremy's tower. At least there, I'll have pleasant memories around me while I have to look at your despicable face."

He chucked her chin. "Now, now, mustn't call your benefactor and future lover bad names." He leaned over and whispered lewdly, "And I promise you will see much more of me than my face." To the guard who had come out, he said, "Cleg, this woman has the court's permission to spend the night with the condemned prisoner."

"Which one, Your Grace? There's two."

The moan from Greymalkin came from her wounded, withered heart.

"The one known as the Falcon. Make sure she carries no weapons in with her."

"Do you want me to search her, Your Grace?"

"No, Cleg." Lord Lunsford licked his lips. "That privilege is being kept for your superior.

353

Take us into your waiting cell and leave us."

Greymalkin spoke up. "I must speak with Isobel before she goes."

"Why, old woman? Do you really think you can slip a sleeping potion into the guards' liquor as you did before?"

"Please let us have a private word together . . . Derek." Annabel softened the name, tasting the bile of it on her tongue. He relented and allowed her and Greymalkin to go off a few yards to speak in private.

"You'll be using the tower for your tryst with Satan's bastard," Greymalkin whispered. "You know about the secret escape tunnel if you need it. Now there's another secret I need to tell you." She told her about the hiding place under the stone.

Annabel nodded and said loud enough that Lunsford could hear, "I'll take very good care of Jeremy's things for you."

"There'll be something there that came to me from my grandmother and which she got from hers. Now it goes to you and will go with you through the centuries."

"What is this gift—a dagger to plunge into my new lover's heart?" Annabel's smile was bitter. That thought had already crossed her mind.

"I won't tell you more, but you'll know it when the time comes to use it. I won't see you again, Isobel. With my grandson's passing, I have no wish to go on living."

"You won't take your own life!" Annabel embraced the woman fiercely.

"No, I don't have to. I've only lived to see my Jeremy through this life. Mine was up long ago, this dried old husk of a body blown not by true breath but by the winds of destiny. Good-bye, girl. Don't try to fight your fate, or that of those you love. That would only bring worse tragedy and unhappiness."

"Good-bye, Greymalkin." Annabel watched, tears dimming her eyes as the fog was dimming the gray street where Greymalkin walked away. Her small figure soon was gone, and in the distance a cat gave a mournful cry that was close to keening.

"So your accomplice has decided not to try any of her old witch's tricks. Good. The hangman would have snapped that scrawny old neck like a broomstick."

"Please let me see Jeremy before I go to the Falcon. I only want to tell him good-bye."

"The deal's been struck and your traitor cousin was not part of it. Now, come with me before I change my mind about what I've promised."

In the cold, darkening room, Annabel stood like a stone statue while Lunsford ran his hands slowly, insinuatingly over her body, stopping at the swell of her breasts and pressing the tender area between her thighs, his breath coming hoarse and loud. She wondered bleakly if he would forget his promise entirely, simply ravage her and hold her prisoner until after the Falcon had been hanged at dawn.

But a man knocked at the door, and Lunsford hastily rearranged her clothing and his own and became the arrogant superior to the jailer. "What are you leering at?" he snarled at the rat-faced man whose expression Annabel suspected was a permanent disfigurement rather than a sign of disrespect.

"Beg Your Grace's pardon, but we have the night watch coming in and they'll be wanting to know your special instructions for watching her." His head jerked toward Annabel as he kept his eyes averted from her still half-exposed bosom.

"Special instructions?" Lunsford said softly, directing his words to the jailer but looking at Annabel. "Guard this jail tonight as though the King's murderer were in that dungeon. If one man jack of you goes to sleep or falls down on his job, there'll be an extra rope on the gallows tomorrow at dawn."

"Should we keep an eye on her tonight?" Again, the jerk toward Annabel.

"No, that won't be necessary. For his last night, the Falcon can have his lovebird in the privacy of his cage. Be sure the champagne I brought is delivered along with the lady. I wouldn't want her to think that England doesn't have compassion for even its most treacherous countrymen."

Annabel lifted her skirts as she passed the man, ignoring the soft chuckle from Lord Lunsford, who said sarcastically, "Give my regards to Lord Sheffield and tell him I shan't be expecting him at the dinner we're having tomorrow night in his honor—so to speak."

"I shall tell him nothing about you," Annabel said with a scathing look.

When she'd left, Lunsford called in the other jailer who was in charge of the room full of regulars—pickpockets, petty thieves, prostitutes—and told him, "Put the blond woman I saw you bring in into your 'guest cell,' the one you and your compatriots use to get your payback from the prostitutes you let go early." He held up a hand protesting the other's stumbling denial of such practices. "Spare me the righteous denial. I know what goes on here. I've been on the King's Newgate Review Committee since I entered politics. Get the girl and have her take a bath, but don't dawdle."

While Annabel was having her final night with her lover, he would distract himself in a way that would provide some vicarious amusement.

* * *

As soon as Annabel was on her way down into the dungeon, she forgot all about Lunsford and everything but seeing the Falcon again. Before the jailer unlocked the last gate leading to the bowels of the prison, she pulled out a note. "Please, if you'll give this to Master Jeremy secretly, I'm sure he will reward you."

The jailer eyed the paper suspiciously. "If His Grace hears of it, I'll be tacked up on the wall for the buzzards." But he mumbled, "Maybe I will, maybe I won't," and tucked the letter in his pocket. "Come along now. I've got my orders and they don't include dawdling out here in the hall."

When Annabel passed the first cell, its occupant rose and, his eyes accustomed to the dimness as hers were not, stared at her as if he were seeing an apparition. He moved to his cell door, his mouth working silently and his mind screaming out that it could not be true, the girl he'd watched drown in the sea could not be walking past his cell like a pale ghost sent to torment him.

He tried to yell at the jailer, but could not make a sound. Terrified, Captain Pollack stumbled into the corner of his cell and drew himself into a fetal position, rocking back and forth. It was she, it was the one I killed, she's come here to have her vengeance. The walls closed in on him and he clawed at his face and eyes, trying to tear away the vision he'd just seen. There he sat, shaking and shivering, awaiting vengeance from the dead woman who had sought him out in Newgate.

Tremaine was standing tall and straight in the same white shirt and black pants and boots she'd seen him leave in on his fatal mission. He was looking up at the ceiling of the miserable cell as though searching for the sky. At the sound of her whispered "Trey, my darling, it's Isobel," he turned slowly, not believing, and a look of incredible happiness spread over his face.

"Isobel! Isobel, is it really you?" He moved forward, still not trusting his vision, then stopped, seeing the guard who was opening the cell gate. "It's some kind of trick. Don't come to me, my darling, it's one of their tricks to incriminate you along with me."

"Stand back, Sheffield, away from the door. The guvner sent this bottle of fancy whiskey, don't ask me why, him being the one wanting you in here so bad." The jailer placed the bottle by the door, and not removing his eyes from the prisoner, quickly slipped back out, rattling the keys nervously in the lock.

"You can see that they're still afraid I'll fly the coop." Tremaine's arms swept out, indicating the wretched cell. "Although I cannot understand why they think I would wish to leave such magnificent quarters."

359

"Trey," Annabel whispered, her voice breaking at the thought of how soon he would be leaving his cell behind, "we have so little time together. Forget this horrible place, forget Lunsford. Think only of you and me and how much we love each other."

His eyes burned like sooty coals. "I have thought of nothing else. God knows, my memories of you have kept me from clawing my way out of this hellhole."

"Then why don't you take me in your arms?"

They moved toward each other slowly, like marionettes being manipulated by the strong destiny that had brought them together. Then the Falcon stopped dead still, his arms dropping to his sides as though the puppeteer had dropped the strings. "Wait. Lunsford would never let you come to me like this unless you had made some unholy bargain on my behalf."

Annabel ached for him to hold her, to make her forget tomorrow, remember only the night. "Trey, you must believe that whatever I promised is part of a future that has no meaning to me anymore. All that matters to me is that we have these few precious hours together."

"I can't have it. I can't have you sacrificing yourself to that filthy bastard for me." Tremaine walked to the bars and shook them, calling, "Jailer! Come here at once. The lady wishes to leave."

When the man came in the door to the outer cell, he looked at Annabel in disgust. "The man doesn't want you, it seems."

"You dolt, I want her more than my life's breath. I just won't have her subjected to another moment of this miserable cell."

"No," Annabel said fiercely, not looking at the jailer but at Tremaine. "I won't leave, and if you make me, I'll confess to every crime that's been committed in the last year in London and they'll have to put me in another cell, maybe worse than this one."

"Isobel, Isobel, have you always been so stubborn?" The Falcon rubbed his forehead, but a little twitch of humor was showing at his mouth, the first sign Annabel had seen of the real Tremaine Sheffield, the real Falcon. To the jailer, he said, "Go on, get out of here. I'm sure you want to get some sleep so you can enjoy my hanging tomorrow morning."

Annabel shivered and ran to put her arms around her lover. "To answer your question, yes, I always have been this stubborn. How could you think I could leave you now? Oh, my darling, I have missed you so!"

"And I you." The Falcon turned and pulled her so tightly against him she could hear his heart beating. "It's been a short time since the week in the hideout, but I swear it seems like a lifetime ago."

"To me, too. I dream about being there with you again—and other things."

"You haven't told me what you promised in exchange for this time together."

Annabel rubbed his chest where the curling black hairs peeked out from his shirt. "I've already made plans to get out of my part of the bargain. I'll be out of the country before Lunsford knows what hit him," she lied.

His arms tightened around her and he sighed, burying his face in her hair. "Please promise me that Lunsford will never have you."

"I promise," she whispered. She had already decided that. "Now, promise me something. Forget that this is a prison cell and we're having our last night together . . ."

"We just got married and are on our honeymoon night." Tremaine fell into the spirit of it and kissed her, swinging her around the room in his arms. "The music is playing—what was it you loved so much that night?"

"Beethoven. But he's much too serious for our honeymoon night. I'll take Chopin."

"Who?"

"Ah . . . sorry." Chopin was only eight years old and, though he was performing at that age, had not appeared in England. "Uh, I forget. It doesn't matter anyway. As long as I'm in your arms, anything can be playing and I'm dancing on air."

"That's not what you said the first time we danced." Tremaine looked down into her gaze, his eyes sparkling at the recollection. "Feisty little Yankee."

"Southerner, please. You Brits call all of us 'Yankees' and that's very off-putting for people from Georgia."

"Well, I shall call you something else very shortly that might please you more. Dear me, will it ever get to be bedtime? Oh, the music is stopping."

"Do let's have our champagne in our room. It's on the house, you know."

Tremaine held out his arm and Annabel put hers through it daintily, swooping up the champagne bottle as they minced across the dirty floor to the straw mat in the corner. "You know, I really do like this hotel. It has a certain . . . character. Only blue-blooded rats are booked in here."

"Yes. But best of all," Annabel said as she handed Tremaine the champagne and waited till he opened it, clapping when the cork popped, "it has marvelous room service."

They sank as one to the mat which had miraculously become a floating cloud of wonder. As their lips touched, Annabel felt the room go around slowly and hypnotically, like a magical merry-go-round. When her arms circled her lover's neck, bringing him down to her once more, she whispered, "We must come here again sometime."

Tremaine lifted his head and asked her, "By the way, what is room service?"

She laughed softly. "You're about to find out—and I don't mean the champagne."

Making love to Tremaine was a bittersweet experience. Annabel almost could not bear the intensity of their physical need for each other. The closer their bodies entwined, the more she wanted, until she felt like a bottomless urn that could not be filled.

Tremaine felt the same way. "My darling," he whispered to her after he had caressed every inch of skin that needed no moonlight to make it gleam, "I feel like a barbarian, but I cannot get my fill of you, cannot kiss these breasts, these lips, these exquisite thighs enough." He tangled his hands in her hair and gazed down into her eyes. "Right now, crushing you into this damned straw—"

"Deluxe mattress," Annabel corrected with a smile. "We're staying in the best hotel, remember?"

"Even your strange phrasing will not get me off the subject of loving you. Isobel, will you love me always, as I will you?"

"Always, my darling," she whispered. After their long kiss, she put her finger on his scar and traced it gently. "I can't bear to think about you on the gallows. Nor Jeremy. Oh, Trey, I keep hoping this is just a bad dream and I'll wake up back in my bed in . . ." She stopped, feeling a whirling confusion about where that bed was.

"That's another thing," Tremaine said sternly, not noticing her midsentence halt. "I don't want you watching the execution. Promise me, Isobel, that you will leave here when they come for you and not stay for the . . . end."

"How can I do that? Don't ask me to leave you to face that terrible gallows without me nearby!"

"I'm asking exactly that. It won't do you or me any good. We're making our farewells now and I don't want you remembering me any way but as I am now." His kiss was fervent and awoke in her an even deeper longing. Annabel felt her lover rising against her and knew her own craving was building to match his. "Ride Lady Godiva out by the river and watch the swans and think of me. Look at the first star when it rises in the heavens and make a wish for us to be together again. See the sunset bathe the world in color and know that we will one day see it all together again."

She was going to cry because that very moment she could hear the stirrings far down the corridor and knew that she and Tremaine had only moments left. "How will I know you, Trey? I know we will meet again, somehow, somewhere, but how will I know you?"

He stroked her face, brushing off the tears. "You'll know. There'll be a symbol, a sign from me. Believe me, you will know."

Their embrace was feverish, and in the midst of it Annabel heard the ominous tolling of bells foretelling the dawning of the day.

The guards came for her and she was quickly herded down the corridor, away from Tremaine, away from the Falcon.

The cell at the end where she had heard some prisoner mewling in his corner was bare.

Captain Pollack, gone raving mad over the sight of the woman he thought he had murdered, had been hauled away to Bedlam.

Chapter Twenty-One

"Guvner, you told me if she tried any funny business to let you know." The jailer, who had put Annabel in the private room to await Lord Lunsford, handed him the note meant for Jeremy. "She tried to talk me into giving the young one this."

Lunsford adjusted his monocle and opened the letter. "No doubt some last minute attempt at an escape. Good work, my man. Now guard the lady well until my coachmen come for her to take her to Sheffield Hall. And make sure she doesn't escape to make a scene at the hanging." He looked out at the shadowy gallows where the final preparations for the execution were being completed. "I want her well away from here when her lover feels the last embrace he'll ever know—that of the hangman's noose."

"Yes, sir. I'll keep a close eye on her."

Lunsford looked up sharply. "Not too close, mind. I swear if you lay a hand on the woman, I'll flay you myself. Go! Tell Miss Isobel that I will join her at the designated rendezvous this evening."

When the man had gone, Lunsford read the letter to himself, his brow furrowing at parts that made no sense to him. "Is it in code? Perhaps the little baggage has managed to arrange a last-ditch rescue and these phrases are instructions. Hmmm."

Dear Jeremy, this letter sadly must take the place of a final farewell. From the beginning, I have loved you like the cousin you took me to be, and I know you loved me in return, as purely and completely as a man can love.

I know things that will come to pass that you do not know. I cannot tell you why I have this foresight into the future. Just accept the fact that I do. My arrival in England could never be explained in rational terms, but know that I am here for a purpose that is higher and more vital than a mere visit to my mother's homeland and family. I no longer question the fact that I was meant to know you and your poetry, as well as those whose names will be prominent in literature in years to come. Thank you for sharing all those special moments with your wonderful friends!

Your name will be as famous as theirs one day, I swear it! I will share your pride when your beautiful poems are loved by countless numbers of poetry lovers.

I also was meant to meet Tremaine, the Falcon, whose terrible fate, along with yours, I could not alter. My grief at losing him is different from that I feel at losing you, my cousin, but no greater.

Keats's epitaph will read (don't ask how I know this) "Here lies one whose name was writ on water." Well, that is not the way it will turn out. As for your name, it is written in eternal permanence in my heart and will be on the lips of generations to come. Love forever, your cousin Annabel.

"Annabel?" Lord Lunsford stared at the signature and shook his head. "Definitely some sort of code. Well, that young miss will have no chances to work her trickery for her precious Jeremy and Tremaine." Jealousy boiled in his heart as he thought of how she had turned the

Falcon's foul nest into an overnight paradise. "But she's mine now."

He heard the sound of the coach carrying the woman away. It was time to carry out the execution that he had eagerly awaited ever since the Falcon had been captured.

As Annabel wept in the coach that was speeding her away from London, Derek Lunsford laughed and lifted his wineglass to the two limp figures swinging from the gallows. "Good show, fellows! Not a sound or a twitch. I shall give the hangman a handsome bonus."

The men who trundled up to retrieve the bodies in their cart were reminded that Lord Lunsford had asked that the Falcon's be buried immediately with no mourners and no fanfare. They mumbled their understanding of the instructions, grumbling about the extra work, and set off down the cobbled streets.

Thus were the bodies of the legendary Falcon and his young stepbrother Jeremy ferreted away by compatriots in disguise. Their bodies would never be found, nor their secret graves, though Lunsford, when he learned of the theft, would issue orders to search Kent from fence to weald.

The legend was born that the Falcon had not died but could be seen riding his black stallion through the dark shadows of the copses of Kent and the surrounding counties.

* * *

Lord Lunsford had given his men instructions to turn the Falcon's mistress over to the Fenmores, and had sent an extra man along as the girl's personal guard.

Felicia could not hide her fury at the arrangement. When Annabel was shown into the great room where she and Newton were dining, the red-haired woman could hardly speak.

"Well," Annabel said, looking at the splendid spread of food from the Hall's pantry and the rare wine that came from Sheffield cellars, "I see that you are not stinting on your meals, though both of you could stand to lose a few pounds." Her grief had rendered her nearly senseless when she had walked in the door to the place that held so many memories. It had been a great relief to feel anger at the Fenmores' crass greed.

Felicia glared at her and put down a forkful of Maude's famous sweetbread. "This is our house now, Miss Sarcastic, and I'll not stand for your insulting me or my brother. We met our part of the bargain, and you have no further hold on us. Unless, that is, you're one of those classless Americans who don't have enough honor to keep their word."

Annabel's peal of laughter was devoid of humor. "Honor? You dare use that word in conjunction with the deal we made? Lady Fenmore,

371

I just left a hanging, a hanging that took the lives of two of the most honorable, wonderful, courageous human beings that have ever lived. You've got your mouth full of pork, Newton. Does mentioning something so unpleasant as a hanging make you want to puke?"

He choked and spewed food all over the table and a disgusted Felicia. "For God's sake, Newton, if you must overstuff yourself, at least swallow the food."

The sickness inside Annabel was coming back, not from these horrid people, but from the terrible loss of the men she loved. She had to have a time to grieve before Lunsford came.

The Falcon's parting words came back, and some of the sharp pain abated. "I suppose we must bury the hatchet for the time being since your friend Lunsford seems to have decided I'm to be looked after by you two. Would it upset you terribly if I took my bouncer here with me for a ride on Lady Godiva? I shan't run away and get you in trouble with Lunsford since I did make a promise."

"Exactly what was his deal with you anyway?" Felicia asked, her eyes narrowed in suspicion. "What do you have that he could possibly want?"

Newton Fenmore, halfway through his goblet of wine, choked and sputtered, and Felicia jumped up, frantically applying her napkin to the red stains on her dress. "You clumsy ass! You've ruined my dress."

Annabel pointed out wickedly, "Actually, Felicia, you should have white wine with pork . . ."

"Oh!" She flung her napkin down in disgust and flounced toward the stairs. "Go riding. Go anywhere you like. All of you, go to hell!"

"I would like to go riding with you, Miss Isobel," Newton said, rubbing uselessly at his vest front.

"Oh, Newton, I don't think Lord Lunsford would like that since Felicia won't be along to chaperone us. And Paul Bunyon here has instructions from his boss that nobody is to lay a glove on me."

Newton looked puzzled. "Isobel, you do have the strangest way of talking sometimes. But of course I shouldn't want to give Lord Lunsford any cause to be put out with me."

"No, I shouldn't think you would," Annabel agreed sweetly. "Well, Tarzan, are we ready to go for a little ride along the river? I'll have Perkins saddle up our gentlest horse for you and I promise, no tricks."

Annabel's bodyguard, she had discovered very quickly, was not blessed with a full complement of brains. He grinned at everything she said, most of which he would not think funny at all if he could comprehend it.

She could hardly wait to get out of the house and atop Lady Godiva, whom Perkins had saddled for her in record time. He whispered as they worked together on the leather straps, pulling and tightening, "I can't tell you how sorry we all are, Miss. There's been some talk of a new uprising. And I can guarantee you that just because the Falcon's been brought down, that don't mean we won't keep on with his cause."

"He knew that," Annabel said, her tears starting afresh at the reminder that she was not the only one grieving over the loss of the Falcon. "He would want you to take care of yourselves and your family first, though."

"We will. I think your escort is getting a little nervous about us. Here." Perkins gave her a lift up into the saddle, and she smiled down at him, her eyes still bright with tears.

"Don't wait, Perkins. This may take all afternoon. I've got a lot of grieving still to do."

He patted her boot and had some tears of his own when he said brokenly, "There's never been another like either one of 'em. I can't believe they're really gone."

She couldn't, either. The rest was up to her now. Jeremy would live on through his poetry someday, and Tremaine—well, she wasn't sure what was going to happen. But he had promised her that they would be together again someday.

The Falcon did not break his promises. Annabel gave Lady Godiva her head and galloped along the river, stopping occasionally to let the lumbering bodyguard catch up. "So Perkins put you on Old Blue, did he?" She looked at the nag he was astride. "I didn't think that horse had but three legs."

She laughed when he quickly bent over to look, nearly losing his seat in the process.

It felt good to laugh again. She could swear there were answering echoes from the river.

Annabel joined Maude and Todd for a tearful reunion in the kitchen. Over tea, she told them everything that had happened, and they cried unashamedly while her appointed bodyguard stood by looking uncomfortable.

"Oh, Miss Isobel, if you only knew how sad it's made everyone out here to think our own master has been hanged, and him the finest man in the country. Young Master Jeremy, too. Is there any justice in England? People are saying that there's got to be changes made, that the people have got to do something to get them rotten scoundrels out for good."

"That's what the Falcon wanted, so if people won't forget him and what he died for, his death will have made a difference in their lives."

They were interrupted by an elderly woman accompanied by a young maid who said they'd been commanded to take care of the lady who was expected to dine with Lord Lunsford that evening. Annabel rose, shushing the alarm this caused in Maude and her husband. "It's all right. I have old business with Lord Lunsford which I agreed to take care of over dinner." She kissed the couple warmly, trying to make light of what they all knew was not a simple dinner invitation. "Please stay here at Sheffield Hall as long as you can," she begged. "I would like to think of this place being in your hands for as long as possible."

They promised to stay if the Fenmores would keep them on and, amid more tears, said their good-byes.

Annabel went with her attendants, bodyguard not far behind, to be readied for the evening that she had promised would belong to Lord Lunsford.

"Miss?" The young woman who was charged with helping Annabel was firm in her choices of wearing apparel. "Lord Lunsford sent this for you to wear." She held out a shimmery red gown whose cut, Annabel saw immediately, was much more daring than the rather demure dress she herself had chosen from her closet.

"Well—Wendy, is it? I really hadn't anything quite so fancy in mind, so I'll stick with this dress." They were in Annabel's old bedroom, which Felicia had not yet commandeered in her role as mistress of Sheffield Hall.

"It's quite pretty," the girl said about the plum-colored silk that covered Annabel's shoulders and bosom. "But Lord Lunsford was quite insistent that you wear this. He had it especially sent out for you."

Annabel was about to take a stubborn stand but then she saw the desperate look on the girl's face and realized she was no doubt being coerced. "Oh, all right." When the gown was in place, Annabel silently looked at herself in the mirror and wanted to weep. She looked like a sacrificial lamb on its way to the altar.

"You look very beautiful," Wendy said sincerely. "No wonder His Lordship is so taken with you. He also sent these for you to wear, saying they would be perfect with your ensemble." The girl dimpled. "Lady Fenmore was not happy about my requesting that she release them for your use."

Annabel stared in disbelief at the infamous garnets that had caused so much grief. But this was a night when she must be numb to all emotions. She sat unmoving as Wendy fastened the necklace around her neck and clipped the earrings on. "They look like dark blood," Annabel murmured, staring at herself in the mirror. "Dark blood."

The older woman came up and finished dressing Annabel's hair, oohing and aahing over its texture and sheen. When she had finished, the two stood back and looked pleased, though Annabel glared at her image, feeling the urge to pick up something and shatter the glass.

"Oh, my, if you aren't the most beautiful lady ever. Lord Lunsford said you're his niece from America and he intends to show you off all over London one of these days. I just wish people could see you tonight!"

So that was what he was telling people. Annabel smiled a grim little smile and obligingly took the hand mirror they were holding out so she could see the back of her elaborate coiffure. "I don't think this is the night your employer has planned to parade me in front of his friends." At Annabel's request, the man guarding the door was called in. "Well, Bruno, what do you think? We need a man's opinion of how I look."

Annabel's bodyguard grinned and blushed until even Annabel had to join in giggling with the other women.

On the balcony, which had joined her bedroom to Tremaine's, Felicia Fenmore stood watching and fuming. Seeing how beautiful Annabel looked, she clenched her fists in fury. "That bastard will never have her! I'll kill her first." She took out the shiny, jeweled knife that she'd secreted in her cape pocket and moved toward the door to her rival's room.

The bodyguard just then moved toward the balcony, his bulk shutting out the light from the bedroom, and Felicia moved back into the shadows.

She waited, breathing hard, for her chance.

Annabel stood in the turret of Jeremy's tower, watching the last of the sunset and thinking about the man she loved. She felt the tears starting again as she saw a graceful swan lift its wings and prepare to fly along the water. "Fly, my darling, into the sun. Fly!"

"If that isn't a beautiful picture for a man to see, there is none in the world."

Annabel whirled around at the sound of Lunsford's voice. "Lord Lunsford! I had thought, perhaps, you had decided to be a gentleman and realized how deep my grief would be after this morning's dark happenings."

He feasted his eyes on her where she stood, slim and lovely against the panorama of river and sunset. Then he rubbed his hands together at the sight of the elegantly set table for two in the middle of the room. "Ah, but this evening is planned to help you get over your sorrow. Is this not beautiful? I had your favorites made, all of them, and the setting is, as you wished, of your own choice."

Annabel shuddered. She could almost hear Jeremy's voice, his laughter in this room. How could she have chosen this place to have her despised rendezvous with his greatest enemy?

Because this is where it began and must end, a voice said somewhere deep inside.

"It is very beautiful. I hope the Fenmores will maintain the place as it's been kept for almost three hundred years."

"Ah, if you mean you hope they won't turn it into one of their garish abominations, I'm afraid you're wasting your time. Felicia and Newton have their usefulness, but when it comes to taste . . . speaking of taste, please try this." Lunsford came over to her and held a glass of wine under her nose. "Sheffield's cellar has some exquisite treasures. I've traded some of that idiot Fenmore's notes back to him for some of the wine down there."

Annabel didn't move to take the glass or to drink. "Surely you know how despicable it is, your manipulating the law to have the Fenmores assume ownership of Sheffield. You're English by birth. How could you be part of such a loathsome scheme to deprive a fine old family of its estate?"

The man finished his wine and then hers. "My dear Isobel, you're American by birth.

Your countrymen had no qualms about taking what had been lost by the weak. Now, please let us not be enemies, you and I. Together, we can bring together two great cultures, perhaps even—who knows?—teach our children someday about how England and America can join together to rule the world."

She moved back from him, repelled. "Children?"

"Yes." He drained his glass and refilled it, then looked at her as though she were a specimen under glass. "Children. You come from good blood. You're strong, beautiful, bright, young. I've given it a great deal of thought. My wife is sickly, not able to bear me any more children—the one we have is not likely to survive—and I don't want my line to end with me."

"Oh, that would be a pity," Annabel said sarcastically.

He honestly thought she meant it. "Well, yes, since I'm the last of the Lunsfords on my father's side. I can tell you that any children we had would receive the best of everything, the best care, top schooling, nannies with credentials that would equal yours."

"I don't believe it."

"Oh, come now, surely you know that if I selected you to be the mother of my children, I

381

would follow through on my word about what you could expect from me."

"No, that's not what I mean. I mean, I don't believe that you have the gall to stand there talking about my bearing children for you to bring up as you see fit. Doesn't it mean anything to you that I utterly and completely despise and detest you and would not bear your child even if it were left to us to repopulate the earth?"

She stood there, spitting the words out like darts, and one by one they missed the mark. Greymalkin had been right. Derek Lunsford was Satan's bastard.

His laugh was straight from the devil's parlor. "I knew I picked the right woman that first night I met you."

"You didn't even meet my mother, did you? Those were lies, part of your ruse to compromise me."

"In fact, I did see her once, in a matinee, when I was quite small. She had a bit part and would have been forgettable had she not had exquisite breasts that even a small boy could fantasize about."

Annabel restrained herself from slapping his grinning face. She wondered what his monocle would look like on the backside of his arrogant face. "Apparently, your perversions started at a very young age."

"And never stopped amusing me. Which brings me to tonight. I know you think if you keep postponing dinner and allowing me to drink that you will be saved from your . . . ah, obligation. But let me assure you that I can consume wine till dawn without any physical effect."

"Well, bully for you. That's a worthy accomplishment shared by drunks all over the world."

"Oh, you do have a sharp little bite, don't you? Like a tart wine that mellows once one rolls it on the tongue, about the mouth . . ." He moved toward her, his lips wet, his eyes dilated from wine and desire. Annabel moved slowly around the table, which sat directly over the secret hiding place that Greymalkin had told her about.

"I should think you would pursue me in a more romantic fashion, Lord Lunsford. After all, you have my promise. Without my heart, though, your prize will be a lump of unmoving clay."

"I don't think so," he boasted. "Women find me . . . quite exciting. You will, too." He reached suddenly across the table and captured her wrist in an iron grip. "Enough games, my darling. You cannot get away from me so easily this time— by your own bargain."

"Then at least let us begin this monstrous farce by eating the food Maude went to such lengths to prepare. I have not eaten in two days and I feel faint."

"Of course. I shall enjoy watching the delicacies pass through the mouth whose sweetness I shall taste later on in the evening." Lunsford's hand loosened and he guided her around to her chair, which he held out for her with a flourish. "Wine? I think you'll like my choice." At Annabel's stiff nod, he filled her goblet. "Ah," he said, seating himself and lifting his glass to hers. "Nothing quite compares to an evening in the country with a beautiful woman, delicious food and drink, and a night filled with anticipation of rapture."

She felt a little sick, but forced herself to eat the dinner, which was, in fact, delicious. If she were to escape the fate that seemed to be in store for her, she must have her strength. "You speak only for yourself, Lord Lunsford. All I anticipate is the coming of daylight when I shall be free of this horrid liaison."

"By daylight, you will belong entirely to me and thoughts of your precious Falcon will have faded into oblivion." He lifted a strawberry from the fruit dish and put it into his mouth. Annabel turned her head, thinking of another night that seemed an eternity ago. "Umm. These berries are exquisite. Please have one."

Annabel put her hand over her mouth, almost gagging. "I'm violently allergic to the fruit,

Lord Lunsford. I'm surprised Maude forgot that strawberries make me ill."

"Allergic?" Lunsford was perplexed. "Oh, another of your odd little repertoire of American words. Actually, I find the way you talk quite charming. I shall look forward to hearing more about your country."

Annabel said heatedly, "Lord Lunsford, I should very much appreciate your dropping these ridiculous remarks about our future together." She flung her napkin to the floor, deliberately covering the spot where the loose stone was to be found. "Please leave me alone for a few moments to collect myself."

He patted his mouth daintily. "Oh, but of course. I expect that you want me out of the room while you . . . arrange yourself." He got up and, at the door, turned and said with a hateful smile, "By the by, I shouldn't try using the secret staircase out of here. It was discovered when your cousin's treasonous writings were found. I have a man posted at that entrance just in case you have . . . ah, second thoughts about breaking promises."

"Very clever of you," Annabel said, not letting him know that this news upset her. Though she had not made a plan to escape, she had kept the knowledge of the hidden exit in the back of her mind. Now that was closed to her. "I'm sure you've thought of everything."

"Everything," he echoed softly. "After all, I have thought of nothing else but having you since I first laid eyes on you. You have your few minutes alone, my dear. Use them well. After all, you have no way out. Why not enjoy yourself?"

Annabel wanted to fling something at the door closing behind the man. "Monster! Rutting, filthy monster!" Then she thought of the Falcon and how he had promised always to protect her. "But not now, my darling! No one can save me from this awful night."

As she sat, feeling hopeless, a clear message came into her mind: Don't forget Greymalkin's secret. She went over and picked up the napkin that covered the stone she sought, in case Lunsford surprised her kneeling under the table. The loose stone came up easily. There she saw a very old gray bag. When she picked it up, it felt heavy, as though it held something metal.

In her eagerness to see what it was, she missed the oilskin packet that Jeremy had hidden out of view.

"Oh!" She lifted out a heavy pendant like no other she had ever seen. The huge moonstone gleamed, catching the real moonlight in its mysterious depths and reflecting up into her eyes. "The moonstone! Oh, Greymalkin, how did you have it when it was the thing that brought me here?" Her mind was boggled by all the confusing implications, but she knew that she held in her hand the one ticket to her fated return to another time. She held it tightly under her chin. "Now?" she whispered to the empty room.

"Not yet," whispered Greymalkin's voice. "When the moon strikes the stone, blinding your enemy momentarily—then." Annabel placed the moonstone beneath the cushion that Lunsford had earlier arranged with coy insinuation.

Felicia Fenmore was having a difficult time convincing the man guarding the tower's secret entrance that she had been given permission by Lunsford himself to join him and his guest at dinner. She begged and pleaded, but the man would not budge.

She finally gave up and left in a tantrum. But her jealousy was too powerful to be controlled. She went to the front door and, on the verge of delivering angry knocks, discovered that the door was ajar. "The bastard was so eager to get his new mistress bedded that he left the damned thing open. Well, Lord Lunsford, we'll see just how far you've gone with the baggage."

She tiptoed up the stairs, reaching the top landing just as the door to the turret closed—but not entirely—on the man she sought. So, he had not seduced Isobel yet. Felicia's blood boiled that he had made such elaborate arrangements for his tart's comfort. The remains of the elegant dinner were easily seen through the crack of the door, as were the silk pillows and sheets that made the window seat a moonlit bower. "He's wooing the wench, damn him! He never wooed me, just dropped his pants and . . ." The vulgar picture whipped up her fury. Which one should she kill? She fingered the stiletto in her waistband. Actually, it would be less dangerous to kill Isobel. She could go to prison and rot for killing Lunsford. Besides, with Isobel out of the picture, he would turn back to her.

Or would he? There was a good chance that he'd kill Felicia in his rage at being cheated of his little baggage. Felicia decided she needed a less risky plan for replacing Isobel as Lunsford's love interest. As she watched through the slotted door, she saw the candle wavering uncertainly as Lunsford passed it. "The bastard, he's taking her dress off like some drooling bridegroom, not ripping it off as he does with me."

He caressed the girl as Felicia silently fumed and cursed. His endearments were further fuel to the rejected mistress's ire. "He never called me anything sweeter than 'slut.'" But she was caught up in vicarious fascination by this new, gentler lover who was showing the kind of tenderness that Felicia had pretended to disdain.

As she watched, a forgotten kind of passion rekindled in her heart and body. *Why, I love the bastard*, she realized in amazement. She could not bear to watch as Lunsford lifted Isobel, in her snowy shift by now, and deposited her lovingly on the moonbeam-drenched bed.

Felicia covered her eyes, from which tears had begun to seep, and sobbed silently and hopelessly.

Then a crack of late summer thunder sounded, shaking the tower to its base and causing Felicia to open her eyes to a blinding flash of brightness coming from the turret. When she looked into the room, the candle was smoking, blown out, and the moon that had lit the room was behind a cloud.

"Isobel? Isobel, where are you?" Lunsford was groping in the darkness, along the now-empty bower, around the room. "Come on, darling, I wasn't going to hurt you, I was just losing my control. It won't happen again, my darling, I promise I will be patient and gentle. Isobel, damn you, where are you?"

Isobel's gone, Felicia said to herself. No doubt she'd somehow worked out her escape plan with the dimwitted bodyguard who'd succumbed to the girl's charm even as he'd guarded her.

Felicia smiled as she dropped her dress and let down her hair. She stepped into the room and with a sweet meekness that implied surrender whispered, "I'm here, my love. I was frightened by the thunder and by the feelings you're causing in me."

With a cry, she was scooped up and taken to bed.

Before daylight came, Felicia slipped from Lunsford's arms, content that he would not know that his arms had held the wrong woman all night. She had been careful to keep her responses demure and inexperienced. Actually, she had enjoyed the role of sexual ingenue and could tell that Lunsford had liked it as well. "Too bad I can't let you know it was me, sweet," she whispered to the exhausted man who, she felt, may have been deluded, but had not been cheated.

The garnets lay in a gleaming pile on the table. Glancing back to make sure Lunsford was still sleeping, Felicia hastily poured the jewels down her bodice. Why on earth, she wondered, hadn't that stupid girl taken the stones with her?

"Well, I just hope that troublemaking little minx is a long way from here by now." Felicia looked up at the fading shape of the moon. "Who knows? Maybe she was a witch, after all, and is on her way to the moon."

She had no way of knowing that she was very close to being right.

Chapter Twenty-Two

Annabel was back in her redecorated turret room, which was no longer a whirl of sky and sea but the place she had left for adventures that she would never be able to understand or explain.

"Moonbeam?" The cat she had left in her twentieth-century world uncurled itself from the window seat and yawned, then meandered over for a pat and rub. "Did you go, too?"

The cat stretched and blinked, then yawned again and struck out for the little kitchenette off the turret room. After Annabel had fed the little creature, she went back to the window seat, half-expecting to have a furious Lunsford come bursting in demanding that she pay her dues.

She tried to put it all together, how it had happened at the last. There had been someone else, she was pretty sure. At that last moment, during the great burst of light, she had seen someone at the door, someone watching through the cracked opening.

Felicia. It had been Felicia Fenmore.

Annabel wandered all over the turret, then down to the main room. She didn't even know what day it was, how long she'd been gone, what had happened in her absence.

There was a spill of mail through her front door slot, including a week's worth of *London Dispatch*. "So that's all I was gone. Six days. Dear God, how could that be?"

There was a big manila envelope from the Institute with dear sweet Bernice's initials on the return address. Annabel tore it open and read the note accompanying a bundle of Xeroxed pages. "Annabel, I lucked out in the Archives when I was searching for some documentation for our presentation of the Fenmore manuscripts. There were some obscure items about his sister and his Parliament sponsor who was well known during the time for his domination of the government-backed Corn Laws."

Annabel stared at the brief item describing the demise of Lady Felicia Fenmore, "whose death at 32 years of age came after a long, painful bout with a disease that in today's world would be diagnosed as syphilis."

Syphilis! Annabel thought of her narrow escape from a similar fate and shuddered. Then she read the next piece.

Lord Derek Lunsford, Fenmore's long-time sponsor and mentor, who wrote a preface to the famous poet's first published collection, was killed while riding through the country in Kent in August, 1823. One of the chief prosecutors in the "Tolpuddle Martyrs" case, in which six Dorset men who tried to organize agricultural laborers into a Trade Union were tried and convicted, Lord Lunsford was survived by his wife Elizabeth. His only son died in 1819.

Annabel sat there, pages in hand, staring out at the river whose swans might have been the same as those back in Jeremy's and Tremaine's world. "Poetic justice," she murmured, thinking about Newton, who was the only one who had not been punished during his lifetime for his wicked ways.

"Somehow I think he probably is suffering in hell, knowing he wasn't really a poet. Poor Satan, having to listen to that God-awful poetry." How the puffed-up little peacock had loved comparing himself to Keats and the other Romantic Age greats!

Annabel still couldn't believe she was back in her own time. She looked down to see that the moonstone, no longer full of fire but quietly murky, had made it back with her. She laughed when she saw that she was still dressed in the shift she'd been wearing while Lunsford was trying to seduce her.

"Funny, I think he may have really loved Isobel," she said to the cat.

She looked through the rest of her mail and then came out of her languor into action at one note and then another. The first was from Roman, who was due back that very evening.

The second was an announcement of the dedication of the Fenmore manuscripts, with ceremonies led by Dr. Morris Keller. Participation was expected from members of the National Poets Society, the Foundation for the Arts, and other distinguished personages from the academic and literary world.

She had to get moving if she were going to set the record straight about whose poetry Newton Fenmore and his descendant were taking credit for. "Don't worry, Jeremy," she said aloud to the room where he'd penned the works that were in the act of being officially stolen from him, "I'll set things straight or die trying."

She went into the shower and luxuriated in

the modern convenience for quite a while. There were some things to be said for the twentieth century, she decided.

It seemed so strange to be listening to the radio, to be back in her time, yet in the same place. Every moment Annabel expected to hear someone riding up in a coach or on horseback. She looked out at the river every time she passed the window and expected (longed?) to see a masked rider on a black stallion.

At least when she went up to the main house for dinner, she would not encounter the Fenmores as lord and lady of the old Sheffield Hall. "Newton and his gambling finally paid off—to his loss."

She'd forgotten about the modern convenience of an answering machine. When she played back her messages, she had two from Morris Keller, who sounded irritated that she wasn't at home. "I know you're out in the county researching my relative, but I would appreciate your returning my call as soon as you can. After all, I'm your thesis adviser and I need to be kept apprised of what's going on."

Oh, boy, would he love hearing what she had discovered about his forebear, Annabel thought. But she called him and was sweet as pie on the phone when he answered. "Dear me, Dr. Keller, the past week has flown by and here I am, almost back where I started."

"Well, Miss, it's time you got serious about your thesis and gave your committee some pages."

"Oh, I will. In fact, I shall probably have an exciting new modification of my proposal in your hands by early next week." She had a lot of work to do, work that Morris Keller would not be happy about. "How are the plans for the dedication coming?" she asked sweetly.

"Swimmingly. I don't like being in the limelight, of course, but there's a great deal of excitement in the academic world about my giving my ancestor's original works to the Institute. Sort of a full circle kind of thing, don't you know? And we've had Keats's handwritten notes on Fenmore's poems authenticated, along with Byron's and Shelley's, which of course makes them even more precious historically."

"Oh? You have a handwriting expert available? There are some notes I've run across, nothing like what you have, but valuable nonetheless to my thesis, that I'd like to have verified."

She wrote down the name and number that he gave her. The poem she'd found before her journey through time was the only original piece she had of Jeremy's, but if she could establish it as his work, and the notes truly those from Keats . . . "Thanks so much. I'll see you in your office bright and early Monday morning."

"Perhaps dinner before then? I know a quiet little place where many of the literary greats dined regularly. It would be my pleasure to take you there."

After tea with Keats, dinner with Byron and Shelley? Ha. "I take it that the missus is off in York again," Annabel said wickedly. "No, Dr. Keller, I'm really tired from all my traveling. You do need me bright and bushy-tailed for the big presentation coming up, don't you?"

Morris Keller had to be related to Lord Lunsford as well as the nerdy Newton Fenmore, Annabel decided as she rang off. What a horrific combination!

Reentry into the modern world was tough. Annabel dressed and took a short walk along the river on her way up to the main hall, thinking how sad it would be to enter the house and not encounter her old friends. She even missed the spoiled Lady Fenmore, who had, after all, saved her in a way from a fate worse than death.

Thoughts of Tremaine and Jeremy brought tears to her eyes, as did memories of Lady Godiva and the rides they'd had. But it was time to shake off the past. She took a deep breath and entered the front door to Roman's. The din of laughter made her smile. How Jeremy would have loved the camaraderie here! He would have been off in a corner quaffing ale and talking poetry, no doubt.

"Miss Annabel!" Armand's Gallic features lit up as she walked back into the kitchen. "We have all missed you so much, wondering when you would come back." He shook his pastry roller at a young girl who was taking the chef's famous crusted pâté from the oven. "Mon Dieu, be careful when you set it down. The crust must cool, not be touched." He rolled his eyes at Annabel. "New help, always new help. I tell Roman if he would let me send for my family, we would have no more amateurs in the kitchen."

"What's for dinner?" This was a joke between them, started the night Annabel had first visited the kitchen.

"Ah! I have added your grandmother's cream-soaked chicken and shushpuppies to our regular menu."

"Hushpuppies," Annabel corrected him with a grin.

"Whatever. And the cobbled apples with latticed cheese." Armand made an exaggerated sound of appreciative smacking. "You Southerners have palates that are almost French, the sauces, the rich breading . . ."

"Armand, I could stay back here talking recipes with you all night, but I haven't even seen Roman. Did he get back?"

"Oh, yes. He told me that you and he would be dining in his room and that I was to pull out all my most alluring cooking tricks to make yours and his homecoming special."

Annabel blushed. "He said that, did he? Well, in the meantime, I'll have a drink in the pub. I haven't had any really cold beer since I left." She had explained her week-long absence by saying that she'd been doing research in another county.

"These provincial cafes are colorful but they leave much to be desired, do they not?" he said.

Try those that were around in 1818, Annabel thought.

The bartender made a great fuss over her appearance, and she soon had several beers in front of her from regulars who greeted her as though she were a long-lost friend instead of a relative newcomer to the area.

When a muscled arm snaked around her to relieve her of one of the many mugs, she caught her breath and turned her head. "Roman." His cheek with the scar was so close her lips grazed it. "How was your trip?" she asked throatily.

"Long. I missed you. God, how I missed you." He lifted her hand and kissed it. "I couldn't wait to get back, that's why I cut my trip short. How was your foray into the past?"

Annabel almost choked on that. If he only knew! "I . . . learned more about my subject than I could have ever learned from the archives at the Institute. I missed you, too."

"Did you really? I was afraid you might be swept off your feet by some handsome swashbuckler in my absence. Maybe that's why I hurried back here."

How could she tell him about what had happened? If her feelings about Roman were as strong as she believed them to be, didn't she owe it to him to confess what had happened with another man, even if it was in another time? "I . . . usually keep my feet on the ground. Roman, I have so much to sort out about my poet Newton Fenmore. Why, do you know I discovered that he never even . . ."

The bartender leaned over, phone in hand, just then to whisper something to the pub owner. Roman took Annabel's half-drunk beer from her hand and put it on the bar. "Armand says dinner is ready and that if we're not up there immediately, he will give it to the cat."

She went up with him, her heart pounding at the feelings she was undergoing at seeing him again. Why isn't this wrong? she wondered. Why didn't she feel wrong about the emotions evoked at the sight of Roman when she had not long before spent the night in the arms of the man she loved with all her heart and soul?

When they entered his suite, she realized that she was in the bedroom of Tremaine Sheffield, a fact lost on her before she had entered the original world of Sheffield Hall. "I never asked you how you happened to choose this room to make your own. There are other larger bedrooms."

Roman led her onto the balcony where a candlelit table awaited them. He uncorked the champagne with a strong, sure hand before answering, "I'm not quite sure. When I leased this place, I came up here and felt such powerful vibes, not just from the room itself, but from this balcony, from the bedroom next door. . . . I just had to be here, that's all. Champagne?"

She took the glass he held out and waited till he stood beside her at the railing overlooking the maze before pursuing some of the questions that were making her mind dizzy. "You never told me, either, how you happened on this house in the first place. It's out of the way, not in a highly populated area that would be conducive to a pub and restaurant. What made you pick Sheffield Hall for 'Roman's'?"

He laughed and touched her hair which was like glistening onyx, striped now with moonbeams. "Aren't you the little Miss Curiosity? Are you doing your research on this Fenmore guy, or is it me you're trying to find everything out about? Hey, it was kind of a funny thing, actually, my finding this place. Hell, this part of England is full of broke aristocrats trying to lease their family estates to rich Americans. I had a fistful of addresses that the real estate broker had given me to take a look at before getting down to business."

"But you found this one. How?"

"Patience, Griselda. I'm getting to that. I was driving all over Kent, to hell and gone, and came to the turn-off, the one where I have my sign now to help other unwary travelers find the way here. There was an old woman standing there, motioning to me. I thought she was stranded or hurt or something, so I pulled over."

Greymalkin. "Did she say anything to you?"

"Well, she mumbled something about feeling as if she might faint, and I thought, Lord, she could die on me right here, so I asked her if there was some place I could take her. She pointed down the road, and when we got to the gates of the estate, she motioned for me to stop close to the old tower. She was crying, not making any noise, but I could tell she was upset. I asked her if I could get her a drink of water or something and she nodded. I got out and went to my car trunk, found the thermos I had back there. By the time I came around to her side, she was gone."

"Gone?"

Moonspell

"Vanished. I looked for her all over, but no luck. That's when I found that cat that you're so crazy about, by the way. Maybe that's why I leased the place that very day. The cat needed a home and so did I." Roman shrugged, looking a little embarrassed. "Don't tell any of my old football buddies about this when you meet 'em. I'm supposed to be a tough guy."

Annabel smiled. "I wouldn't dream of telling them what a pussycat you are. Now, shouldn't we do something about that absolutely divine-smelling dinner Armand's gone to so much trouble over?"

"Not before we do this." Roman put his glass down and took Annabel's from her and took her in his arms. She felt as though centuries melted together with their lips as they kissed.

Roman felt it, too. When he raised his head, he said shakily, "Is it my imagination, or am I really standing here holding a woman that I thought existed only in my dreams? I swear, Annabel, I can't understand how I found you, how you came into my life by chance, the woman I always looked for but never could find."

"Chance?" Annabel smiled up at him, stroking his cheek. "Chance is just fate's way of making the game of love more exciting."

They would have liked to have stayed in each other's arms all night, dinner forgotten, but both sighed simultaneously at the sight of Armand's feast and the thought of what he would say if they neglected it. Annabel said with a grin, "We're here to stay, you and I, but chefs like Armand are hard to replace."

Roman agreed as he pulled out her chair. "You're right. But I'm not giving you up to any French temperament for the rest of the night—understood?" He reached out and held her hand tightly, stroking her tender palm as he added softly, "I'm in charge of the dessert tonight, not Armand."

The pub was closing as the two late diners finished their final course. Annabel could hear the sound of cars leaving the parking lot soon after the ringing out of "Time, gentlemen!"

"Now that it's getting nice and quiet around here, I wouldn't mind a stroll in the garden. I have a poem I'd like to read to you. That is, if you like poetry?" This addendum was asked anxiously. Annabel wasn't sure that anyone who didn't like poetry could ever be a permanent romantic interest for her.

"Elizabeth Barrett Browning, especially." Roman chuckled. "Once when I was football captain in college, I recited 'How Do I Love Thee?' in the huddle and, boy, were guys ready to get outta there. I got some funny looks for the rest of my college career, even earned the nickname the 'Rhymin' Fullback.' "

Annabel laughed along with him. "You know, I realize that the era of 'sensitive, caring' men is fading out on us, but I really do like a lot of things about you. You're kind of a Renaissance man crossed with a gladiator."

"I like that."

"Being the perfect blend of macho/gentle?"

"No, the part about you liking a lot of things about me. What about my hair?" Roman pulled out a tousled curl. "Would it blow my image if I told you neither the curl nor the color is natural?"

Annabel's mind went crazy with images. . . . Of Tremaine's dark hair rumpled under the mask of the Falcon, long thick locks tickling her nose. Of her finger tracing the line of the scar which he had teasingly told her was the outline of the Rhine River. Of dark eyes gazing into hers as two lovers reached ecstasy together. "No, it wouldn't. Do you mind telling me why, though?"

"I did it during a period when I wasn't sure who I was. I can't explain it. I felt as if any day I would turn a corner and see something, meet somebody who would make everything clear. Maybe that's why I tried so hard to be everything, to involve myself in every kind of sport, every kind of hobby. The hair color and perms were part of my search for Roman Forsythe and what the hell he was doing here."

She longed to tell him about similar feelings that had culminated in becoming another person in another century. But she knew he couldn't possibly believe what had happened, no one could. She could hardly believe it herself. "One thing he's doing here is making me very eager for that walk in the garden."

They went downstairs, stopping by the kitchen to pay their compliments to Armand, who beamed with pleasure. "Ah, you ain't seen nothing yet," he said with obvious pride in his growing grasp of Americanisms.

Annabel dragged Roman outside before she burst into laughter. "Poor Armand! He told me he's learning English from old movies. He's working his way through Al Jolson to Humphrey Bogart."

"Just so he doesn't discover James Cagney and John Wayne. Hey, is this a great night, or what?"

They strolled hand in hand through the garden. "I like the quarter moon best of all," Annabel said, looking up. "The full moon has too much influence on us earthlings."

Roman put his arm around her and led her to a stone bench in a circle of flowers. "Read your poem to me. It's not Poe's 'Annabel Lee,' I hope? That one's much too sad, and I'm feeling anything but that."

Annabel giggled as she unfolded Jeremy's poem, the one that had started her quest for the real poet behind the work she was writing about. "I was named for that unfortunate lady. Have you any idea how much flak I've had to take in my profession for having my name?"

He squeezed her hand. "I think it's a wonderful name, suits you to a tee."

She read the ode "To Isobel in Her Garden" slowly and with much emotion. When she stopped, a fat tear dribbled down her cheek. Roman was very quiet; then he pulled her into his arms and gently kissed away the wetness on her face. "That means a lot more to you than just another poem by your poet, doesn't it?"

Annabel nodded. "Roman, I've discovered something terrible, something that might destroy my academic career forever. But I have an obligation to set the record straight." She sat up and sniffed, getting herself back in control. "I want you to hear this other poem and tell me what you think."

She read Newton Fenmore's "Milkmaid's Lament" from his final volume of poetry. When she finished, Roman was again quiet, but then he laughed. "It's a joke, isn't it? That's not by the same person who wrote 'Isobel.' It couldn't be."

"That's the point I have to prove. If I could only get my hands on Fenmore's original poems,

407

the ones from the same volume that Isobel's ode was published in. Dr. Keller has been extremely reluctant to let me see those. He says that they're so precious that we mustn't handle them before they are donated to the Institute. But I now think that he *knows* his ancestor was a fraud, and that comparing the handwriting on this poem to that of the other originals would prove it." Annabel sat, thinking hard. "There's another way, too! Both Fenmore and the true author were published, Jeremy through his underground newspaper and Newton through his work in the government."

"Do I detect a Nancy Drew caper coming up?"

"No, more like a P. D. James's Cordelia caper. I'm not doing this for fun and games, Roman. A man's life work was stolen from him, and I intend to see to it that plagiarism is proven."

"Where do we start?"

Annabel stared at him. "We? You mean you and me?"

"I don't have a mouse in my pocket, so I guess that is what I mean. You and me. Us."

Annabel felt the presence of Jeremy so acutely, she could almost hear his happy laugh. She was sure he had heard and appreciated Roman's critique of the milkmaid poem. "Dr. Keller can turn out to be a nasty enemy. This isn't your mission, you don't have an ax to grind."

"I have always wanted to be a beautiful woman's sidekick in rooting out evil. So, where do we start?"

Annabel grinned wickedly. "Elementary, my dear Watson. We start in the tower, where Jeremy wrote all his poetry."

"Sound idea. Maybe we can find some more of his poems like the 'Isobel' one."

"That wasn't exactly what I had in mind," Annabel said, her smile warming Roman to his toes as he got up with her. "I was thinking more in terms of seeing how romantic you are when it comes down to repeating history."

She didn't have to repeat herself.

Chapter Twenty-Three

There was no ghost of the loathsome Lord Lunsford in the tower that night. In fact, when Annabel awoke in her lover's arms the next morning, she felt happier and more complete than she had ever been.

She and Roman had moved to the more comfortable bedroom downstairs after their initial romantic interlude in the turret. Counting stars and identifying constellations had led to more exciting activities that called for more space than the narrow window seat provided.

Annabel raised herself up on an elbow to look at the man lying beside her. He was boyishly vulnerable with his ruggedness softened by sleep. She smiled at the tousle of long curls, seeing the peeping darkness at the roots. "What will you look like when your hair grows back to its natural state?" she whispered to herself, not wanting to wake him before she'd had a chance to relive the romantic night in her mind's eye.

It had been like a dream, being in Roman's arms. The memory of making love with the Falcon in the prison cell had miraculously blended into the current circumstances.

"He said that I would know, that there would be a sign that he was back with me." But there had been no such manifestation during the lovely time with Roman. In fact, the intensity of the night had all but blotted out anything other than the moment of ecstasy.

"Hey. You awake already?" Roman stirred sleepily and reached for her. "I was dreaming about you."

"No, you were not. I saw your legs kicking like a hound dreaming of chasing rabbits. And you distinctly moaned at one point, 'Monica. Monica, my darling.'" Annabel tickled his lips with a feather from the pillow.

"No doubt that was the name of the rabbit. Hey, you." His eyes opened wide as he pushed her hair away from her cheek. "Last night was wonderful."

"For me, too." She kissed him. "But we can't lollygag around in bed. I have some work to do today. The presentation's just a week away, and I have to get that proof I need for sinking Keller's Good Ship Plagiarism." She kissed him again and swung her legs over the edge of the bed. "First coffee, then Operation Sink."

"After we're married, I hope you aren't going to start every morning off with all this energy that could be better directed toward making me happy."

She paused in the act of pulling on a loose sweater and jogging pants. "What? 'After we're married'? I don't recall having been consulted, much less seeing you on your knees posing the question that usually precedes the Wedding March."

"I'm an ex-football player. Getting down on my knees is hard work. Does getting up on my elbows count?" He had her laughing so hard she threw his robe at him and went off to make coffee.

"Trust me. I have contacts," Roman said. They were on the roundabout from Maidstone to London and Annabel didn't trust anybody on that mad-mouse intersection. "Brillo, my bookkeeper, can crack safes without even thinking about it."

"Your bookkeeper is an ex-felon?"

"Think about it. He can spot a scam or a loophole that a gnat couldn't squeeze through.

He'll get into your friend Keller's safe without leaving a sign. Isn't that what you want?"

Annabel was dedicated to her cause but wasn't sure she needed to break laws to realize its culmination. "Isn't that illegal?"

They were stopped at a light on the outskirts of London. Roman put the car in park and leaned over to give his tense companion a kiss. "Pardon me, but I thought you wanted to get this sleaze."

"Why do they call him 'Brillo'?"

"Wait'll you see his hair, you'll understand."

"I have to get in touch with the handwriting expert," Annabel said. "Dr. Keller gave me the name and number of one."

"My sweet naïve darling, you do not go to the fox's accomplice to find out who's stealing eggs from the henhouse."

Annabel couldn't help comparing the busy London streets they were driving through to the London of Isobel's time. "That's a mixed metaphor, I believe. You think, then, that the handwriting expert is in Keller's pocket? I only have the one poem signed by the actual poet, Jeremy Harker Simmons. The handwriting on it should, if my theory is right" (*as I know for a fact it is,* Annabel thought to herself), "match that of the originals Keller has."

"You have to get your hands on a sample of Newton Fenmore's handwriting."

"I've got a trusted ally working on that. She may even have the goods sometime today." Bernice was probably the most efficient researcher in the whole Institute. "I may be wrong, but I think that Morris Keller destroyed those boxes of the later manuscripts, the bad poems by Fenmore that were published much later. I think he recognized that they were not by the same poet and didn't want it found out."

"In other words, your boss is a crook." They were turning down a narrow alley on a street that Annabel would not have felt safe on without her fullback along. "Don't be alarmed. Brillo knows every hood in London. Probably served time with most of 'em. Here we are."

"My God." Annabel looked at the dirty, narrow staircase leading up into a dilapidated office building. "He's been watching old detective movies like Armand. If he pulls out a bottle of bourbon from his desk and has a platinum blonde as a secretary, I swear I'll have to laugh."

"Come on. And while we're at it, I'll call an old friend of mine who's retired from Scotland Yard. He was the best forgery expert in the business. If we get our hands on the manuscripts, you can bet your boots Stone will tell you what's what."

Annabel followed Roman up the dingy stairs. "I don't believe this. Even in America, we don't have real gumshoe detectives except for those who follow cheating spouses."

The man inside the office quickly lowered his feet off his desk when his visitors walked in. Annabel saw right away how he'd gotten his nickname. His gray, bristly hair covered his head in tight, kinky curls that really did look like steel wool. "Blimey, Forsythe, you told me she was a looker but you didn't say enough." The man held out his hand to Annabel and she shook it. "Not too hard, Miss. These hands used to make my living for me."

"I hope you haven't lost your touch, Brillo," Roman said, brushing off a huge yellow cat from the only other chair in the room so Annabel could sit down. "We need a safe cracked, and you're the only one I know who can do it and not get caught. Plus, you're good about keeping your mouth shut."

"Have you two done business together before?" Annabel asked suspiciously.

Roman laughed. "No. As I told you, Brillo keeps my books and, believe me, nobody—but nobody—can pilfer even so much as a roll of toilet paper from my business without this fellow putting a finger on it." He got down to business. Annabel saw Brillo's eyes widen when he learned where the "heist" would take place.

"Hey, that's a bloody government building." He rubbed his hands together and said gleefully, "I've never cracked a bloody government safe. But where's the profit in a bunch of papers?"

Roman had not given the man any more information than he had to. "We're not stealing for profit, Brillo. This is a matter of righting a very old wrong. The less you know, the better. Annabel will be with us and will make sure we take only what we need to make our case."

"In a way, you'll be paying off your debt, if you have one, to England," Annabel pointed out.

After Roman had called his retired Scotland Yard friend, Brillo pulled out a half-empty bottle of whiskey from his desk.

Annabel couldn't help it; she burst out laughing, and soon Roman had joined in. Brillo, although not understanding the cause for hilarity, laughed as well. "You Americans are so bloody jolly," he said as they all drank to the mission ahead.

Bernice was waiting in Annabel's office when Roman dropped the girl off. "I couldn't wait for you to get here. Bingo! I found an entire file of Parliament measures proposed back in your boy's term. There were four bills handwritten and signed by Fenmore."

"Bernice, you're wonderful. I just hope that Roman's friend will be able to tell something from the copies you made."

"Copy?" Bernice's eyes gleamed with triumph. "I could go to jail for it, I suppose, but I managed to swap the copies the librarian made for me with the originals." At Annabel's squeal of delight, the secretary held up her hand. "There's more. Your Jeremy Harker Simmons apparently became something of a folk hero along with his cohort, the Falcon. There was a whole shelf of his political writings that some of his followers preserved after his death. The archivist said they could not be taken out of the building, but just about that time, she got a phone call and left the stack on the library table."

"And you relieved said stack of at least one article." Annabel hugged the other woman. "Oh, Bernice, I hate like the devil involving you in this."

"Look, I don't know exactly what you're up to and I don't want to, but I do know that Morris Keller is an ass and if you're using that copy of the key to his office I gave you to show him up for what he really is . . ." Bernice grinned. "I'm all for it."

"Where is the darling man, by the way? I'd really like to avoid seeing him today if I can."

"Where do you think? Out trying to cozy up to the editor of a national journal that plans to feature the presentation in its next issue. Keller likes getting his picture in prestigious publications as the descendant of a great nineteenth-century poet."

If Annabel had her way, he would have his picture plastered on every post office wall around the country. Or did they do that in England?

When Roman came by to pick her up, Annabel was beside herself with excitement. She had compared the writing on Jeremy's treatises to that of the poem he'd written for Isobel, and they were identical. "And those stupid bills that Fenmore wrote when he was in Parliament are totally different. He even used his seal, so we've got him, Roman! Once your friend authenticates what I already know is true, we'll have Dr. Keller between a rock and hard place. He'll have to own up that Jeremy Harker Simmons's work was stolen by his ancestor and passed off for his own. He'll be the laughingstock of every academician in England—America, too."

"How are you going to handle this? Morris Keller, from what you tell me, is cunning and immoral. If you back him into a corner, he's liable to turn nasty. I've known some of these academic types who think that having a Ph.D. next to their name is tantamount to being Zeus."

"I'll confront him with our proof and give him a chance to save face at the dedication ceremony. He can announce that while the poetry was mistakenly attributed to Newton Fenmore, a final preparation of the original papers uncovered the true author."

"Hmm." Roman still looked worried. "I don't like it. At first when you told me what you think he did, I thought it was all ego-driven. But, Annabel, this man is more than an ego-maniac. If he were a real scholar, he would take pride in upholding the moral standards of his profession. If he were just an egotist, he'd be happy to donate the works with all those famous poets' scribblings on 'em to the Institute. But his motivation goes deeper. I just wish I could know more about the man and get a handle on what makes him tick."

"He doesn't know about you and me."

"Are you sure?" They were pulling into a parking spot not far from the hub of the theater district. "Do you think you could use a spot of beer and maybe a sandwich?"

Annabel agreed enthusiastically. She was starved. When they went into the pub that Roman had chosen, she looked up at the address and the tavern sign and burst out laughing. "You devil, you! 'The Sherlock Holmes' and it really is on Baker Street."

Annabel threw her arms around Roman and gave him the biggest kiss he'd had in the past twelve hours.

"Do you really think Holmes would have done that to Watson?" Roman asked when he finally could catch his breath.

Bernice confirmed to Annabel that her superior would be out to dinner with yet another notable from the academic circle, so it appeared to be the best chance to pull off the burglary that night.

"Roman, you can still back out of this," Annabel assured her accomplice as they waited for Brillo in the shadows of the back corner of the Institute parking lot.

"I'm in it with you all the way. I'm just a little worried that Keller might decide to check the safe tomorrow before we've had a chance to get the authentication done by Stone. If he raised a row, you or Bernice could be in deep you-know-what and the whole thing could blow up in our faces."

"Bernice said he told her that they would be preparing the display cases Thursday, three days from now, and that it would be best not to handle the fragile pages before that morning."

Annabel checked her watch. "Are you sure he'll show up?"

"Brillo will be here, trust me. The man is as addicted to this kind of excitement as you are to poetry and I am to you." Roman kissed her. "Scared?"

"A little. No, make that a lot. I just hope the schedule for the security guard's check of offices hasn't changed." Annabel checked her watch again, getting nervous. "He should be here by now, Roman."

"He is." Roman pointed to the dark figure coming toward them. "Brillo, you're five minutes late. Are you slipping?"

"I checked out the back of the Institute, mate, made sure there weren't no surprises. You ready?"

"We'll go in the side door," Annabel told them. "I have a key. If anyone shows up, both of you make yourselves scarce. I have access to the building day and night, and nobody would think it out of the way for me to be working in my office at night. But they might think it odd if I showed up with you guys."

The building was a graveyard, the hall lights turned to dim. "We're in luck," Annabel whispered as they crept along the hall. "Most everybody went to the public readings in Trafalgar Square. Some of our grad students were doing a presentation of concrete poetry."

"Yuck. That stuff that has a train choo-chooing and nothing else, or somebody trying to immortalize the sounds of asthma."

Annabel laughed softly. "You've really got it in for contemporary poetry, don't you?"

"I just don't like people who string unrhyming sentence fragments together and stick in a four-letter word or two and call it poetry."

"Shh. This is it." Annabel took out the key Bernice had made for her and gave a sigh of relief when the door to Morris Keller's office opened with ease.

"I've got my light," Brillo said. "Make sure the shades are down." He swiftly moved to the safe in the corner. Annabel marveled at how quickly the man moved in the dark—like a cat. "Oh, blimey, and they call this a safe. A tot could get into it." He knelt as Annabel peeked through the corner of the window covering and Roman acted as sentinel at the cracked door. "No wonder our government is in deep trouble," he muttered as he gave one turn, then another, then another, his ear to the safe door. "Look at this," he said in disgust as with a delicate pull, the safe swung open.

Annabel had seen a light outside and was relieved when the car, apparently holding two romancing students, moved on. "You've got it?" She went over and bent down to retrieve the sealed box labeled CONFIDENTIAL. "I'm sure this is it." It was about the same size as the box the highwaymen had stolen from Jeremy on the coach near Canterbury.

She opened the metal box and felt her heart melt on seeing the paper lying atop the others. It was the copy of the poem to Isobel that Jeremy had taken with him to Italy, except that the name was "Felicia" and had obviously been changed. "Surely your friend Stone can prove this sacrilege," Annabel said. "Why, you can still see the faint imprint of the original title." She got up and glared at the other two. "That bastard Keller! He had to know!"

"Shh. I thought I heard something." Roman put his hand on Annabel's arm and they stood there listening, holding their breath. Then they relaxed. "Just another car. Still, the sooner we're outta here, the better." He looked at the box holding the precious manuscripts. "You know, just as a safety precaution, why don't we leave the box and fill it with blank paper? That way, if Keller checks the safe in the morning, he'll see the box and won't suspect anything."

"Good idea." Annabel went into Bernice's adjoining office and took a box of typing paper, emptying it and replacing the pages with the contraband sheets. She put the blank paper in the metal box, and Roman replaced the tape holding it shut. "There. He'll discover the manuscripts are missing but maybe not before we're ready for him to."

Outside, they let out sighs of relief. Brillo said slyly, "I say, we make a good team. I read something the other day about a display of famous jewels at the British Museum . . ."

Roman and Annabel let it be known what they thought about that notion, and Brillo cheerfully faded into the dark on silent feet.

"Whew." Annabel leaned back against the seat, feeling her adrenaline returning to normal. "I hope Jeremy knows the kind of trouble we're going to for him. Are we taking these over to your friend's house right now?"

"After this." Roman leaned over from the driver's seat and took the manuscript from Annabel's lap and placed it carefully on the floor at her feet. He then pulled her into his arms and kissed her. After a moment or two, he grumbled, "The trouble with English cars is that they don't have proper backseats. I don't know about you, but life as a cat burglar is pretty exhilarating for me. Makes the ol' blood start pumping, like a close game with the score tied and us with goal and two."

Annabel pushed him away, laughing. "I can see that I'm going to have to break down and learn about football. Come on, Roman, if a bobby happens along and sees us necking, we'll wind up in the pokey. Let's go see your Scotland Yard man. Then we can fool around."

"Promise?" Roman cranked up the car.

"Well, as Brillo pointed out, you're not getting anything out of this deal but my appreciation. And I think I know how to show that."

Roman swerved to miss a car that was turning into the Institute's parking lot. "Duck!" When Annabel came back up from the floor, Roman was looking into the rearview mirror. "I didn't get a good look, but I'm pretty sure whoever it was didn't see you."

"What kind of car was he driving? Not a black Mercedes?" Annabel's heart pounded crazily. If Morris Keller went to his office at this time of night and discovered the papers missing, he could have a warrant put out for the miscreants within the hour.

"I was too busy getting out of the way to tell. Well, our best bet is to get on with the business at hand and hope to hell that wasn't Keller."

Their euphoric high dispelled by the incident, they rode in silence to Inspector Stone's flat on Bleak Street.

"Forgery? Ha! Don't bestow the name of a skilled art to this botched and blatant theft." Inspector Sydney Stone scoffed and bristled under his magnified light. He had just finished examining the copy of the original "Isobel"

426

poem while his visitors sat dranking very old brandy and waiting for the verdict. "Why, anyone beyond primary could see that the original title of the copied ode was obliterated and another substituted. As for the handwriting on the original manuscripts, they match perfectly this Jeremy fellow's hand. See the 'f's with the curved bar? The 't's with a curled base, the heavy ink on emphasized lines?" Stone rose from the desk and took off his spectacles. "This Newton Fenmore must have been a damnably stupid fellow, to think that he could pass off these works as his."

"He was," Annabel said promptly. "I mean, he must have been. Inspector Stone, will you be able to give me some sort of affidavit as to your findings?" Annabel's sense of relief, compounded with the effects of the brandy, made her feel weak in the knees. Up till now, she had not been sure she would ever be able to prove what she knew to be fact. But the former Scotland Yard man bore a sense of authoritative confidence and knowledge that she knew would stand up against Morris Keller and other detractors. "And if it came down to going to court, would you be willing to testify?"

The man's slate-gray eyes looked at Annabel reprovingly. "My dear young woman, I made law enforcement and the ferreting out of those who defied it my life's work. I hate a thief more

427

than I despise the heinous murderer. Stealing a dead man's words is stealing his very soul. At least if he's killed, he retains his soul. Of course, I will supply an affidavit. And those who have current authority to see that this case is ended in justice will be behind me every step of the way."

"Sydney, I owe you one." Roman rose and held out his hand. "Just let me know when."

The older man's eyes twinkled. "Well, I should think a wedding invitation to a lonely old sleuth would be a start toward the debt. Young lady," he said, turning to Annabel, the merriment turning to seriousness, "I don't know exactly where you fit in with all of this, but I admire your grasp of what is important in this modern world of deteriorating principle. As a tired old lawman, I salute you as a youthful beacon of hope for restored morality."

Annabel wanted to cry but she simply put her arms around the stiff shoulders and hugged the man who was helping her return Jeremy Harker Simmons and his poetry to their deserved place in literature.

Chapter Twenty-Four

Annabel and Roman left Sydney Stone's flat with the understanding that they would contact him the next day about the affidavit and other legal steps that would nail the coffin shut on Morris Keller's claims to his ancestor's poetic fame.

"I want Jeremy's work to be kept safe in the tower, with me," Annabel told Roman when they were on the road back to Maidstone. "Somehow, it's come full circle, the way it should have, and I think he'd want it that way."

"This Jeremy of yours must have been some guy." Roman leaned forward to wipe off the mist from the windshield. It was getting late and the famous English fogs were obscuring the back roads to Sheffield Hall. "Sometimes I get the feeling that I've met him somehow."

Annabel didn't say anything to that. She was clutching the box of Jeremy's writings to her chest, thinking about the letter Isobel had tried to get to him in prison. She hoped he had seen that note, had known at the last before he died that his name would one day be almost as famous as his friends'. "Thank goodness we're almost home." She laid her head on Roman's shoulder. "Home. Do you feel that way about this place, too?"

"I have from the first moment I saw it." Roman pulled up in front of the tower. "Don't you think it would be best if you slept up at the main house tonight?"

"I would like to be alone tonight." She looked up at Roman anxiously. "I don't mean that I don't want you with me, it's just that . . ."

Roman kissed the tip of her nose. "You don't have to explain, my darling. I know how important all this business has been to you and that tonight was . . . well, tonight was a biggie." He started to get out, then stopped, his hand on the door handle. "Hey, Annabel, there's something I thought about and maybe you should, too. You've worked really hard on your academic credentials. If things don't work out the way they should, if Keller somehow comes out smelling like a rose in all this, where does that put you? You'd be discredited, your work would have gone for nothing, you'd have a hell-uva time getting another place in an academic institution. There's a huge ol' boys network in these schools. I know you're aware of that."

"Am I ever." She kissed him. "You're sweet, but I'm going forward with it, come hell or high water. I'm committed, let the chips fall where they may."

He kissed her back. "I knew you'd say that, which is one of the reasons I love you. Hey, what happened to my show of appreciation night, Holmes?"

Annabel turned to laugh at him from the door to the tower. "Tomorrow night, sweet Watson." She blew him a kiss. "Good night, sweet prince! And flights of angels sing thee to thy rest."

"And thee," Roman murmured as he watched until she was safely inside the door before he drove off.

Several yards down the lane, unilluminated by headlights, a dark car's engine started up its throb and moved cautiously, ominously, toward the space vacated by Roman's vehicle. The figure inside got out carefully, easing the car door shut without a sound, and looked up to the turret where Annabel had just lit up the room atop the tower.

431

The man waited for a few seconds, then went to the door of the tower where he had earlier wedged a matchbook so that the door now opened to his nudge.

Upstairs, Annabel stretched and yawned, wondering if she had enough strength left to undress for bed, much less lift the heavy stone to the old hiding place in the turret floor. "No," she said to the temptation to leave that till morning, "I'll sleep better if I know dear Jeremy's poems are at last safe again."

She put the box in the secret hole and rearranged the rug over the loose stone. "There . . . Oh, my goodness, what was that? Roman?" The creak on the tower stairs was a familiar one, halfway up. She smiled, getting to her feet, and with a teasing reprimand on her lips, went to the turret door. "Now, Roman, you're being very naughty, coming back after I told you that we'd make up for lost time tomor—"

The words froze on her tongue as the door swung open and there stood Morris Keller, his bulk in the doorway ominously threatening. "Is this a bad time?" he asked with a terrible smile.

"Dr. Keller! I . . . I was just about to get ready for bed. I'm so sorry I missed you in town today, but your secretary said you were tied up and . . ."

He came in and pushed the door shut behind him. "Bernice is a fool and so are you. Where are they?"

"Bernice? Roman? Why, I guess they're both . . ."

"The manuscripts. I know you took them. I saw you bring them in here right before your boyfriend left. Very clever of you, leaving the dummy papers in the safe, but not smart using my secretary to get a key to my office. She sneaked the wax imprint easily enough but stupidly neglected to wipe it off." He smiled again, the terrible smile. "I've done that a few times myself so I know the signs."

Annabel decided it was time to let him have it with both barrels. "All right, I'll admit that I took the manuscripts. We can make a deal, you and I, since we both know that it's all over. You can still come out with your academic integrity intact if you agree to publicly acknowledge that your ancestor, Newton Fenmore, was not the author of the acclaimed volumes that bore his name."

"And why would I do that? Because some little twit of a graduate student has some wild-haired theory that the poems were written by an obscure poet whose name nobody's ever heard of?"

"No, because I have the manuscripts and the proof that Fenmore—and you—are frauds."

He moved a step closer to her, and she moved back. "Proof? I happen to know that the handwriting expert I referred you to hasn't laid a glass on said manuscripts since I first had him authenticate them."

"I've just had the manuscripts examined by an independent expert who will swear to the forgery. Why, Dr. Keller? Why would you prostitute your academic reputation, your credentials, to perpetuate this lie about your ancestor being a great poet?"

"Why? You little know-it-all, coming over here with your brazen Yankee gall, acting as if you invented scholarliness, going behind my back at every turn to try to discredit me—how could you understand 'why'?" Annabel was horrified to see that the man's eyes were glazing over in his fury, saliva coming out of the corner of his sneering mouth. "I didn't get where I am through some giveaway scholarship, or get high grades because I had the right curves. I scratched and struggled and fought my way to where I am, and if you think I'm going to let a little twit like you ruin what I've worked for, destroy the prestige I've earned, you've got a lot to learn."

"Dr. Keller, please think about what you're saying. I'm not the only one who knows about the manuscripts. In fact, there's a man from Scotland Yard who's prepared to testify that

Fenmore could not be the author of those poems."

"You've been reading too much Agatha Christie, my dear. Oh, I know you've probably involved my lumpish secretary and your lover in your little ploy to gain attention in academic circles, but without the manuscripts, you have nothing."

"But I have the manuscripts, Dr. Keller," Annabel said softly.

He gave that slow, awful smile again. Maybe Felicia's insanity had not been solely from her venereal disease and had come down through the generations, Annabel thought suddenly. "Oh, yes, you have the manuscripts." He looked around the turret. "Charming room. After the Sheffields and your pet poet were hanged for treason, my ancestor adopted this turret for his own study. You can almost feel the history in here, can you not?"

"Dr. Keller, there's no point in this. I've offered you a chance to clear the slate and go on with your life, but if you refuse, I'll have to pursue the matter in a different way."

"The manuscripts . . ." It was as though he had not heard her. He was still looking around the room. Annabel forced herself to keep her eyes on him and not on the hiding place he sought. "They're in here, of course. I can feel that. These old English structures have so many centuries of blood and human suffering soaked into their stones, don't they?"

She started edging toward the door. He stopped her cold with a sharp, "I wouldn't do that if I were you." She stared at his hand which he'd kept secreted in his jacket pocket until now when it emerged with a mean-looking derringer. "It's not nice to leave in the middle of a conversation."

"Dr. Keller, nothing is worth going to prison for. You can start over somewhere else, build a new reputation on something real and honest, not an ancestor's lies."

"I like it here," he said in a steely voice. "Too bad that you won't give me the manuscripts back like a nice girl. But I would have destroyed them anyway since you've meddled this much in my affairs." He pointed the gun at her. "Get away from the door, my dear. I'm not a violent man, but you have stretched my patience."

She moved toward the window seat as he indicated. "What are you going to do?"

"I'm going to allow you to accompany your precious Jeremy's manuscripts into Dante's Inferno." Annabel shivered at the high-pitched laugh that was almost a giggle. "Get in, pretty maid. Too bad you never found me attractive. Most of my graduate students have been quite taken with the, ah, extracurricular opportunities I've provided. No extra matriculation fee, naturally." Again, the maniacal giggle.

She numbly climbed into the window seat as he held the lid open. The slam and sound of the latch closing grimly resembled the last sealing of a coffin lid. Dear God, how long before Roman comes back to check on me in the morning! Her claustrophobia was a sporadic condition that she prayed would not choose this time to appear.

He was still in the room. She could hear him moving about. What was he doing? He wouldn't find the manuscripts, that much she was confident about, but why wasn't he leaving? What had he meant when he said he was going to "destroy" the papers?

Dante's Inferno! She smelled the smoke just as it struck her what he planned to do. She started beating on the window-seat lid and yelling, coughing in between as the acrid fumes began permeating her hideaway.

Hideaway. Annabel put her sleeve over her nose and mouth and with her free hand started tugging at the bottom of the space.

This was the entrance to the old secret exit that Greymalkin had shown Isobel!

It wouldn't open. And then Annabel remembered how, when she and Roman were renovating the place, he said he had plugged up some drafty places so that she would be snug and safe in her tower. She sobbed out loud.

"Oh, Roman, where are you? Falcon, Falcon, I need you right now!"

The smoke was filling her nose, making tears stream from her eyes. And then she heard the voices, the miraculous shout of the man she had been crying out for . . .

"Annabel!" he cried, flinging up the lid. "Oh, my God, are you all right? Dammit, Stone, why did you have to make us wait so long? She could be dead." Roman lifted Annabel out of the window seat. Inspector Stone followed them down the stairs to join the uniformed men waiting outside. Through a dim haze of smoke, Annabel saw Morris Keller sitting in the back of one of the police cars.

But her concern was directed elsewhere. "The tower! Oh, Roman, Jeremy's poems! The manuscripts are up there!"

"Calm down, darling." He held her close, soothing her, wiping off the sooty tears. "The fire's almost out, and the box you brought with you is full of junk, not manuscripts."

Annabel looked up at him in shock. "What? You mean . . . ?"

Stone answered, "I mean, Miss Poe, that when you came to me with your story, I wasted no time calling the Yard about Dr. Keller's peculiar preoccupation with his ancestor's alleged literary works. It turns out that the investigation that has been under way at several government-funded institutes has uncovered a ring of thieves who peddle rare manuscripts at huge profits to underground collectors. Dr. Keller was the ringleader."

Annabel was still confused. "So the manuscripts in the safe, the ones we took and showed you, were forgeries."

"Very good ones, too, contrary to what I said in my office. Keller planned to present those to the Institute, thus getting the bonus of having his name connected with literary greatness while simultaneously selling the real things at astronomical prices."

"Are Jeremy's poems really that valuable?"

Stone smiled at her. "Pages with note after note penned by Keats, Lord Byron, Percy Shelley, even a funny little ditty with Mary Shelley's name underneath? What's that American phrase—'Are you kidding?' "

"So Keller wanted the fake ones burned so the forgery couldn't be proved." Annabel turned to Roman. "You knew all this and didn't tell me?"

He shrugged. "Stone said it was best if you didn't know that Keller was on your trail and that we were on his."

Annabel didn't know whether to hit him or kiss him. She opted for the latter. "So where are the real manuscripts?"

"Safe at Scotland Yard," Stone said. "Unless, of course, you entice your safecracking friend to help you liberate them before we return them to the Institute for the dedication Thursday."

"Will Jeremy finally be acknowledged as the author?" Annabel asked anxiously.

Inspector Stone grinned. "Read Thursday's tabloids and find out. London papers are going to have more fun with this story than they did with Charles's cellular phone and your Elvis's appearance in a kidney-pie eatery near Winchester Cathedral."

Sleeping was out of the question that night. Roman took Annabel back to the main house and tried to sneak into the kitchen, but Armand, sleepy but cheerful, showed up just as the eggs were being cracked on the edge of a frying pan.

"Mon Dieu! I thought I heard the mousetrap, but instead it's you, interfering with my domain."

"Armand," Annabel said, by now beyond her second wind and sincerely hungry, "we do not want pâté, we do not want omelette grande, we do not want anything but just plain ole bacon and eggs and, God help me, grits."

"Well, yuh just tell me whut yuh want, pilgrim," the chef said, putting an apron on over his candy-striped pajamas.

"Oh, Lord," Annabel groaned. "He's found the John Wayne oldies."

They were married in the maze, two days after Roman had signed the contract to buy Sheffield Hall, intact, with surrounding grounds.

After the ceremony, he took her off to the side to tell her that she had a special wedding gift awaiting her.

"Roman, you've given me so much!" Annabel told him, laughing, and still unbelieving that so much happiness had come so soon after the turmoil following the night in the tower. "I don't know if I can stand any more. These were presents enough." She fingered the moonstones in her ears that matched the pendant she'd worn with her wedding gown.

"It's only just begun. I plan to give you everything, including the moon and the stars. But come with me now. I think you'll like this present."

She shook her head at him, but followed as he led her, hand in his, to the stables. "Wait'll you see what I've found for my darling bride."

Annabel moved slowly toward the horse that stood immobile in the first stall. "Lady Godiva?" she whispered unbelievingly. "Can it really be you?"

The mare whinnied and threw her fine head up and down, rolling her eyes and, Annabel could swear, grinning from ear to ear. "So horses can do it, too," she whispered, fishing out a mint from the wedding table as she nuzzled a very old friend.

"Don't make me jealous. Look at what I've got in the next stall."

Mordred. "Hey, fellow. Be careful with the guy riding you. I want to keep him around for another century or two, you know."

Their wedding night was spent in the suite that would only hold beautiful new memories from now on, Annabel decided. She had a little jagged thought about Tremaine, about the Falcon, as she waited on the balcony for Roman to join her for their first magic night as husband and wife. But she loved her bridegroom and knew that they would be happy together for as long as they lived.

Roman had sounded a little funny when they'd retired after the reception, but Annabel had thought it a charming bit of shyness. She waited for him to come out to her so she could tell him so.

And waited. And waited.

"Roman? Are you all right?" She banged on the bathroom door. "Darling, I'm not going to hurt you, I promise." She waited. "Roman?"

He said in a muffled voice, "Go back out on the balcony. I have a surprise for you. The guys back on the ole team sent me a wedding present."

Annabel grinned and went back out on the balcony.

At a sound from the door to the bedroom, she turned and saw . . .

"It's my old Falcon football helmet. The guys sent it to me, saying I might need it again sometime."

Annabel's heart went crazy as she looked at the emblem of the fierce falcon with his spread wings and saw a long-ago image that blended into this one, making her feel like the most loved and protected woman who had ever lived.

"You were a Falcon," she whispered. "Why didn't I know that?"

"You asked me once if I played for the Atlanta Braves. I just didn't quite have the heart to point out the difference."

She held out her arms. "You're at first base with me, darling."

"Make that 'first down,' sweetheart," the Falcon said with a smile.

"Play it again, Sam," Annabel said.

TIMESWEPT ROMANCE
TEARS OF FIRE
By Nelle McFather

Swept into the tumultuous life and times of her ancestor Deirdre O'Shea, Fable relives a night of sweet ecstasy with Andre Devereux, never guessing that their delicious passion will have the power to cross the ages. Caught between swirling visions of a distant desire and a troubled reality filled with betrayal, Fable seeks the answers that will set her free— answers that can only be found in the tender embrace of two men who live a century apart.

_51932-1 $4.99 US/$5.99 CAN

FUTURISTIC ROMANCE
ASCENT TO THE STARS
By Christine Michels

For Trace, the assignment should be simple. Any Thadonian warrior can take a helpless female to safety in exchange for valuable information against his diabolical enemies. But as fiery as a supernova, as radiant as a sun, Coventry Pearce is no mere woman. Even as he races across the galaxy to save his doomed world, Trace battles to deny a burning desire that will take him to the heavens and beyond.

_51933-X $4.99 US/$5.99 CAN

A TIMESWEPT ROMANCE

Timeswept passion...timeless love.

A TRYST IN TIME

EUGENIA RILEY

Devastated by her brother's death in Vietnam, Sarah Jennings retreats to a crumbling Civil War plantation house, where a dark-eyed lover calls to her from across the years. Damien too has lost a brother to war—the War Between the States—yet in Sarah's embrace he finds a sweet ecstasy that makes life worth living. But if Sarah and Damien cannot unravel the secret of her mysterious arrival at Belle Fontaine, their brief tryst in time will end forever.

___3198-1 $4.50 US/$5.50 CAN

TIMESWEPT ROMANCE

TIME OF THE ROSE

By Bonita Clifton

When the silver-haired cowboy brings Madison Calloway to his run-down ranch, she thinks for sure he is senile. Certain he'll bring harm to himself, Madison follows the man into a thunderstorm and back to the wild days of his youth in the Old West.

The dread of all his enemies and the desire of all the ladies, Colton Chase does not stand a chance against the spunky beauty who has tracked him through time. And after one passion-drenched night, Colt is ready to surrender his heart to the most tempting spitfire anywhere in time.

__51922-4 $4.99 US/$5.99 CAN

A FUTURISTIC ROMANCE

AWAKENINGS

By Saranne Dawson

Fearless and bold, Justan rules his domain with an iron hand, but nothing short of the Dammai's magic will bring his warring people peace. He claims he needs Rozlynd—a bewitching beauty and the last of the Dammai—for her sorcery alone, yet inside him stirs an unexpected yearning to savor the temptress's charms, to sample her sweet innocence. And as her silken spell ensnares him, Justan battles to vanquish a power whose like he has never encountered—the power of Rozlynd's love.

__51921-6 $4.99 US/$5.99 CAN

TIMESWEPT ROMANCE
TIME REMEMBERED
Elizabeth Crane
Bestselling Author of *Reflections in Time*

A voodoo doll and an ancient spell whisk thoroughly modern Jody Farnell from a decaying antebellum mansion to the Old South and a true Southern gentleman who shows her the magic of love.

__0-505-51904-6 $4.99 US/$5.99 CAN

FUTURISTIC ROMANCE
A DISTANT STAR
Anne Avery

Jerrel is enchanted by the courageous messenger who saves his life. But he cannot permit anyone to turn him from the mission that has brought him to the distant world—not even the proud and passionate woman who offers him a love capable of bridging the stars.

__0-505-51905-4 $4.99 US/$5.99 CAN